SACR...

D0174577

PRAISE FO...
BALLAD...

'Everything you already love about Vikki Wakefield—plus a spine-tingling supernatural mystery. *Ballad for a Mad Girl* is brilliantly creepy and thrilling.' Fiona Wood

'There's a dark side to being the funny one in the group. This is a piercing, creepy tale about a wild girl who could lose herself to a ghost. Vikki Wakefield's writing never fails to give me chills.' Emily Gale

'A ghost thriller with a literary feel from an Australian author we love.' *Readings*

'*Ballad for a Mad Girl* is brilliant, edgy and unsettling. Grace is a tough and sympathetic anti-heroine. I felt her grief and, even when I cursed her curiosity, was compelled to follow her to the story's satisfying, cinematic end.' Simmone Howell

'I'm obsessed with Vikki Wakefield's words. Seriously—I'd be happy reading her grocery list.' Danielle Binks, *Alpha Reader*

'Fans of intelligent, unflinching, spine-crawling thrillers will love this book.' *Books+Publishing*

'Vikki Wakefield is one of Australia's best YA writers. I couldn't put down *Ballad for a Mad Girl*.' Cath Crowley

FRIDAY BROWN

'When I finish a Vikki Wakefield novel I get a tiny ache in my heart because I'm already missing her gutsy characters.' Melina Marchetta

'*Friday Brown* will haunt you long after you've turned the last page...It will break your heart then put the pieces back together in a new way. I absolutely loved this book.' Libba Bray

'*Friday Brown* is every superlative you can throw at it. It's a masterpiece...There are no words to describe this novel adequately. There is only humbled, awestruck, heartbroken silence.' *Mostly Reading YA*

'Vikki Wakefield writes the tough stuff...Her characters are so vivid and endearing, or vicious and infuriating that she makes you feel everything down to your bones.' *Alpha Reader*

'The gripping story and rich characters took me to places where I didn't expect to venture... I devoured each page.' *Australian Book Review*

'This is a pull-no-punches story about learning the truth and growing up, full of the preciousness of friendship and love.' *Herald Sun*

'This novel is Australian young adult fiction at its best. *Friday Brown* will blow your mind.' *Viewpoint*

'A tense, multilayered tale about loyalty, memory and survival...Lyrical, suspenseful and haunting.' *Kirkus*

INBETWEEN DAYS

'An utterly gripping read with authentic,
complicated and relatable characters.'
Sydney Morning Herald

'Memorable, intriguing, perceptive and often
very funny, this is an unforgettable YA novel and
a most unusual love story.' *Magpies*

'Vikki Wakefield writes stories that will
break your heart…A gritty, heartfelt read for teens
and adult readers alike.' *Readings*

'I just adored *Inbetween Days*—really complex,
raw, beautiful characters.' Melissa Keil

'Wakefield has never sounded more like Harper Lee…
Inbetween Days is Australian YA gothic. It's at times bleak and
tender, with touches of romance threaded with heartache…
Another "must-read" from one of Australia's best young adult
authors writing today…I adored this book.' *Alpha Reader*

'Vikki Wakefield has done it again. She's gone
and taken my breath away with another exquisite book…
Without a doubt, Wakefield is one of Australia's
best writers.' *Unfinished Bookshelf*

'Vikki Wakefield…proves again that she's the mistress of YA
twisted relationships and disturbed characters, all memorable,
all sketched with compassion, wit and insight, the adults as
well as teens.' *Australian Book Review*, Books of the Year 2015

'Wakefield gives her fictional landscape the same haunting
quality that she achieved with her first novel, *Friday Brown*,
and her writing is full of insight and feeling.' *Age*

Vikki Wakefield's first YA novel, *All I Ever Wanted*, won the 2012 Adelaide Festival Literary Award for YA Fiction, as did her second novel, *Friday Brown*, in 2014. *Friday Brown* was also a CBCA Honour Book in 2013, and was shortlisted for the prestigious Prime Minister's Literary Awards. Vikki's third novel, *Inbetween Days*, was Highly Commended in the 2016 Barbara Jefferis Award, and was a 2016 CBCA Honour Book. Vikki lives in the Adelaide foothills with her family.

vikkiwakefield.com

BALLAD FOR A MAD GIRL

Vikki Wakefield

TEXT PUBLISHING MELBOURNE AUSTRALIA

textpublishing.com.au

The Text Publishing Company
Swann House
22 William Street
Melbourne Victoria 3000
Australia

Copyright © Vikki Wakefield 2017

The moral rights of the author have been asserted.

All rights reserved. Without limiting the rights under copyright above, no part of this publication shall be reproduced, stored in or introduced into a retrieval system, or transmitted in any form or by any means (electronic, mechanical, photocopying, recording or otherwise), without the prior permission of both the copyright owner and the publisher of this book.

Cover design and illustration by Astred Hicks, Design Cherry
Page design by Imogen Stubbs
Typeset by J&M Typesetting

Printed in Australia by Griffin Press, an accredited ISO/NZS 14001:2004 Environmental Management System printer

National Library of Australia Cataloguing-in-Publication entry:
Creator: Wakefield, Vikki, author
Title: Ballad for a Mad Girl / by Vikki Wakefield
ISBN: 9781925355291 (paperback)
ISBN: 9781925410327 (ebook)
Target Audience: For young adults
Subjects: Teenage girls—Fiction.
Life change events—Fiction.
Families—Fiction

 This book is printed on paper certified against the Forest Stewardship Council® Standards. Griffin Press holds FSC chain-of-custody certification SGS-COC-005088. FSC promotes environmentally responsible, socially beneficial and economically viable management of the world's forests.

For my mum, Jules
and for biscuits
(because I can't say no to a dare)

ONE

I've been having hateful thoughts again.

I wish I could cast them out like an airborne curse or summon a superpower through sheer will. I'd choose telekinesis over flying any day—slam some saucepans, smash a few ornaments, shatter a window. I'd drag my dad across the floor, slide him up a wall, pin him to the ceiling, and laugh like a maniac as I stroll out the front door.

It's this house. Over a year and I still can't get used to it. It's everything we're not: sweet, tidy, *suburban*— a two-storey shoebox with a homemade plaque on the toilet door and the puke-worthy scent of potpourri in every room. It stinks of happy families. We were once a long, low farmhouse with whispering walls; we were junk and brawling dogs and sprawling yard. Our sun didn't set behind a row of cardboard houses and we never had to play musical cars to get out of the driveway. That was before. Now I can spit from the back doorstep and hit the fence; now I sleep so close to strangers I hear them breathe.

They're the polite thoughts. The hateful ones I mostly keep to myself.

My room is the only thing I like. When we moved in, I claimed the master bedroom, upstairs, far away from everyone—it has a window seat and an ensuite bathroom, shiny fake floorboards and a view down the street over the cloned roofs of the other houses in the estate. The bed was a bribe. I traded my rickety single and hundreds of acres for a king-sized bed that's bigger than our new backyard.

It's balmy tonight. Filthy black outside. The footpath beneath my window is spotted with old chewing-gum; the lace curtains twitch to a faint breeze. I'm sitting on my bed—watching *She's the Man*, painting my toenails, killing time—trying not to think about the things I'm missing. For the past hour, cars full of teenagers have been coming and going. Going, mostly, with the music up and the windows down.

My friends are out there, somewhere. I grip the brush so tightly it slips, leaving a bright red streak on the sheet, and my thoughts go from bad to worse: right this minute, if I had three seconds to make a wish, I'd swap the family I've got for the one I've lost. And I'd erase the last two years while I'm at it—or maybe that counts as two wishes.

At nine o'clock, Pete texts. I lunge for my phone, and knock over the bottle of nail polish. The streak turns into a puddle.

Grace? Pick you up?

I sigh and pause the movie. *Grounded. Again. You know that.*

Straight back: *Pipe challenge!*

I wait until I've finished the toenails on my left foot. *Who?*

Downstairs, Dad bellows at the television. The outside sensor light goes on, which means he's let Diesel out for the night and he'll be in bed soon. Diesel is the inside dog, the only one we could keep.

We're all here. Gummer Mitchell Amber Kenzie Me. You. Come on, it's Saturday.

Kenzie. I didn't really expect her to stay home in sympathy just because I got caught and she didn't. Wait, no. I did.

Dad never gives me a parole date—he keeps me hanging. If I ask when I'll be allowed out, he adds another week, and if I'm more than five minutes late home after school, he adds two. My brother Cody is twenty—three years older than me—and apparently a grown-up. Dad couldn't save the farm, couldn't stop Cody from dropping out of school, couldn't stop Mum from dying—pulling on my reins is his favourite thing. I'm the one person he still thinks he can control.

3

Grounded, on a Saturday, the only night anything ever happens in Swanston—Swamptown, if you're a local, and you don't get much more local than fifth-generation Swampy, like me. It was twenty kilometres to town when we lived at the farm, but living in the estate makes it harder to pretend I'm not missing out on anything.

Pete takes my silence as a yes. *Pick you up at the end of your street in 15.*

He knows getting out isn't high-risk—I mastered the roof-to-tree trapeze act a week after we moved in—but getting caught is a problem. Dad's antennae will be twitching. I've never missed a pipe challenge. The last two years I've been the first to cross. I hold the record time, and the only way to keep it is to turn up, go first, and psych out the challengers.

Make it 30 minutes.

I wander downstairs in my pyjamas. This house is open-plan, so I can't sneak into the kitchen or raid the fridge anymore without running into whoever's in the lounge or dining-room. Dad is sitting on the couch, watching the late news. I open the fridge and stand in the square of light, letting the air chill my skin.

Dad lowers the volume. He stretches his arms behind his head and shoots me a glance. 'You get your home-work done?'

I nod and grab a can of Coke.

If Dad was any sterner his face would crack. He's got a long line running through the middle of his forehead, as if somebody ironed a perfect crease there. He wasn't always like this: slow to forgive, quick to anger. It used to be the other way around.

'No caffeine before bed,' he says.

'Fine.' I put the can of Coke back and swig from the milk carton.

He switches the television off and stands. 'I'm working tomorrow. I'll be gone early, mending fences all day, so I won't be home until late. Can you cook dinner?'

'On Sunday?'

'So cook a Sunday dinner.'

'I meant that you're working all weekend.'

'I take what I can get,' he says, frowning. 'And make sure you stay in. Don't give me something else to worry about, okay? Cody will check.'

I hide a smile. Cody won't check. 'Night.'

My record will fall tonight if I'm not at the quarry. I can't live with that. Dad makes me feel bad for things I haven't done, so I might as well do them and deserve the punishment.

Back upstairs, I brush my hair and teeth, climb into bed, and lie facing the wall. Ten minutes later Dad knocks, opens the door and says goodnight again to make sure I'm there. I wait another five, then slip out of bed. I put on shorts and a tank, tie my hair in a ponytail, grab my tote bag and slide my feet into a pair of Skechers.

Good grip, no slip, out the window.

Diesel waits below, a bark in his throat. It's a familiar game. He keeps my secrets in exchange for liver treats.

I sneak along the fence next to the neighbour's rose-bushes and step out into the street. Three houses along a man sits in darkness on his porch, cigarette glowing. He barely glances at me as I tiptoe past. In my other life, the man on the porch would have a name; he would have called out to me and I would have waved back. All of these people living in the same street and nobody seems to know each other.

I jog the hundred metres to the corner. Gummer's black Ford 250 is there, tinted windows, engine running, headlights off. Pete's green station wagon is parked behind it.

I open the back door of the wagon, clamber over Mitchell's long legs, and land in Kenzie's lap.

'Hey, you,' she says, smiling. Reluctantly, she lets go of Mitchell's hand and makes space for me in the middle. 'There's more room in Gummer's truck.'

'Nuh-uh.' I fumble for the lap sash and snap the buckle as Pete revs the engine. 'I like it right here.'

Gummer's always wasted. He drives like an old man. Pete's a lunatic but at least we'll arrive this century.

Pete laughs and mumbles something crude about leaving Amber and Gummer alone together.

I flick the back of his head. 'Don't even think about it. If they get together, that leaves me and you, and that's taking this cross-pollination thing too far.'

Kenzie nudges my elbow. 'Stop it.'

'So how come you're allowed out?' I ask her. 'That's hardly fair.'

6

'You know I could set fire to our lounge room and my folks would only ask me to move out of the way so they could see the TV.'

Kenzie is fifth-generation Swampy too, but her parents are close to sixty. She's the youngest of seven. It's like they've run out of patience and don't really want her around, so they let her run wild. She has a tongue piercing and a belly-button ring, an infinity tattoo behind her right ear and nine studs in her left. I'm a shorter, skinnier, cleanskin version of her: same long, dark hair, hazel eyes, narrow face, high cheekbones. We're so alike people take her for my older, more rebellious sister. But Kenzie only looks like trouble.

Mitchell reaches across me and grabs her hand. They're new at this. We all are. Sometimes I think it would be better if we just stayed friends. We've been a tight group since primary school, but when it comes to Kenzie and me, Mitch is an extra—he has to know that. It is and will always be Grace and Kenzie, Kenzie and Grace.

I wriggle myself a bit more room.

Mitch drops Kenzie's hand and shifts closer to the window.

'Why are you all in the back? What am I, a taxi?' Pete mutters, taking a corner on what feels like two wheels.

I check the back window. Gummer's way behind.

'You scared, Grace?' he adds, catching my eye in the rear-vision mirror. 'High stakes tonight. Gummer's got a hundred on you beating your own time. Me and Amber put fifty down, each.'

'Double your money, Doughboy, you faithless cheapskate,' I hiss, and he laughs.

'Grace isn't afraid of anything,' Kenzie says, linking her arm with mine. 'But it's your own stupid fault if you lose. She doesn't have anything left to prove.'

There isn't a corner of Swanston we haven't explored in our boredom. It feels like a big town—four schools, six pubs and over ten thousand people—the heartbeat of surrounding hectares of farmland. Everything comes in shades of brown, beige and grey, with a fine layer of dirt, as if the town was flung to the ground by a passing tornado. During a heatwave it shimmers like a mirage. Swanston smells like old boots, mouldy hay or wet dog, depending on which way the wind blows, and there is a swamp, but it's a joke—a mosquito-infested bog behind the Colonial Museum; it stinks like a sewer during the cooler months and dries to a foul crust in summer.

We pass through the middle of town with its wide streets and heritage-listed buildings. The main shopping strip, Centennial Park and Swanston Cemetery are all in a row. Don't ask me why the first settlers decided it was a good idea to bury the dead right where most people go about the business of living—maybe back then they kept them close because cars weren't invented. Maybe they visited every day.

I don't visit. Dead is dust; only the living care if you leave flowers.

'So what's the plan?' Kenzie says.

'I'm making it up as I go.' I wink and she smiles—Kenzie knows better than anyone that Grace Foley is always good for a laugh.

Pete takes the shortest route, zigzagging through the backstreets past the overland train station. He turns onto the freeway. The quarry is about three kilometres out of town—disused now, but it would take a thousand years to fill a hole that big. As we're turning off the freeway onto Yeoman's Track, a sheet of lightning illuminates the endlessly flat landscape.

'Yes!' Pete slaps the steering wheel and snakes the car.

I slam sideways into Mitch. Dust swarms through the air vents, and I whisper a prayer, thinking a wasted Gummer is looking pretty good right now.

Another flash and the crater shows itself to our left: vast, black, deep. At the western end, the quarry narrows into a steep gully that peters out several kilometres away; where the gully begins, a massive underground bore-water pipe connects one side to the other. Every year they fix the barricades at the entrance to the quarry; every year someone with a bull bar simply drives through the fence.

Pete finds a parking space between two other cars at the edge of the quarry. He licks his finger and holds it up through the open window, testing the breeze. 'Perfect weather,' he says. 'And a decent crowd, but there are more of them than us. They called it late on purpose.'

There are fifty or sixty Year Elevens and Twelves.

I'm guessing at least fifteen or so, including us, are from Swampie Public; the majority are Sacred Heart Private students. Pete's right: they've deliberately called the challenge late so we wouldn't have time to rally our troops. Our schools are next to each other. We have to share their library and their gym, and we're fiercely competitive—in sport, in ethos, in extracurricular everything, right down to who hangs out in which car parks and cafes, and who turns up to which party.

Kenzie and Mitch get out. I stay in the back seat.

Pete opens the boot and passes around a few beers. He won't offer one to me. I don't drink.

He hands me a can of raspberry lemonade. 'You ready to put the scaredy Hearts back in their box?'

'*Omm.*' I cross my legs and pinch my fingers.

'Right. Psych.'

Gummer and Amber haven't arrived yet. I'll need them with this hostile crowd. I hope they haven't pulled over somewhere—I wouldn't put it past Amber to try to seduce Gummer. She has a bad habit of testing our friendship one way or the other. She's probably dazzling him with skin, perfume, legs—in the last year she's changed, transformed into cartoon proportions, and Gummer is clueless.

'You better not fall tonight,' Kenzie says, leaning through the window. 'What's wrong? Are you scared?'

'*Shh.* Psych.' I'm waiting for the buzz I get before every prank, every performance. The only thing that scares me is the dead silence that follows a flat joke.

'Come *on*, Grace,' Kenzie beckons.

She wants it to be over. I wonder when this all stopped being fun for her. In the last year Kenzie has changed too—now she's serious about her schoolwork. And perhaps she's serious about Mitchell after all? Is everything else silly and juvenile for her now, including me?

Losing Mum, leaving the farm—that was bad enough. Now I'm failing school and my friends are all hooking up.

I summon the hateful thoughts—the unfairness of it all makes me mad, and anger makes me feel like I can do anything—but tonight, as much as I try, there's nothing. I can't feel.

Gummer's arrived. He's nodding at Pete, but he looks stunned. Amber appears, holding a bottle of cheap champagne. She hovers close to Gummer, glancing at him from beneath her lashes, and I know she's struck again. It might not be a death blow to our friendship, but it's close.

I climb out of Pete's car.

Pete gives a lazy finger to the Sacred Heart crowd and herds the Swampies into a cluster. 'Thirty-six point five seconds is the time to beat,' he calls. 'Sick 'em, Foley. Show those immaculate conceptions or immature conniptions or whatever they call themselves.'

I get a round of applause and take a bow, but my heart's not in it.

Kenzie won't look at me.

I turn my attention to the pipe, my old friend. There

11

are fan-shaped grilles each end, but they don't stop us. There's a rope ladder underneath, so it's easy enough to scoot down the bank of the gully and climb back up on the other side of the grille. The smallest, like me, can simply slip through sideways. Most straddle the pipe and shuffle along it. A few have mastered the tightrope walk, but I have an advantage: I'm light and quick. It's forty metres across, as wide as a horse's back, and fifteen metres down. When I'm standing in the middle of that pipe, knowing that something terrible happened here, knowing that there's only air between me and death, I feel it: life is sharper, brighter, more intense. It's a delicious kind of fear.

And I'd rather be terrified than feel nothing.

'Wentz is going,' someone says.

Noah Wentz, Sacred Heart's poster boy. He's crossing the pipe like a dog scratching its backside on the carpet.

The record holder *always* goes first. The Swampies start yelling and throwing empty beer cans.

'Let him go!' I yell, waving a hand. 'Some challenger. You dragged me out here for this?'

I ignore the barrage of rude gestures from the Hearts and make my way to the pipe. Wentz has reached the other side, still on his arse, and he's trying to stand to half-hearted applause. It's a crap time.

The gully looks bottomless tonight. Some say Hannah Holt is buried in the gully, her uneasy spirit slipping from crevice to shadow, sniffing for fear, and when she smells it she'll pull you down by the ankles with her teeth. We all know the stories are spread by grown-ups to keep us away from the quarry, but this is the first time I've ever thought about Hannah Holt, or William Dean, before I've crossed. I can't help wondering whether he closed his eyes when he jumped, or met the rocks with them wide open.

'Over a minute,' Pete shouts. 'Don't bother,' he says to me, but Wentz is coming back, on his feet this time, and he's moving fast.

'Who's timing?'

'I got it.'

'How can he see where he's going?'

Wentz blinks in the glare of a dozen sets of headlights and a haze of dust. Why he would choose to attempt the record on the return is beyond me. But his arms are loose at his sides as if he's going for a stroll around the block. At over six feet, almost a foot taller than me, his steps are longer. He's making it look effortless, and effortlessly walking the pipe takes a whole lot of practice.

The Sacred Heart students, anticipating a record time, swarm the grille.

'Damn,' Pete says. 'I think he's broken it.'

'Is it legal? Can he do that?' Kenzie groans. 'Grace, don't even think…'

'I got this,' I tell her. Now, the buzz.

'Thirty-two flat,' Gummer says, leaning over Pete's shoulder. 'If you're going to beat that, Gracie, you need a death wish.'

It's my turn. I've never really been tested before.

It can be done, two steps for one.

Wentz holds out his hand as I pass. We brush knuckles. We'll never be anything but rivals, but it is an impressive time. The Hearts step away to give me space, but step up their insults to rattle me.

'Practice run first,' I declare. 'I'll challenge on the return.'

Wentz nods to accept and Pete slaps my back, but Kenzie makes a strangled sound and walks away. The image I take with me as I slip through the grille is of Kenzie taking Mitchell by the hand and leading him to Pete's car.

'Be careful,' Amber calls.

The first section of pipe is slick with beer and spit. I kick off my shoes, step across the wetness and begin moving—evenly, but not too fast—feet turned out, arms outstretched. Beneath, the steep sides of the gully drop away. I block out the shouting, stare ahead at the distant midnight sky and keep the pipe in my peripheral vision. The stars give enough light if you trust them, but looking down can give you the sense that you're not moving at all.

I've done this a hundred times, maybe more.

A gusty breeze tugs a strand of hair into my eye. I blink it away. I'm twenty metres out now, almost to the halfway point where *school sucks* and *Jeff loves Denise*. There's a ragged concrete join in the middle that'll trip you if you don't know it's there—I bend and perform a walk-over to clapping and cheers.

14

There's a sudden hush. Heart speeding, I finish the distance at a jog, all windmill arms and graceless feet, to clutch at the grille on the far side. Just enough to press close to Wentz's time but not quite enough to beat it. Pete calls out my time but I'm not listening; it doesn't matter. I never meant to win first time around.

I set my feet in a starting position and lean forward, squinting. The headlights on the other side are brighter than I expected but I'm ready, sparked with adrenalin, fear at my back. I let go of the grille, moving with the breeze, pulled into a slipstream. The concrete is cool and alive, like a serpent. I run, touching down lightly on the balls of my feet, no thought of slipping, knowing that Wentz's record will fall only minutes after it was set and Sacred Heart will lose again. I laugh and the breeze dries my teeth.

Don't look down. The pipe is only an inch from the ground. It's not convex, it's a bridge, a mile wide. It's not far.

My feet are sure, my breathing steady. I try to focus on the faint glitter of stars so I won't be blinded by the headlights—but it's as if they've heard me: one by one, the headlights turn off. The universe disappears. An old scar on the cornea of my left eye—always with me, like a tiny drifting cloud—is all I can see.

I stop, steady myself, blink. Stretch my arms and wait for the edges of the world to come back. Fear is in front of me now, and to the side, above and below.

Sabotage.

'Turn on the lights!' If I can just hear a clear voice,

see a single beam of light, I'll find my sense of direction.

Where have the stars gone? Where is the sky?

I've forgotten the time—I've already lost—and I'm thinking about falling. A low whistle: something small and hard hits the back of my head. I drop to a crouch, feel for the pipe and straddle it with my palms pressed flat. The concrete hums with vibration.

'Are you crazy? Are you trying to kill me?'

No reply. Another near-miss missile; a beat later, the sound of whatever it was skittering onto rocks.

'Kenzie?' The breeze snatches my breath and blows it back like a ghost. 'Pete?'

After long seconds the stars reappear. Has the sky darkened? A soft blue-tinted mist has swallowed the edge of the quarry, the cars, the people. *Can they see me? Do they know I'm stuck?* I fumble in my back pocket for my phone but it isn't there—it's still in Pete's car. I can barely feel my feet but I dare to look down. They're dangling; they seem far away, and in the dim light my ankles are crisscrossed with welts and scratches.

I call out, gagging on a wave of bile. The fear—I'm dizzy with it. My thighs are numb and tingling from the freezing pipe; my hands are losing grip and sensation. I drop my eyes to the gully below: a dragon's yawn, and the rocks, the rocks like teeth. A lone shadow separates from the rest before the mist snatches it away with cool fingers.

'Grace!'

I hear them now, screaming from the other side, but

I'm so tired. I want to close my eyes and slip into the sweet, powdery blue. I glance down: I can just see my hands. Where they grip the pipe, there's a single looping word and a tiny drawing of a black bird—hundreds of times I've crossed the pipe, but I've never seen it.

Hannah.

I trace the word with my finger. It shimmers. A sharp impact near my ribs knocks me sideways and the pipe seems to buckle and twist. My legs lose grip. Close by, someone is sobbing as if their heart could break.

I see a shape through the mist, a hand solid enough to be real. To reach it, I have to let go.

TWO

'Good morning,' I croak.

Kenzie is perched on my window seat in the sun, knees up, arms folded around her legs. She's wearing a red-and-white polka dot dress. It hurts my eyes to look at her.

She turns around. 'It's afternoon. Cody let me in. I've been waiting for you to wake up.'

'Afternoon?'

'Near enough. It's almost twelve.' She unfolds herself and swings her feet to the floor. 'How do you feel?'

'Like I've just woken up. I think I'm having the vapours.'

She smiles. 'Do you think your dad knows you were gone?'

I shrug. 'I doubt it. You know he sleeps pretty hard.'

'What happened last night, Grace? You were really freaked. You scared me.'

I sit up. My head is throbbing; my throat is burning. My teeth feel sore and loose, like the time I had braces and the wires were changed. I taste rottenness in my spit. I reach for my phone on the side table and knock over a glass. Water spills onto the carpet.

Exhausted, I fall back onto the pillow. 'Where's my phone?'

Kenzie fetches a towel from my bathroom and soaks up the mess. 'Are you sick or something?'

I nod, but the truth is that my memory of the night before is as elusive as a half-remembered dream. Thinking about it makes my head pound harder. I touch the base of my skull—there's a tender lump the size of a plum and my fingers come away crusted with rust-coloured flecks. Fury gives me the strength to swing my body out of bed.

'Somebody threw something.' I hold out my hand as proof. The flecks are gone.

'What? No.'

'They turned off the headlights. It was so dark. I couldn't see.'

'Grace, the headlights were on the whole time.' She shakes her head, her mouth set. 'I wouldn't let that happen.'

'The mist...'

'There was no mist. A few spots of rain, that's all.' Her expression is gentle.

I start pacing. It's all coming back. 'Everyone was yelling and I couldn't concentrate. Maybe I slipped. Maybe I hit my head. Did I fall? Something hit me and I fell.'

'No,' she says firmly. 'You got halfway and you stopped. Nothing happened—you just froze.'

'They were all shouting and screaming…'

'*You* were shouting. You put your arms over your face and *you* screamed. For a second you wobbled, but you got your balance again. We only yelled at you because we were afraid you were going to fall.'

'I don't remember it like that,' I say. 'That's not what happened.'

'There were fifty people there, Grace. They all saw what I saw. I wouldn't lie to you.' She puts her hand on my arm.

I jerk away.

'It's okay if you got scared. I don't know how you do half the things you do. I mean, it was fun when we were younger. But my mortality got the better of me that time you dared me to backflip off Morley Bridge.'

The stubbornness kicks in—a gut emotion in my spider-webbed brain. 'I wasn't scared.'

'Fine.'

'Fine.'

She pauses for a beat and says, 'I thought you were going to jump.'

I snort. 'Don't stupid up the place, Kenz.'

She picks up her bag from the seat and scrolls through

her phone. 'Mitch is wondering if you're all right. I told him I'd let him know.'

'So let him know I'm *fine*—apart from the hallucinations.' I'm still in the same clothes I was wearing last night. There are watery red stains near my left armpit. 'Look,' I say, stretching the fabric. 'Blood.'

She leans close and sniffs. 'Raspberry lemonade.'

I check my legs and ankles, but there are no scratches. The stubbornness curls up and dies. 'Then someone must have spiked my drink. And where's my *goddamn phone*?' I fumble in my bag and look under the bed.

She sighs. 'Noah Wentz had to go out there—it took him fifteen minutes to talk you into crawling back on your hands and knees. When we got you in the car you were sobbing your heart out, and halfway along the freeway you started screaming. You didn't stop until you were almost home. Amber led you back up to your room and put you to bed—she said when she left you, you were crying in your sleep.' Kenzie slings her bag over her shoulder and kisses my cheek. 'And that's the truth.'

I shake my head. 'Noah Wentz? Oh God, I'll never live this down.'

Kenzie drags the corners of my mouth up with her fingers. 'Smile. It'll be okay. It's Year Twelve—it's making us all jumpy. Sometimes it terrifies me to think everything has been leading to this.'

'To what?'

'You know…study. Exams. The tunnel narrowing and all that.'

That's what terrifies her?

'It's this house,' I say.

She presses another kiss to my cheek. 'I'll see you tomorrow.'

She's gone.

I'm still pacing, but I'm back somewhere on that freeway. My head hurts. Pete is silent, grim, speeding. Mitch is staring out the window, gripping Kenzie's knee. Every detail is so clear I can count the bones in his knuckles. Kenzie is in the middle with her arm across my shoulders; she keeps turning me by the chin so she can look at my face, but I'm transfixed by the freeway markers rushing past in a red and white blur. Pete's phone is ringing repeatedly. I'm looking for a fixed point to focus on because everything is moving way too fast— and I find it. My head whips around. I'm out of my seat belt and clambering onto the parcel shelf with my face pressed against the glass. Kenzie pulls me back. It's gone in an instant, and nobody has seen what I have seen: something—someone—is crawling in the ditch by the side of the road.

Now I remember screaming.

In the morning I think about skipping school, but Kenzie shows up early and offers to walk with me. Usually we meet at the midway point between our houses, Reilly's Auto, where Cody works part-time, and we talk nonstop the rest of the way. Today, we make the twenty-minute journey in near-silence—Kenzie, texting Mitch, and me, dazed, anxious and dog-tired from a second night of strange dreams.

When we arrive, kids who've known me since primary school are acting as if they don't know me at all. Someone nudges my backpack. Something hits the back of my head. My armpits gather sweat but I don't turn around.

'I heard Pete found your phone.' Kenzie links her arm with mine.

I nod. 'He rang the house last night.'

'Phew.'

Kenzie seems more relieved than I am. Lately, her phone is always in her hand in case Mitch calls, and I'm pretty sure she can text him blindfolded. She even sleeps with it under her pillow. My phone is an old one of Cody's. I lose it all the time. I go out and leave it at home; I forget to charge it. I get anxious when I don't have any messages or when I have too many messages, and it's a constant reminder that I can't call the one person I desperately want to talk to: Mum.

She lowers her voice. 'Ignore them. It's yesterday's news. It's going to be fine.'

For a moment I believe her.

'Well.' I let out a shuddering sigh. 'Do you think they know how shitty it feels to crawl into one of our dingy boxes when it's all free-range and chandeliers right next door?'

A solid, eight-foot wall separates Swanston Public and Sacred Heart. They made it arty by placing a thick

Perspex panel every thirty metres or so, just to give the illusion that it's all friendly, that we're not segregated according to how much money our parents can afford to blow on our education. The wall keeps two castes of baboons from tearing each other apart.

Despite their chaste checked uniforms and shiny shoes, Sacred Heart students are no classier than we are, and we Swampies are no less imaginative for our Home-brand educations. Mooning, flipping the finger, pasting vicious slogans and spitting are common from both sides. The risk-takers will smear unmentionable fluids; the talented will install insulting sculptures under the guise of art; the above-it-alls will saunter past, their noses in the air, without realising they're part-of-it-all. We ran out of fresh ideas a long time ago.

Well, I didn't run out of ideas—I've sabotaged Sacred Heart's divine order no less than fourteen times in the past year. A month ago I switched both the small and the medium-sized axolotls in their Science room for a colossal one called Rex, sparking the rumour that Waldorf swallowed Statler. (One day I'll return them—they'll think Waldorf coughed Statler back up—but for now they both recline in a tank in the corner of my bedroom.) I cancelled the bus bookings for the Year Eleven camp in July, leaving forty-seven kids and forty-seven suitcases stranded in the car park for five hours. Many times, I've started rumours that became truth, set up hoaxes that fooled everyone, perpetrated pranks that became legend. I've never needed the glory—just the laughs. As long as my friends think I'm funny, I'm happy. And I don't discriminate: Swampie Public isn't exempt.

And neither, it seems, am I.

'Let's just get it over with,' Kenzie mutters as if it's both our names, not just mine, written across the first panel.

Aarghchgh! whatever that means, is written in brilliant red texta, along with a crude drawing of a stick figure, a noose around its neck. Underneath the figure: *Grace Foley choked.* Behind the Perspex, three Sacred Heart students have staked their claim and perfected their poses: one crouches and rocks in the foetal position while the other two re-enact Munch's *The Scream*, their school ties knotted around their throats. As Kenzie and I pass, they double over, laughing.

The next panel has just one word: *TRAITOR.* No pictures and nothing on the other side, which in itself is unsettling. The word is written on our side, a punishment reserved for the worst kind of loser or the most heinous of crimes—committing an act that improves the standing of Sacred Heart, including hanging out with them, having unconsecrated relationships or letting them beat us at anything.

Kenzie puts her arm across my shoulders. I want to shrug it all off, stick out my chin, strut. Make like it's yesterday's news. But I can't. There were only a few Swampies at the quarry on Saturday night—already it's clear that the story arrived at school long before I did, and it's only gathering dirt.

'Did you hear what happened on Saturday night?'

25

'Noah Wentz broke the pipe record. Grace Foley choked.'

'Foley freaked.'

By the time we reach the end of the wall, Amber and Pete have caught up to us. Having them beside me makes me feel better until Pete opens his mouth.

'Have you seen the video?'

Kenzie growls, 'Not now, Pete.'

Amber digs her elbow into his ribs.

'What video?' I stop. We're a minute's walk from homeroom. I could just turn and go. I should. Just go.

'Well.' Pete hesitates. 'There's more than one, including mine. I honestly thought you set it all up, Grace. I thought it was a joke.' He hands me my phone.

I peek at the screen. There are more notifications than I'd usually get in six months. 'Maybe it was,' I say, feeling queasy.

A couple of younger kids barge around the corner and skitter out of our way. One hisses, 'Loser.'

Pete blushes. 'I don't know what to say. Sorry?'

Amber steps in. 'Pete, if you send that video to anyone else, I will end you. It's bad enough that the Hearts have posted it all over the place.'

I groan and cover my face.

'Like I said, I thought it was one of her pranks,' Pete says.

'She doesn't remember what happened,' Kenzie says quietly. 'Watch the video, Grace. Maybe it'll all come back to you.'

I check the time on my phone. It's burning a hole in my pocket with all those messages and notifications. 'We're going to be late.' On cue, the bell rings. 'I'll see you guys at recess.'

Amber and I share homeroom. As we walk, I can tell she wants to ask me a million questions, but she says nothing until we reach the door. 'There's a GIF,' she says. 'It's pretty funny. I shared it, but that was before I knew…' She shrugs. 'That's why I was so hard on Pete.'

I see it now. The only way out of this is to go along with it. 'It was a joke, Amber,' I say dryly. 'It was an act, okay? You know I like to keep everyone guessing. Between us?' Which means it'll be all over school by lunchtime.

She buttons her lips and opens the door. 'That was pretty risky,' she says admiringly. 'To hand Noah the record like that.' She touches her mouth when she says his name.

I make it to nine o'clock before I decide that today absolutely qualifies as a pyjamas and shame day. After homeroom, I sign out and leave via the teachers' car park to avoid the wall. Fifteen minutes of scorn and scandal is enough.

'Did you hear? Grace lost her nerve.'

'Gummer lost a hundred bucks.'

'Grace Foley lost her record.'

All this stuff about losing, and nobody could tell that I was only worried about losing my mind.

*

The GIF is funny, or it would be funny if it wasn't a close up of me. I'm screaming, on loop, lit up like a silent movie star, all pale face and gaping mouth. The caption reads: *I see dead people*. Original. It looks like I'm acting. Overacting, even. I watch it fifteen times but it doesn't show me anything. The zoom is out of focus and behind me it's dark; I can't see anything below my chest.

When I've had enough, I slam down my laptop screen and pace. Waldorf and Statler are pink and white aliens at the bottom of their tank, glowing, as if they're radioactive. 'Should I look? Guys? What do you think?'

The videos are even easier to find—three pop straight up on Facebook. Over four hundred comments on the first. I find Pete's and click Play.

The video begins as I'm coming out of the back bend. So far, so good. The finish is shaky, but I already knew that. Behind me the sky is clear, shot through with stars; the cars' headlights beam straight at the pipe. I think of the time I lost out there, unable to see, not knowing that fifty people could see me as clearly as if I was performing under a spotlight on a stage.

It happens just like Kenzie said: I run, I stop, I falter and regain my balance. Finally, I straddle the pipe and start screaming, seemingly for no reason. There's no mist; nobody throws anything. The video zooms. It slips out of focus for a second and, when my face fills the frame, I'm muttering—that's when I remember finding her name, but my hands are out of the frame.

When it zooms out again, Wentz is coming for me. He's crawling, calling, holding out his hand, but I'm in another place. I appear to convulse and slip sideways. My eyes roll back.

In the corner of my room, Statler moves across the floor of the tank the way only an axolotl can move—as if he's moonwalking, all the time in the world. I know I could watch him for an hour and he'd only make it halfway. But what if his reality is different? What if, for him, it's only a few seconds' journey and he's moving at the speed of light? The tiny tank is his universe. Just because I can't see it—I'm not experiencing it—does that make his reality unreal?

I look back at the screen. Pete's video doesn't show what happened to me. This is like trying to decide which half of myself to keep: the sane half that accepts proof when I see it, or the crazy half that wants evidence that I'm not going mad.

I replay the moment when I convulsed and almost fell. Wentz's hand is outstretched, but he's still too far away to help. I slip. *Rewind.* Wentz is calling out, waving, trying to get my attention. *Rewind. Play.* He reaches for my hand. I convulse, slip. *Rewind. Play.* Out goes his hand, he waves, I slip. *Rewind.* I slip, recover…Wait.

Rewind. Play. I slip. No, *I'm hit.* Near my ribs there's a ripple, an indentation in my white T-shirt, and even now I suck breath as if something unseen has knocked the wind out of me. Like it did on the pipe.

Rewind. Wentz is too far away. No matter how many times I go back, he won't reach me in time.

Rewind. I was wrong—it's not a convulsion. I'm hit, I slip, and then it seems as if I'm...*tugged in the opposite direction*. Like a puppet.

Over the next two hours, I watch three more videos. None is as clear as Pete's. In a way, they're worse: I get a playback of the Hearts' commentary and they think it's all pretty funny, making fun of the funny girl.

This time the joke's on me.

THREE

Swanston Primary, Grade Three. The first day. We were
allowed to sit next to whoever we wanted for the first
term but the seat next to me stayed empty. I didn't know
anyone—I'd gone to a separate, smaller Junior Primary.
I was a farm kid who sometimes played with other farm
kids, and my brother was my best friend; I spoke the
language of trees and dogs and cattle, not kids with
glitter hair ties and brand-name sneakers. I spent recess
and lunch wandering around the yard without making
eye contact or speaking a word, waiting to be invited to
join in the other kids' games.

It didn't go so well. I wondered why the girls were all
in pairs, arms linked, as if their twin might be claimed if
they let go.

I remember feeling scruffy, different, bad-tempered. I don't remember noticing if there was anybody else like me. I stared at my feet and wished the day away.

My memory of the second day might not be so strong if it wasn't for Amber Richardson. Ten minutes into lunch, I looked up from my feet. I heard laughter. A crowd of kids had clustered around the bench nearest to the girls' toilets, and one boy was honking like the old goose who guarded our front dam. I stood on tiptoe, trying to see past them all, so much taller than me, with jostling bodies and mean elbows. I pushed my way to the front to find one girl sitting on the bench, crying, and two older girls barricading the toilet door.

Amber was skinny and limp-looking. Her freckles were pale orange against the hot pink of her face, and her knees were pressed together, ankles apart, toes turned in. The honking boy had picked up a stick; he was trying to lift her skirt, and I realised—with equal parts horror and fascination—that there was a slow drip coming from underneath her dress, and a puddle on the ground.

Before I could think, I stepped forward and put my foot on the stick, snapping it in half. I picked up both pieces and handed them to her. Honker gave me a dead arm for my trouble, but the crowd broke up, Amber scuttled into the toilets, and I wandered off.

Kenzie was the first friend I found.

I remember her standing in the classroom doorway wearing hand-me-down clothes, looking as if she might puke on the carpet; I remember offering the seat next to me. I can still picture the way she sat—so still, so serene—but her hands were shaking. I shared my lunch because she'd forgotten hers.

Kenzie says she found me. She swears it happened when she had to switch classes to even up the numbers, and our teacher pointed to the only spare seat.

That's Kenzie—always oversimplifying. She thinks I overdramatise everything. I guess it doesn't matter whose memory is real.

Kenzie and I stalked the playground in the second week, scooping up loose classmates. Pete Testa was first. He only had six rotten front teeth but he managed to tell us a long story, punctuated with bubbles of spit—something about Milo in his milk bottles and honey on his dummy. And although Pete was funny-looking, even then he was popular. But he still hung around with us.

Gummer was always by himself. Spookily quiet, a head taller than the next-biggest kid, he didn't seem to mind being alone, curled up inside the tunnel in the playground, reading his retro magazines. When we asked him to join us, he didn't even look up—it took him a full week to make up his mind.

Amber was last. She trailed behind us for the first few weeks. It was months before the others stopped calling her names, but she put up with it. Me, not so much. I defended her with fists and foul language—Kenzie, with her sweet voice and calm control.

We were the leftovers. Only it didn't feel that way. It felt like we chose each other carefully, to make sure all our odd shapes fitted together.

Kenzie and I had big dreams until we realised how small our lives really were. We'd lie on my bed and talk for hours about getting out of Swamptown—moving three hundred kilometres to the city, opening a cool wine bar with mismatched chairs and couches, the walls papered with the pages of Gummer's magazines. Our friends would come. We'd rent apartments in a building called Oasis or Nirvana with a fifty-metre pool, a gym and a rooftop garden; we'd spend our nights apartment-hopping, reclining on balconies, drinking cocktails and passing plates of fancy food. Kenzie would wear the fifties-style dresses and bright lipsticks she likes. I'd swan about, an androgynous artistic type, wearing shifts made from sacks and waving my expressive hands. Sometimes the wallpaper would change or we'd add a couple of rich boyfriends, but the dream remained the same. And we'd giggle and sigh and fall asleep smiling because everything is possible when you're twelve.

Now when we lie on my bed we talk about Mitchell being too shy to do anything but kiss Kenzie. If we do revisit the old fantasies, things have changed: Kenzie and Mitch share an apartment and I'm living next door (with a connecting hallway, but the thought of popping in and finding them playing Mr and Mrs Stow makes the dream fizzle out like a wet sparkler).

We talk about Amber making some arcane bargain with the devil last year and trading in her loyalty for popularity—or I talk about it, and Kenzie tells me she

34

loves me a little bit less when I judge.

Pete wants to drop out of school because his folks think he's only good for making pizza, but he's the one with the best chance of getting in with the in-crowd and out of this town. Everybody likes Pete. He scores laughs without trying. I think it has more to do with his expressiveness than his execution—he cracks himself up. It's contagious, like listening to a baby giggle. I'll spend months planning a prank, but Pete will do something unexpected, off the cuff, and everyone loses it.

Gummer's real name is Oliver Gomersall. He was Oli back in primary school, and for a while we called him Wally—he used to wear thick, black, lenseless frames because he read a psychological survey that showed how those who wear glasses are seen to be more intelligent. Later, he read that people who wore glasses without lenses were mocking hipsters. Then he discovered that people who genuinely needed glasses privately mocked those who wore glasses without lenses, so he threw them away. He thinks everything through, from every angle. He reads a lot, mostly books about true crime and conspiracy theories. Now everyone calls him Gummer; now he *needs* glasses but he refuses to wear them. He's kind of complicated. And these days Gummer is stoned *all* the time, tuned out to a life the rest of us can only dream about. His parents own the biggest station this side of Swanston— he could ditch school or switch schools if he wanted, but he doesn't seem to want anything. Apart from the Ford he drives, you'd think Gummer was homeless, the way he survives on free meals and couches.

And now when Kenzie and I are alone enough to really talk, it's all about the here and now and what *is* instead of what *could* be. Sometimes I want us to go back to being twelve and start over, to not let that dream slip through our fingers.

I sometimes wonder if dreams are like dandelion seeds: once you blow them off they take root somewhere else, with somebody who still believes.

Kenzie phones me late, after Mitchell has taken her home. She's stopped calling me when she's with him. Lately she calls less and less.

'Hello?'

'It's me.' She pauses. 'Kenzie.'

'Well, I know that.'

'Then don't say hello with a question mark,' she says. 'I wanted to know how you are. You left without telling me today.'

'I'm fine.' *I'm scared. I'm not feeling like myself. I have this awful sense that I'm suddenly carrying the weight of a thousand terrible histories and my hands are not my hands; they're shaking and the veins are moving like worms under my skin.* 'How are you?'

'You're lying. I'm coming over.'

'No, don't do that.'

'Then tell me the truth.'

'I'm cold. My chest feels weird.'

'Is it tight? Can you breathe?'

'In, out, right? In and out.'

'Grace, you're scaring me!'

I don't know where my next words come from. 'My heart is a room with an unwelcome visitor.'

'Stop it! It's not funny!'

'It's not meant to be. I'm so tired, Kenzie. I'm going to sleep now.' I hang up.

My phone rings another four times, then the house phone downstairs starts up.

Dad comes upstairs. 'She's here, Kenzie. She's fine.' He leaves the door open.

I roll onto my side. In my chest it feels like there are no ribs between my heart and my skin. I'm all shakes and jitters, but when I place my palm over the space where my heart should be there's the barest beat, so slow it's as if I'm hypothermic. Amber once said a panic attack made you feel as if you were going to die, but I just feel as if my bones are put together all wrong, and somebody else is breathing for me.

My heart is a room with an unwelcome visitor?

The heart is meat and gristle. That's all it is. Meat and gristle. Breathe. Breathe. I can't keep my eyes open; I'm conscious of a hole—a deep black nothing on the other side—and if I close my eyes I might fall in.

Morning is normal. Dad's truck is idling in the driveway. He and Cody are talking in the kitchen, a friendly conversation, something Dad and I never have.

'Grace!' Dad yells.

37

I drag myself out of bed and stumble to the top of the stairs. Diesel is curled up on the bottom step. He's never mastered stairs; until we moved here he'd never seen them. He watches me go up like I'm ascending to a heaven not for the likes of him—wistfully, with a touch of indignation. I'm sure he thinks it can only be done on two legs. He's probably practising in private.

He raises his head and pricks his ears.

'I'm up,' I call. My eyes are gritty and my skin feels clammy.

'Get ready for school. It's late. Your brother said he'll drive you.'

Great. Cody never stops talking. He puts every single thought into words; apparently he has a lot of them, but I need to be alone with mine. I toy with the idea of pulling another sickie, but there's a Biology test today and this time I studied for it. I need a decent mark to pull up the indecent ones.

I wipe beads of sweat from my upper lip. Maybe I'm sick. A virus. High temperatures can cause hallucinations and convulsions.

I shower and put on my crumpled school dress, my fingers fumbling with the buttons. The cotton is scratchy against my skin and the hem falls above my knees—too short to pass regulations, but Dad insists he won't waste money to replace a perfectly good uniform. It's only a matter of time before Principal Moore notices and I get a detention. I'm looking forward to the battle between him and Dad; Dad's as stubborn as a three-legged camel.

38

Gina, Dad's truck, pulls out of the driveway.

Eight-fifteen. I have less than ten minutes to put on make-up and shovel down some breakfast.

I reach for the light switch in the bathroom and hit smooth wall. Stupid—it's on the other side, not something I should forget. And the toilet seat has been left up, which means one of them has used it. I tie my hair in a high ponytail, wipe my face with a cool flannel and check my skin: blotchy, smudges under my eyes. They're hazel, but today they look green. One pupil is slightly larger than the other. I grab for my make-up bag and knock it off the counter—I know I'll waste more precious minutes picking up the scattered tubes and bottles, then proceed to waste precisely that amount of time thinking about picking them up, followed by the realisation that I've been standing in front of the mirror holding a razor.

What was I doing before this?

Make-up. Right.

'Grace!' Cody calls.

'Two minutes!'

Cody is uncharacteristically silent on the drive to school. He won't look at me. My brother takes after Dad: muscled, blond, tanned. I'm pale, fine-boned and dark-haired, like Mum, except her hair was shorter.

Like she *was*. I wonder if it still hurts Dad to look at me. He told me it did, once.

'What's wrong?' I ask. 'Are you pissed off at me, too?'

'You mean, Dad? He's not pissed at you, Grace. That's how he always is.'

'Not with you.' To cover the whine in my tone, I say in a hick accent, 'Y'all are bestest buds now, drinkin' brews in the shed. Probably lightin' each other's farts.' Cody always found anything to do with farts funny.

He doesn't find it funny. 'We're working on the car. It's taken *this* long for him to even look at it, so back off.'

This long. He means since Mum died. And the car—of all the things we left behind on the farm, all the untainted memories, we had to tow the carcass of Mum's red '78 Celica to suburbia, to a house only she could have loved. The back verandah is scattered with its innards and even the kitchen stinks like petrol and grease. It's like Dad's still working on Mum's bucket list after she's gone.

'Take it easy on him, will you? And be easier.' He adjusts the rear-vision mirror and turns up the volume on the radio. 'Because if you want the truth, you're bloody hard work, Grace.'

'Oh, I'm a girl so I should be easy.' I fold my arms over my chest and turn towards the window. 'It's only dumb pranks. You did worse.' Cody's changed sides. He's forgotten how to speak sibling.

He laughs. 'You think hot-wiring a teacher's car and parking it three streets away is a prank? You got off easy. I would have been charged for theft and probably expelled.'

'Kenzie hot-wired the car. I just drove.' I'm smirking but I don't want him to see. 'And I'm grounded. That's not getting off easy. Kenzie got off.'

'You've been grounded for half your life. Doesn't

40

stop you going anywhere. And Kenzie is a sweet kid—
you're the evil mastermind.' He pulls into the student car
park. 'I'm just saying, Dad's got a lot on his mind. Give
him a break, huh?'

I sigh. 'Yeah.' As I grab the doorhandle, he puts his
hand on my arm. I jump. We're not touchy-feely people.
'What?'

'Your face...I have to ask.'

'What's wrong with my face?' He's noticed. I knew
it. My eyes have changed.

'It's just...' He squirms. 'You look like something
from *Rocky Horror*.'

I lean across him and flick down the visor. I normally
wear mascara, concealer, lip gloss. That's it. But I look
like a clown. No, like a three-year-old has coloured me
in. In the dark. Green eyeshadow, black skids of eyeliner,
red over-sized mouth. No foundation, just clumpy puffs
of powder on my nose and cheeks. My hair is parted on
the side—me: middle part, always—and tied with a blue
ribbon.

I rip the ribbon off, reach into my bag, pull out a
packet of wet wipes and start scrubbing at my skin. Cody
watches me, lost for words again.

Nothing is normal.

Amber slips into her seat beside me in homeroom. She
used to be a tomboy, like Kenzie and me, but while we
quietly grew into our bodies and gave in ungracefully to
looking half-pretty and smelling nice most of the time,

Amber turned into an explosion of girl. Now her hair is long, straight, dyed a deep red. Her dress was new this term but it's already been shortened to above the knee; when she sits down, it rises to mid-thigh. Like an older sister, Amber has a sneaky way of bending school rules often enough that they're slackened for the rest of us. The shy girl who pissed her pants on the first day of Grade Three is long gone.

'Tamara Fraser is having a party next Saturday,' she says. 'She made a point of telling me no Swampies allowed.'

On any other day I'd see it as a challenge. 'Why are you even talking to Tamara Fraser?'

'Have you been crying?' she says. 'It looks like you've been crying.'

'No. I'm just not wearing any make-up.' My skin is dry and itchy where I've scrubbed it.

'Want to talk about it?'

'About what?'

She shrugs. 'Nothing.' She bites her lip. 'Okay, so Noah Wentz told me he doesn't think you were faking.'

A lightbulb goes on in my head. 'You've been consorting with the enemy.'

'Consorting?' Amber smiles dreamily. 'I have *loved* my enemy.'

She knows any girl with a beating heart has lusted after Noah Wentz at some point in her life, if not for all of it. Swampie Public doesn't have an equivalent god, so we've all lusted, we've all wanted him, but always from afar. This is treacherous new ground.

'You're trashy,' I say. 'It should be your name all over the wall, not mine.'

It's loud enough for everyone to hear over the noise of the hut we call a classroom. There's sudden quiet.

I clap my hand over my mouth. I've never said it aloud to her—only to Kenzie. Amber is a puzzle we all figured out long ago; she's predictable, bossy, broken, but harmless. And honest. Loyal. Loving. Trashy is a label other people give her because it's easier than trying to work her out.

Amber leans away. She seems half-irritated, half-pleased.

When did such a simple friendship get so complicated? I wonder what the others will think of me when she tells them—and she will. I've broken code. We're not the most popular, we're not cool, but we don't need anyone else. We have each other. We are—or we were—complete. Six virgins with no ambition except to survive high school and move on to Phase II—Nirvana with the rooftop garden—at least with our friendships intact, if not our virginities.

At this rate I won't survive high school. I'll be a dead friendless virgin.

FOUR

None of the crew is waiting around after school to walk with me or offer me a lift. Everyone has something pressing to do, except me. *Straight home*, Dad texted. *No excuses. Grounded means grounded this time. Embrace thine infinite boredom.* For once I'm okay with being grounded—after a whole day of avoiding people, batting away insults and steering clear of the wall, I'm close to tears and raw all over.

I blitzed the Biology test. I'm riding high on the relief that follows near-perfect recall of twenty-five facts about the endocrine system, as if a long-buried crypt had been opened in my brain. But then I remember what I said to Amber and my mood crashes; I'm imagining a fast and furious text relay where I'm bitched about, blacklisted and sentenced to eat lunch in exile for eternity.

I let myself into the house. Diesel's lying in his bed by the back door. He has his favourite soft toy tucked under his body, like he's hatching an egg, and there's another in his mouth. Six years ago we went to the shelter, took one look at his skinny black body and tiny paws, and brought him home. He was bits of this and that, and he stayed skinny and tiny for a few weeks, but then he grew. He didn't stop growing for two years. Cody says he's the love-child of a moose and a hyena.

Diesel's always carrying something around—if it's not a toy, it's a sock, a shoe, or somebody's underwear. He won't greet a stranger at the door without the security of having something in his mouth. If he decides he likes you, he'll offer it, drop it at your feet or in your lap; if he hasn't made up his mind, he'll test you. He'll spit out whatever he's carrying and wait, mouth open, almost smiling, and it's a race to jam something between his jaws before he latches onto a limb instead. He doesn't break skin; he just hangs on until you offer a sacrifice.

We keep a basket of odd socks near the front door.

I throw my bag onto the kitchen counter and grab a banana. I skin it and lob the peel into the bin. Crack shot. Except now I'm standing with a slimy, skinless banana in my hand and the sensation is utterly foreign—I always peel in increments, never the whole thing.

I am so confused. My head aches. There's a stabbing needle behind my damaged left eye, and the cloud-shaped scar seems bigger.

I groan. Diesel launches himself to a sit, ears pricked.

Maybe I have a bleed in my brain. A clot. A parasite. Confused. Con-fused. Conjoined. As in combined, merged, melded…except that's not what confused means, is it? It sounds like that's what it means. Stupid thoughts.

I groan again.

Diesel drops his soft toy. He sidles up to my leg and sniffs. He cocks his head and a low growl vibrates in his throat. I reach down to pat him.

And he bites.

There's a sickening pop, more sensation than sound. A fang punctures the base of my thumb. I yelp and tug my hand away. Diesel spits it out as if he doesn't know what it is or how it got there; he drops his head and sways in anguish. For a second, I think *it's nothing, it doesn't really hurt, his pain is worse than mine.* But the pain kicks in when I see the blood. I stare at the wound: it only oozes at first, just a light tickle, a wet trickle. Then it begins to pulse and I can time my heartbeat by it; I'm thinking *I can't remember if thumbs have arteries* and *I know arterial blood is supposed to be bright red but blood is always red* and out of nowhere comes: *blood is black.*

Diesel growls again.

I make the vicious sound we keep for when he pees inside or chews things he shouldn't. '*Baaaad dog. Aaaaach.*'

Diesel drops to the floor and rolls belly up: classic submissive stance. He's sorry, but instinctively I know if I touch him he'll bite again. His ears are flat to his head and his tail is tucked. Like Dad always says about me:

instinct is stronger than good manners.

I cradle my hand and move slowly to the bathroom, turn the tap and run cold water over my thumb. It's weeping but the bleeding has slowed. The flesh around the wound is bruised and puffy. A tangle of veins bulges under my skin.

Diesel has followed me; he peers around the door, sad-eyed, but his hackles are raised. He's on alert, the same way he is when fireworks go off on New Year's Eve. In return, I'm wary of him and what he senses about me. My own senses are off-kilter, spinning like a broken compass. I'm freezing hot and seeing stars in a haze of red; I'm bone-tired but my muscles are restless and twitching. It's as if I'm too full. Something squirms in my intestines like some kind of malignant bloat, and behind my left eye is the relentless, stabbing pain.

I sit on the floor and cover my other eye with the palm of my good hand. The pain eases, the red haze fades to pink, but my damaged eye is playing tricks; the familiar, drifting cloud has disappeared. In its place, a black smudge, dancing across the wall, just out of direct vision. I can't catch it, so I stare straight ahead. The smudge has a life of its own—it darts behind me, and I turn so quickly the tendons in my neck burn.

It's gone.

Diesel slinks away. I unclench my hand—the bite is bad. The blood is turning black.

Dad never hesitated to pop a slug behind the farm dogs' ears if they showed signs of bad character, if they started nipping at sheep or developed a taste for blood. Diesel is as good as dead if I tell, and I know that's not fair. It's something about me that set him off.

'Dad?'

'Yeah.'

He's glued to the late news, beer in hand, still wearing his work clothes, Diesel at his feet. The patch of carpet underneath his boots is worn through to the underlay and the couch slumps to one side, just like Dad. We moved the furniture, but nothing has changed; everything sags. We've given up.

'I cut myself on a nail. I should get a Tetanus shot.'

'How'd you manage that?' He doesn't look up.

'You know...climbing fences.'

'How bad is it?'

'Just a precaution.'

He sighs. 'You have to be more careful.'

'I know.'

He changes the channel. 'I suppose I need to sign something.'

'Probably.'

'When did you last have a shot?' He reaches down and rubs Diesel's ears, shaking his head. 'I should know this stuff, huh?'

'I don't remember. Three, maybe four years ago.'

'Cody can take you.' Diesel growls and Dad cuffs him lightly. 'What's up with you, boy?'

'I can take myself.' I wait. Dad's sitting down and

I have his attention, sort of. I should tell him there's something worse going on with me than a dog bite or a scratch from a rusty nail. I won't mention Diesel. I'll tell him about the freakish pain and the weird sentences I say, the screwed-up thoughts I think, and the things I see that aren't there. Maybe Dad will sign something and they'll plug me into a machine that will make it all stop. 'Dad?'

'Yeah.'

An unholy screech sounds somewhere above my head and I crouch, hands over my ears. Diesel erupts, scrabbling across the carpet, barking, spraying slobber and snapping at air. Dad calmly gets up, crosses the room and stuffs a sock between Diesel's jaws, but he keeps barking and gagging while Dad looks up at the ceiling with his hands on his hips, then down to me, still crouched on the floor.

He grabs my elbow and hauls me up. 'Grace, get the gun.'

I run, skidding sideways on the kitchen linoleum. *The gun? Where's the gun?* I catch sight of my own reflection in the kitchen window and freeze.

'Grace? What's wrong with you? Get the broom.'

The broom. Get the broom.

I get the broom.

The part of me still able to think rationally knows Dad doesn't notice Diesel is barking at me. It takes longer for me to register that the screeching is the smoke alarm. Surely he sees my hair, crackling with static and standing on end as if the world has tipped upside down or I'm the wrong way up, but Dad only says, 'Something must have shorted out.' He reaches for the broom and stabs the detector with the handle until it spills its electronic guts, then he walks out, muttering something about a torch.

I step back into the darkness of the hall, away from the screeching, which has stopped, at least outside my head. My hair settles heavily on my shoulders. I wait, sitting on the bottom step of the stairs—too scared to go up alone and terrified to stay where I am—while Dad rummages in the fuse box outside.

Diesel watches me from underneath the coffee table. This time he's not sorry.

FIVE

Me: *Are you mad at me?*

   Kenzie: *I'm not mad.*

   Me: *Are you avoiding me?*

   Kenzie: *I'm not avoiding you!*

   Me: *Where were you this morning? I had an early doc appt but I waited at Reilly's. You could have texted.*

   Kenzie: *Sorry. I was running late.*

   Me: *Okay. See you at lunch?*

   Kenzie: *Eating at Mitchell's. See you after school.*

It's not hard for Kenzie to avoid me—if that's what she's doing. The teachers got wise to our sneaky disruptions a long time ago and this year we only have two classes together, four times a week.

I wait for her—again—in the student car park after school, conscious that I'm standing there with a pathetically hopeful expression on my face, the only one of us with a licence and no access to a car. Cody won't let me near his Commodore. We had to sell the farm ute and Dad won't let anyone drive Gina. And I don't want to drive a truck anyway. Even Amber, who's already had two minor accidents, is allowed to borrow her parents' car whenever she wants.

My skin is greasy with sweat and my backpack feels as heavy as a wet sandbag.

'Grace!' It's Gummer, pulled over in the bus zone, out on the street. Cars are banked up behind his Ford but he either doesn't notice or doesn't care. 'Want a lift?'

I glance at my phone. No messages. It's twenty to four already, and the cars stuck behind Gummer are starting to ride their horns.

'Coming!'

I throw my bag into the back seat and climb in. The cab stinks of weed and the great unwashed. Gummer is wearing the same HR Giger T-shirt he had on yesterday and the day before that.

'Did you skip school?' I ask. I sound nasal from trying to breathe through my mouth.

He shakes his head. 'I went. I have to keep my attendance up.'

'You have to smoke less weed,' I grumble, and lower the window. 'Let me drive.'

He pulls over.

'Really?'

He grins. 'Yeah. I could do with a nap. Just drive until I tell you to stop.'

We switch places, and he surprises me by doing exactly that: reclining the passenger seat and pulling his beanie over his eyes. I pull out into traffic. The Ford is a great, hulking beast of a thing. I can barely see over the dash. My phone beeps somewhere in the depths of my bag but I ignore it, cruising past Lumpy's, the pizza bar where Pete works, the shopping strip, the cemetery and Centennial Park. And because I'm in a different car and I think it can't possibly hurt me now—it's been two years—I turn down Waites Street and head for the intersection.

Halfway along I change my mind, but it's too late. I can't turn safely—no U-turns allowed. I have to keep going. I can't close my eyes or I'll crash Gummer's house on wheels.

If every second above ground is precious, why does someone spend their last minutes on earth doing something as mundane as shoving groceries into the back of her car? One minute Mum was here and the next she wasn't, carved up by a truck driver on the corner of Waites and Blaine on her way home from shopping. Dad, Cody and I take a three-block detour to avoid passing the intersection and that tiny white shrine—not something we built, not really hers.

Someone tends it, keeps it fresh and white, but not us. Most people probably have a story about the time someone they love didn't come home or went missing for a short time, just slipped from the edges of their vision, even for a moment. Mothers, sisters, brothers, children. And maybe a million awful thoughts took root in their minds, and they were sick with worry, sweating, pacing, waiting for news. But we didn't do that. Cody was asleep on the couch. Dad was outside, priming the pump for the dam. I was practising a card trick in my room. Nobody noticed Mum hadn't come home until the police arrived and everything stopped. Even when Sergeant Miller got us all together, we just stood looking at each other. Dad said to Cody, 'What'd you do?' Cody shrugged and said, 'Nothing worth a home visit,' and I remember thinking whatever it was, if it was bad, I wouldn't be able to go to school camp on Monday.

The lights turn red. The Ford lurches to a stop. It's right there: the white cross, adorned with faded plastic flowers. I rest my head on the steering wheel and suck breath. *Plastic flowers*. The ache behind my eye is back, as if the capillaries are exploding. I'm vaguely aware of a car behind the Ford, tooting.

Maybe I didn't get the grieving part right; maybe I didn't let it out. Like when Diesel gets grass seeds between his toes—Dad said you have to leave the wound open until it drains of poison. With no exit, a single seed could travel all the way to his brain. What if madness is really grief, trapped inside? You think it's gone but it's still in you, worming through your flesh, infecting everything.

'They don't get any greener,' Gummer says. 'Are you

okay?' He sits up, leans out the window, and gives the driver behind a lazy finger. 'Pull over, Grace.' His expression is so sad and stoned and kind, I burst into tears.

Gummer ends up piling his things on our couch. Nobody ever remembers inviting him—he shows up, parks on the lawn, helps himself, leaves his stuff lying around so he has an excuse to come back, and disappears in the morning without thanks or goodbye.

Dad and Cody accept his presence and his stink. They give him beer. They talk to him more often than they talk to me. Cody reckons Gummer is some kind of genius under the stoner veneer; Dad says he puts up with Gummer because he gets a lot of agricultural work from the Gomersalls. I suspect he likes his company because he's easy.

At seven o'clock, Gummer has already eaten everything remotely resembling food from our pantry and fridge. He says, 'Want to go get Pete-za?'

'I'm grounded.'

'Go,' Dad says.

I stare at him.

'What? You think I like having you moping around when *Ice Road Truckers* is on? Go.'

Lumpy's is the best pizza bar in Swanston. It's only the best because of Pete. Every pizza is a custom-designed wood-fired work of art; you only have to say your name over the phone or show your face, and Pete knows what you want. He keeps his uncle Lumpy out

55

the back, sour-faced in a sweaty singlet, spinning bases and stoking the fire.

'Ladies,' Pete says when we walk in. It's quiet for a Thursday, only one couple in a booth at the back. If he's surprised we're here he doesn't show it. 'Are you eating or visiting?' He has flour on his nose.

'Gummer ate all our food,' I say. 'So, eating.'

He selects a small base, spreads Lumpy's special sauce and adds my toppings: roasted pumpkin and capsicum, Gruyere cheese. He'll add a sprinkling of fresh baby spinach after it's cooked. For Gummer, it's a large with BBQ sauce and everything except olives, plus extra mozzarella. Pete calls it The Gumbo. Kenzie likes Hawaiian (The Wallflower), Amber doesn't like pizza (A Travesty), and Mitch always orders pepperoni plus pineapple (Baby Spice). Pete makes himself an Anchovy Pastie, which is disgusting and would probably be a calzone if it wasn't an affront to all calzone.

Mine's called The Disgrace.

'Mitch and Kenzie came in earlier,' Pete says, wiping the counter. 'They've definitely done it.'

It sets off a chain reaction: a spark in my brain that lights a fuse in my blood and ends up burning a hole in my belly. I'm not hungry anymore. 'Shut up, Pete.'

'Charming. I'm only telling you what I know.'

'Shut up, Pete,' Gummer says. He sits down in the booth nearest the counter. 'Grace saw the shrine today.'

'Shut up, Gummer.' I sit across from him, pick up a shaker of Parmesan cheese and tip a pile onto the table.

'It's no big deal.' I pinch the pile into a pyramid.

Pete's quiet until the couple at the back leave, then he turns up the radio and starts dancing to 'Mambo No. 5', trying to whip his own arse with a tea towel. 'I'd like a little bit of Monica,' he says. 'Except there's a rumour she has chlamydia.'

I laugh until my face hurts and for a moment everything is okay.

Gummer says, 'You're burning my Gumbo. And I need to pee.' He leaves the booth.

Pete sighs and slices the pizza. He brings us two glasses of water and slides the trays onto the table. 'One Disgrace. You know I have to get Gruyere in special, just for you? Bon appetit. Do you think Gummer's lighting up in the toilet?'

'Thanks. And maybe.'

'What happened to your hand?' Pete says.

My thumb throbs. The clean dressing is now covered with cheese. I didn't need a shot after all—the doctor said a booster lasted ten years. 'I put a nail through it.'

'For laughs? Or for stupid?'

'An accident.'

Pete purses his lips. 'Phew. Thought you were going to tell me you had experienced the stigmata.'

'Not recently.' I don't like his tone—Pete's always been my biggest fan.

I'm eyeing my pizza and it doesn't appeal. The Gumbo does, however, so I help myself to a slice. Gummer's standing in the back of the shop, talking on his phone.

'Is there something wrong with yours?' Pete says pointedly.

'He won't mind. Gummer would eat roadkill if we locked him out of our houses.' Pete watches as I roll up a second slice and feed it down my throat. 'What? I'm hungry,' I say, mouth full. Three slices. Four. I'm usually the last to finish but now I'm barely chewing. It's as if I haven't eaten in days. There's sauce on my wrists and oil on my chin. I wipe my hands on my T-shirt. Five.

Pete's shaking his head. He throws me the tea towel. 'Grace has her nose in your trough,' he says to Gummer, who's come up behind him. 'It's fascinating and kinda gross.'

'You're eating offal?' Gummer slides into the booth.

Offal is what I call processed meat. I don't eat it, as a general rule. Now I can feel it: my last mouthful clumped at the back of my tongue, grease and gristle in my teeth. One minute I wasn't hungry and now I've eaten like I was starving. I spit the mouthful into a napkin and groan.

'I feel weird.' I rest my forehead on the cool table.

Five minutes ago I had a hole inside me that threatened to cave in if I didn't fill it; now the hole is filled, it's like I voluntarily gorged myself on five slices of evil.

'That was like watching a freakin' pie-eating contest.' Pete laughs.

I look up. 'Quit laughing. I'm not your entertainment.'

Gummer is staring at me with the same sad, gentle expression. 'Grace saw the shrine today,' he says again, as if that explains everything.

58

SIX

Me: *Sorry I missed you yesterday. Sorry I didn't call you back :)*

Kenzie: *No biggie. I only waited for half an hour.*

Me: *Gummer gave me a ride.*

Kenzie: *Lucky you.*

Me: *I thought you weren't coming :(*

Kenzie: *Well I did.*

Me: *Can we talk? Meet you at Reilly's usual time?*

Kenzie: *Can't, I'm already at school. English essay due today, remember?*

Me: *I know. Thanks for the reminder. I did mine. I can help if you want.*

Kenzie: *When???*

Me: *Last night. Couldn't sleep. Stayed up till 3.*

Kenzie: *How very unlike you. Congratulations.*
Me: *Don't be mean :(*
Kenzie: *I have to finish this. Talk later.*
Me: *Okay xxx*

The last class on Fridays is double Art. It's another subject I bumble through. I don't mind art theory. It's just facts and dates and critical responses; either you get your facts straight or your response is perfectly valid even if you don't know what you're talking about. But making art—I suck. We all know I suck. Kenzie's quite good and Gummer's insanely talented—he's been obsessed with Giger since primary school—but I have a serious disconnect between my eyes, my brain, my fingers and the paper.

The art room smells of turpentine and a new brand of Mrs Miskov's incense, something fruity and exotic. Immediately, my headache returns. Mrs Miskov tells us to set up for life drawing. Most of us groan. The studio vibrates with the click-clack-scrape of easels and whispering paper.

Kenzie sets up her easel next to mine. She leaves twice the usual gap between us, crowding Gummer into a corner. He glances at me and raises his eyebrows.

I shrug. 'Five bucks says it's the plastic pears.' Mrs Miskov loves making us draw pears. '"Think of the fruity flesh as the sensual curve of a woman's buttock",' I mutter. '"Pay particular attention to the dimples."'

Gummer snickers. Kenzie throws me a warning look

and turns away, waiting serenely for instruction. I let loose a theatrical sigh at the worst moment: set-up is complete and the class is quiet and still.

'Grace Foley.' Mrs Miskov swishes over to me. A purple bandana pins down her crazy hair and she's wearing one of her long, jingling skirts that make her seem as if she's levitating.

Great. She's going to put me on charcoal ration duty, or worse, pencil sharpening. I've sharpened more pencils in the last five years than there are comments on my school record.

'Choose a subject, Grace.'

'Pardon?'

'A subject for life drawing today. A person.' She smiles and sweeps a semi-circle with her palm. 'Anyone you like.'

Hands pop up. If you pose, you don't have to draw. If you pose, you nap. Arnold Pettigrew puts his hand up. He's bony with see-through red ears and oversized nostrils. He'd be the popular choice for a laugh, but this isn't caricature drawing. I'm not shooting for laughs today.

Amber eyes me steadily from the opposite corner. She wants to model, I can tell, but she won't put her hand up. It's undignified. If I choose Amber, it's nepotism; if I don't, I'm disloyal. And it's clever of Mrs Miskov to make me choose—either way I wear some blame for an hour and a half of silent torture. Damned, whatever I do.

'Grace? We don't have all day.'

'Amber,' I say. I owe her for what I said.

Amber smiles and a few guys clap. She slips off her shoes and wanders into the centre of the studio, swaying her hips. She starts unbuttoning her dress.

'Clothes on, Amber,' Mrs Miskov says, followed by a chorus of boos. 'Strike a pose. One you can hold for a while, please. Grace, hand out the charcoal.'

Amber drags a chair into the centre of the studio and sits, slouching. She presses her knees together, sets her feet apart, and folds her arms. Her eyelids droop.

'Get started. Remember to focus your eye on the negative space. Loose elbows and wrists.' Mrs Miskov leaves the studio.

I take a box of variegated charcoal from her desk and work my way around the room, passing out the sticks. I set aside a few pieces for myself. It's quiet, apart from chalky squeaks and the odd snap and grunt when somebody presses too hard.

I study Amber. Where do I start? Her face? Her legs? What the hell is negative space again? *The only negative space is between her ears.*

Gummer's busy sketching already.

Amber watches me from beneath clumpy lashes. She's left the two top buttons of her dress undone.

I peek at Gummer's sketch to see that Amber has no head—he's started with her chest. The quiet, Amber's intensity, the teacher's absence—it's a moment ripe for comedy. I glance at Kenzie. She knows what I'm thinking. She shakes her head and the moment is lost when Mrs Miskov returns.

Sighing, I turn back to my easel, staring at the blank sheet until black dots begin to dance on the paper. Fifteen minutes already gone. The needle's at the back of my eye. My head is pounding now and my ears buzz with a persistent hum. Surely everyone can hear it? The smell of incense clogs my throat; my arms feel impossibly heavy, as if they're strapped to my sides. I recognise the panic beginning to course through my bloodstream, wrapping its tentacles around my organs. When I look at Kenzie I can't remember a single thing about us; it's as if I knew her once, long ago, and she's nothing more than a fading memory.

Someone is breathing too loudly.

I dip my fingertips in the dust in the bottom of the charcoal box and paint cloudy smears, leaving a ghostly white silhouette in the centre. The dots still dance. If I squint they look like a line of marching ants. Or tiny numbers. All I have to do is play connect the dots. I pick up the stick and follow the numbers: hard, black lines. The charcoal shatters but I go on, trying not to let the numbers get too far ahead, or I'll lose them. I grind each piece to a nub, and when I run out I use my fingers and the corner of an eraser, working the dust, smudging: light here, dark there. An eye. Lashes. A bridge of nose and one slender arm, reaching. Her hand must be pressed against the glass; I can see it clearly in my mind, but I can't quite master the delicate spread of her fingers. I can't find the shape. She glares at me accusingly. Brisk lines to lower her arm and conceal her hand in the fold of her dress; her eye loses its gentleness and becomes hard, glittery. I reach for a fresh stick to cover up the shadow of her hand and work it: vertical dark slashes with lighter sections, and markings like whorls of wood. Horizontal, now. A frame. The image spills over the edges of the paper, bleeding into the board. The numbers have disappeared but I don't know how to stop. *I'm ruining it. Too much darkness.* The hum sounds like a jeering crowd now; the panic is gone, replaced with a deep, unrelenting sadness that seems like the last emotion I will ever feel.

Snap. The charcoal breaks.

'Grace.' A tug on my elbow.

My hands fall. I lean against the bench behind me. Where has the time gone?

'Okay.' Mrs Miskov claps her hands. 'Finish up now. Turn your easels.'

'Grace.' Kenzie is squeezing my arm. 'What the hell?' She peers closely at my drawing and recoils. It's her turn to look at me as if I'm someone she doesn't recognise.

The loud breathing is mine. I created this. Me, but not me. I feel disoriented, as if I've just woken up. Kenzie seems frightened. She steps closer to Gummer and whispers. He looks across. His expression twists into something like disgust. No...it's envy.

Mrs Miskov works her way around the studio, inspecting our drawings. 'Interesting, Jenna. You've shown a lot of improvement. Matt, try varying the thickness of your lines. Great, Tori. Very expressive work.'

Amber's close behind her, frowning, disappointed with much of the work.

'We have to get rid of it,' I mutter to Kenzie. Wherever this thing came from, I want it to go back there. I pick at the tape holding the paper, but Mrs Miskov is waiting.

'I didn't finish,' I say.

'Grace, I'd like to see your work, please.'

Slowly, I turn the easel.

Mrs Miskov gapes and steps back. Her hand flutters at her throat. 'Well,' she says after a long pause. 'This is unexpected. It's quite unsettling, isn't it?' She turns to address the group. 'Notice that the mistakes are still evident. Rather than erasing the line of the arm here,' she points, 'Grace has simply worked over the top, which leaves an impression of movement. Here and here, the lines are overworked. They're a little vicious. A bit more restraint and this might have been remarkable. What do you think of Grace's interpretation, Amber?'

Mrs Miskov's face is seven shades of purple. She's babbling. I know it; she knows it. If I was capable of speech, I'd babble, too.

'That's not me,' Amber says. 'The girl is wearing pyjamas. And either Grace has been practising or...'

'Or what?'

'Or she's passing off somebody else's work as hers,' someone says.

Mrs Miskov appears relieved to be offered an explanation. 'Is that true, Grace?'

Amber is right. The girl's hair is longer. Her face is thinner. Her eyes are arctic, not brown and soft. She's

65

framed by a window, not sitting in a chair. And the angle is all wrong, as if she was observed from below rather than from across the room.

'I don't know,' I say finally. Kenzie. 'Kenzie saw.'

But she only shrugs and makes an apology with her eyes. 'I didn't see.'

'I need an answer, Grace.'

Dozens of eyes are staring me down. I've always loved being the centre of attention, but not like this. 'Dark magic,' I say, and it comes out sounding cheeky and not thoroughly freaked out, which is how I really feel.

'Sometimes you go too far with your pranks, Miss Foley.' She rips the tape from the easel, rolls the drawing into a cylinder, and hands it to me. 'I'll see you after school in the front office. We'll discuss it further there.' She claps her hands. 'Pack up.'

A hand on my arm makes me jump. Arnold Pettigrew. 'That's not Amber,' he says.

'I know.'

'It's that missing girl, Hannah Holt.'

'I know that, too,' I reply, but I don't know how. I feel connected to her in some way, but I don't know her story beyond an urban legend and a blurred image on a Missing poster.

I do know this: she's under my skin.

'Grace, a couple of years back, you left a dollop of red paint the shape of a lipstick kiss on my chair. Do you

66

remember?' Mrs Miskov is leaning over her desk, her hands busy moving the wooden limbs of an artist's mannequin. 'I certainly won't ever forget.'

'That wasn't me.' I'm slouching, sullen. It's half past three and I've probably missed any chance of a ride home.

She frowns. 'I'll admit, I had my doubts at the time. It was juvenile and your methods are usually quite sophisticated. You know, if you put half the time you spend perfecting pranks into learning, you'd be a joy to teach. I'm not the only one who thinks so.' She touches the rolled-up drawing lying on the desk. 'Case in point. Unless…' She waits.

'Unless what?'

'Unless *this* wasn't you, either.' She moves her hand as if to swat a fly. 'I think the best way to sort this out is for you to complete a little exercise.' She places the mannequin in front of me. It's poised in some kind of ballet move, balancing on one foot, arms above its head. She hands me a pencil and a sketchbook.

'I don't…'

'I'll leave you for a few minutes. I'd hate to distract you. Is fifteen minutes enough time to practise your dark magic?' She smiles as she closes the door.

I pick up the pencil and open the sketchbook. She was right to have doubts: I wasn't responsible for the paint on her skirt. That was kids' stuff. I've never pranked Mrs Miskov; I like her, even if she thinks the worst of me. I stare at the mannequin. I feel nothing again. I wonder if this is all some kind of passing sickness—like the year I had hives, suddenly and for no apparent reason—or if I'll have to wonder what's real and what isn't for the rest of my life, if crazy is my new normal.

I draw the figure as I see it—stick-like—and autograph the bottom of the page. Sit back, drumming my fingers on the desk. Stare at the wall. Bite my nails.

Last night, I wrote a thousand-word essay, effortlessly, when I should have been sleeping, and today I've sketched a dead girl. I have a brain tumour—that must be it. Like in that movie with John Travolta, when he has headaches and sees flashing lights and he turns into a genius and invents life-changing technology and learns a whole new language in a single day. But he dies. A tumour is a distinct possibility—an awful one. I'd rather believe in the possibility of ghosts and possession—but ghosts are high on my family's list of No Such Things, along with aliens and honest politicians.

I reach for the drawing, unroll it, and pin down the edges using Mrs Miskov's tape dispenser and stapler. The charcoal has smudged but the girl's face is still eerily familiar. She's unhappy, maybe angry. She has a glint of a challenge in her expression.

I roll up the sketch and shove it into my bag. It's mine, regardless of how it came to be.

I'll just have to accept my punishment. I close the sketchbook with a slap, and the sound sets off the mannequin's sudden collapse, like it has no bones.

SEVEN

On Saturday night, in a desperate attempt to reclaim my old self, I call Kenzie, Pete, Gummer and Amber to tell them we're crashing Tamara Fraser's party. Nothing like a prank to make me feel like everything's right with the world, and Tamara is the worst kind of private school snob. She needs binoculars to bring the view down her nose into focus.

Gummer's in. So is Pete, and Amber doesn't need any convincing. Kenzie and Mitch had plans for a quiet night in—it takes me a few minutes to talk Kenzie into it. She covers her phone but I can hear him: *Why do you let her do this? You promised…Tell her we're busy.* Kenzie spits something sharp and he backs off. It's all I can do not to take a dig at her for letting Mitch murder her mojo, when she says, 'Sounds like fun,' and tells me she's glad I'm feeling better. They'll meet us there at nine.

Cody and Dad are working on the car in the shed, and judging by the *pop-shhh-tinkle* sounds, they're working their way through a carton of beer. I lock my bedroom door from the inside and leave the TV volume loud enough for them to think I've fallen asleep with it on.

For the first time in ages I let Gummer pick me up. He doesn't seem his usual level of wasted—at least not until we park at the end of Tamara's street and he lights up. The house is an elegant two-storey with a miniature replica for a letterbox and a perfect, sloping front lawn. From here, the house twinkles with fairy lights like it's still Christmas, but there's nobody out the front. In Swampie terms it's not a real party unless it spills onto the street.

I text Amber. She replies to say she's already here, inside the house, which confirms my suspicion that she was invited. Pete turns up ten minutes later on foot, since his house is only three streets away, and climbs into the back seat. While we wait for Kenzie and Mitch, a nasty feeling is eating away at my insides. Not nerves—something else.

'That lawn is begging for a burnout,' Pete says.

Gummer breathes out smoke. 'Way to announce our arrival, Doughboy.'

I fan my face. 'Gummer's right.'

Pete says, 'Someone text Kenzie and Mitch. I need a drink.'

It's Kenzie and Mitch now. No more Kenzie and Grace.

'I don't think they're coming.' I get out of the car. 'Let's go. First one to puke on the carpet is a legend.' I'm striding up the driveway, Pete and Gummer close behind.

Pete's laughing, asking, 'What am I if I pee in the pool?'

Gummer says, 'Stupid. The water will turn red and everyone will know it's you.'

Pete snorts. 'That's the whole point, dickhead.'

Gummer's comment about the water turning red makes me giggle. I'm thinking three amigos will have to do. Kenzie thinks she's in lurve. Amber's always had one foot outside the circle, and Mitch thinks he's better than the rest of us.

'Guys, I need a diversion,' I instruct. 'Get everyone to come out the front. Nothing too destructive. Or self-destructive.'

We go in through the side gate and follow the music. A wide path winds through a lush tropical garden, leading to a set of steps and a large deck. R&B, lots of bass, seems to be coming from all corners of the backyard. I can't see any speakers. A couple of Sacred Heart Year Twelve girls are leaning over the railing. They nudge each other and shuffle aside on their heels, leaving the next group to raise the alarm: a circle of nine or ten, boys and girls, sitting under a huge Balinese thatched hut off to one side of the pool.

'Swampies!'

Gummer peels away left and, as faces turn, he raises his hand and spreads his fingers in a Vulcan greeting. He wanders through the open double doors and into the house, grooving to his own beat, followed by a conga line of concerned citizens. Pete heads straight for the outdoor bar and helps himself to a beer. In the ensuing tussle between him and a Sacred Heart white knight twice his size, a glass shatters on the tiles.

I skip back down the steps, duck behind a giant palm, and wait.

'Hey.'

I jump, but it's only Amber. I grab her elbow and pull her behind the tree. She's wearing something short, black and slinky, with high heels that make her seem six inches taller. They sink into the soft dirt.

She slips them off, muttering to herself.

'How come no one yells Swampie when you turn up?' I say.

She just smiles. 'So, spill it. What's the plan? Just don't hurt Noah. I need him in one piece.'

'Traitor. You didn't answer my question. Whose side are you on?'

'My side,' she says. 'The trash and trouble side. Let's face it—they need us and we need them. Otherwise this whole town would choke on its own boringness. Plan?' She snaps her fingers. 'And where's Mitch and Kenzie?'

The buzz in my ears has started up and I feel sick. 'Tamara Fraser's swimming pool is far too blue.' I reach into my pocket.

'Go on,' she says.

'I have a bottle of Rockin' Red Party Pool dye.'

Amber laughs. 'Welcome back, Grace Foley.'

'Hey, I never left.' It's a droning now, like a fever of mosquitos. 'Can you hear that?' I slap at my face.

The music shuts off.

'What? I can't hear anything. Wait, here comes the cavalry.'

Pete's yelling. He's flanked by two senior guys who have him headlocked as they drag him into the house. I bet Gummer's somewhere inside, calmly causing chaos. Amber and I wait until everyone follows, leaving the backyard empty, with hardly a sound but the waves slapping against the pool steps.

She picks up her shoes.

'Where are you going?'

'I'm going to referee. Someone has to make sure nobody gets hurt.' She disappears through the doors. All the noise is now coming from the front of the house.

Every instinct is telling me to get out of there, but Pete and Gummer have kept their end of the bargain—I need to keep mine. It's been a long time between laughs.

I swallow the sour burn in my throat, leave the shadows and creep over to the edge of the pool. Despite the warmth of the breeze, the hairs on my arms are standing on end.

A crackle of static makes me jump. I glance back at the house: every room on the ground floor is flooded with light, but I can't see anyone inside. The static is coming from the speakers. I see them now, impossibly small, six or so dotted in high corners around the deck, the hut and the bar.

The pool is long and narrow, a whirlpool of current stirred by a set of swim jets in the shallow end. I unscrew the cap, kneel down, and tip the contents of the bottle of dye into the stream. For a moment I wonder if it's enough, but the colour hits the current and vibrant red clouds swirl like the blowback of blood into a syringe. Within seconds it settles into an even mix: a brackish purplish red. It's revolting. It's beautiful.

My rules for self-preservation kick in: leave no evidence, exit the scene, tell no one. Bow out before the punchline. I stuff the empty bottle into my pocket and rub my pink-stained hands on my black jeans. Somehow, I've managed to spill dye on myself: a mark that looks like skinned flesh covers my forearm and there's a bloom of red, like a gunshot wound, over my left boob. Swearing, I reach into the pool, rinse my arm and splash water on my chest. The red is spreading now and my palms look as if I've committed murder.

I stand too quickly, sway, and reach for a deck post to support myself. I feel drunk, outside of my body. The bitterness in my mouth is in my veins, too. Staining the pool must have only taken minutes, but it's as if I've been here for hours.

I stagger to the steps, heading for the path at the side of the house. As I reach the deck, the speakers screech a burst of feedback. The nearest one sparks. I duck and weave, but each time I move, the speakers whine and fizz. I'm desperate to leave, terrified they'll hear me, and the worst of it is the voice in my head telling me *look up, look up, something is coming*. I have to leave before they all come back outside, and I have to put distance between myself and whatever is coming before I pass out, throw up, crack up or, *God help me*, look up.

My body hums and twangs with vibration. It's an oddly soothing sensation now. I stop moving. And I look up.

A black shape hurtles from the darkness. It's a bird, small and graceful in flight. Just a bird. But the bird swoops at a sudden and horrifying angle, flying straight into the wide glass doors at the rear of the house. The impact is devastating—it drops like a stone. Shock squeezes my chest, but before I can move to pick it up, there are more flutterings, the rustle of many wings.

Pshoom. Pshoom-pshoom-pshoom. Pshoom-pshoom. Six of them, shooting like black bullets into the pool, leaving plumes of luminous bubbles. When their tiny bodies break the surface, somehow I know they're dead.

I'm released by whatever was keeping me still, left alone with shock and confusion and carnage. I crawl up onto the deck and pick up the body of the first bird. It's broken but still warm.

But I'm not alone.

Kenzie's standing at the side of the house. She's frozen to the spot, staring, dressed in full prank gear—black T-shirt, black boots and jeans. She might have been late, but up until this moment she was still with me. I imagine what she sees: me, cradling a limp crow, the stained pool, the floating bodies, the crimson puddles on the tiles.

I drop the bird. I hold out my hands, truly shockingly red palms up, asking her for…help? Understanding? Forgiveness?

Kenzie shakes her head and turns away. She's crying. She doesn't recognise me anymore.

I don't blame her for leaving—I know how it must look. And I know that whatever horror I imagined was coming might take the shape of a suicidal bird or a vision, a smudge on a wall, a dog bite, a bad dream or the uncanny likeness of a dead girl, but those things are not its true shape. And it isn't coming; it was already here.

Gummer's driving. It's Sunday night, just before dark, and Yeoman's Track is deserted. After the pool prank, Gummer took me home and stayed the night on our couch. I haven't told him about Kenzie. By his count, we're tied one-all against Sacred Heart as we head into the school holidays, but at least we've clawed back some credibility after losing the pipe record.

'This is a bad idea,' he says. 'Why do you want to come back here? Are you challenging?'

'Dad says I am.'

He snorts. 'I meant are you challenging Wentz? You'll need a Heart for an official time.'

'We're here in an unofficial capacity. I need to know if I've lost my nerve.'

'Huh. I'm beginning to question your mental capacity. Pretty sure you've lost your mind.' He makes another snorting sound, drives through the hole in the fence, and skids to a stop near the quarry. He opens the window and sticks his head out, looking up at the darkening sky. And smiles.

'What are you so bloody happy about?'

'I'm thinking if I'm ever going to be abducted by aliens,' he says, 'it would be on a night like this. With a lunatic like you.' He Bluetooths his phone and selects a playlist.

'Gummer?'

'Yeah?'

'What did Amber do to you that night of the pipe challenge?'

He squirms. 'How do you know anything happened?'

'Because Amber's Amber. And because you're squirming.'

He thinks. Eventually, he says, 'I don't know how to explain it. She likes messing with people's heads. It's like she's a kid with a new Nerf gun. She feels compelled to shoot, even though she knows it'll hurt.'

'Nerf gun?' I frown. 'Is that a terrible metaphor for boobs or something?'

'Yeah, I guess.' He laughs. 'Let me put it this way— having Amber try out her moves on you is like swimming through a warm patch in a public swimming pool.'

'How do you mean?'

'Well, it's both pleasant *and* disturbing.'

I turn away and stare out at the quarry. 'Don't you miss the way we all used to be?'

Gummer shakes his head. 'Everybody hooks up. Look at *Friends*. It's in the script—it's inevitable.'

'It's predictable. Wait a minute…you watch *Friends*?'

He shrugs.

'Sex gets in the way of everything. I want to go back to BMXs and murder in the dark.' I get out of the car and scuff through the grit to the edge of the gully.

I've been out on the pipe without a spotter before, but I've never felt as alone as today. Gummer isn't the most attentive human being. He's still sitting in the car, focused on his phone. It takes me ten minutes of playing hokey-pokey before the dust settles and I can muster the gumption to squeeze through the grille. Now that I've looked down, it's like I can't *not* look down. All I can think about is the drop, while Gummer's music rattles my brain like the soundtrack to a slasher movie: My Bloody Valentine, Megadeth, Slayer. For a pacifist, he sure listens to some violent stuff.

I sit down, straddling the pipe. The concrete's still warm. There isn't a breath of wind. A sheep's skeleton is draped over the rocks below, covered with a dirty blanket of shrivelled skin and fleece, and the sinking sun throws a pale orange light. I'm wasting time—daylight means protection. Everyone knows that.

I inch along, working my way to the middle of the pipe, scanning the words of graffiti that might have been there for five minutes or thirty years. About fifteen metres along—I might have missed it if I didn't lean forward and run my eye along the side of the pipe—I find a tiny black bird, sitting on a power line. It's scratched and faded to grey. Once, it might have been black.

Hannah Holt.

Try not to think something and you can't help but think it; the mind is tricky like that. On the left-hand side under my knee, another bird, this time shooting forwards in flight. And two more, just centimetres away from each other, beaks open.

Hannah Holt.

Three metres further, two more birds. They're falling, tangled together.

Hannah Holt.

Finally, here's the word in looping scribble—and the last lonely bird. I whisper her name, seven times for seven crows.

I start to cry.

Seven for a secret never to be told.

I'm crying for somebody I never knew. I'm crying for the mother I lost and for the friends I don't understand anymore, for the funny girl I used to be. But mostly I'm crying with relief, because the fragile possibility of ghosts means everything.

If I can feel the unquiet spirit of a long-dead girl, maybe my mother is still here, somewhere. Maybe she can hear me.

EIGHT

'Kenz, don't hang up! Please let me explain.'

The sixth time I called, Kenzie finally answered. I'm in my bathroom with the bright white tiles, sitting in the bathtub. All of the upstairs lights are switched on, so I can see anything coming.

'There's nothing you can say to make this go away,' she says. 'You went too far this time and I can't get it out of my head.'

'Where are you? Is Mitch with you?' She sighs and I know I've wasted time and words. 'I'm sorry. It's just...'

'I can't do this anymore. You're making me crazy.'

'Please. I think I'm being haunted. Or possessed.'

She sighs again.

'You don't believe me?'

'I think you must have hit your head. And I think you need help.'

I know Mitchell is with her. I know he's squeezing her leg or her hand and he's got that stupid intense expression on his face that makes him look as if he's trying to read her mind. 'If you don't believe me, nobody will.'

'Grace, you're like the girl who cried wolf. You can't blame people if they think you're full of shit. You've built your whole reputation on that.'

'The missing girl,' I say. 'I saw her that night at the pipe when Pete was driving home. She was crawling in a ditch by the side of the road. She's dead—and she's in my head.' Kenzie swears under her breath and I hear Mitch's voice, echoing the sentiment. 'Have you got me on speaker?' I hear a click. Her voice becomes louder and clearer.

'And what does she want from you?' she says flatly.

'I think she wants me to find her.'

'You're not yourself.'

'No shit.'

'I meant you're not *acting* like yourself.'

'I'm not acting at all, Kenzie. I *need* you.'

She barks a laugh. 'This is the first time you've ever really left me out of one of your jokes. I'm not sure how I feel about it. I'm going now.' There's a pause before she goes on. 'Actually, I do. I know how I feel. I'm fed up. It was fun, once—it isn't anymore. Grow up, Grace.'

She hangs up—or she *thinks* she hangs up. She's talking fast, making plans for the holiday break and asking Mitch whether she should cut her hair. I rest my phone in the soap dish and listen to them not talking about me. Outside, moths flutter against the window; downstairs, Cody lumbers around in the kitchen, making the walls shudder. Diesel barks a greeting as Gina pulls into the driveway. I lie down in the bathtub and make myself as small and still as I can be, and Kenzie's voice drones on and on, like if she just keeps talking she won't have to say something that means anything at all.

I acknowledge her presence now—the missing girl, Hannah—but that's not the end. She won't go away. I listen, but that doesn't mean she's able to speak, or I'm able to hear. I accept the proof of something *other*—other than this life—but that doesn't make me any less afraid.

There's a spot in my room that feels different. It's just an empty corner that's thrown into shadow when the lamp is switched on, but I know the corner is occupied. I keep the lamp switched on all night and all day. I can't sleep without it. When I do sleep, she's in my dreams. I can't tell the true shape of her, but I sense her crouching, or maybe she's squatting with her arms curled around her knees. She never stands. She has no face and she's never still. Sometimes she's the darting smudge I saw in the bathroom; other times she's just *with* me, like an unfamiliar emotion that doesn't belong.

I say *she*, *her*, but she's an *it*. Whatever once made her a girl is not a part of her anymore. I don't think she likes me when I think like that—that's when my brain fizzes and things go pop. For no reason, the picture on my TV jams between stations, and the numbers on my digital clock radio have disappeared. Some nights, when my dreams are close to the surface, I can wake in another room not knowing how I got there or what I've been doing.

It's safer to stay awake.

In the evenings, I sit downstairs with Dad and Cody for as long as they're up. I go to school. I laugh and joke and breeze through my schoolwork, but Dad has noticed I have purple smudges under my eyes and my eating habits are weird. Cody says I'm going through delayed puberty. They're both kind and concerned but I think they just want the melancholy to go away—none of us is equipped for tragedy. I arrange my face to show Grace-like expressions and somehow manage to convince my friends that I'm still the same, but Kenzie is lost to me. She can't forgive me for the birds.

The only time I feel it—*her*—gone is when I'm actively thinking about her, searching for fragments of her life, her history. But I'm not fooled. The weightless-ness is not her leaving—it's because she's carrying me.

It's Tuesday, lunchtime. Pete and I are sitting under the row of plane trees on the northern boundary of school. Nobody else has shown up here for days—it seems our group is officially disbanded. With the end of first-term holidays looming, I think Pete feels sorry for me, on my own, with escalating rumours of a Sacred Heart retaliation for The Deadpool Incident.

'What have you got?' he asks, peering at my lunchbox. 'Anything worth trading?'

I have a squashed, half-unwrapped cheese sandwich and a bruised apple. I whip out the sandwich and catch a glimpse of something bloody and twisted as it falls into my lap.

Pete spits out a piece of salami rind and launches to his feet. 'What the hell is that?'

I fling the sandwich away and freeze, eyes averted, hands in the air. 'I can't look. Get it off me.'

'Stand up.'

'No. Get it off me, Pete!'

He snaps a small branch from one of the plane trees, strips the leaves from the end and starts prodding between my crossed legs.

'What is it?'

'Open your legs more.' He gags. 'Shit, that's juvenile. You can look now.' He's dangling the thing from the stick—a chicken's foot with shrunken skin, curled claws, and a blood-caked bone protruding from the end. 'You got punked.'

'Gross. It stinks.' I look around, shuddering. Pranked by one of our own, too. No one from Heart would have been able to get near my locker without help. 'Get rid of it.'

He flicks it over the fence and onto the street.

I gather my scattered lunch and move to another spot. I laugh, making sure the sound carries, and unwrap my sandwich. If I show they've got to me, it's a point to them—the trick is to be good-natured when karma comes your way.

I'm about to take a bite when Pete clubs the sandwich out of my hands.

'Hey!'

'You got double-punked,' he says, pointing with the stick. 'Chickens typically have two feet.'

I get up, leaving the chicken foot sandwich lying on the ground.

'Where are you going?'

'I'm not hungry.'

'I'm not surprised.' He's trying not to laugh.

'I'm going for a walk.' I stomp off.

He follows. 'Wait! Cundalini the chicken wants his foot back.' He cracks himself up. 'Gracie. Gracie, Gracie, you've not got a sense of humour!' he shouts in a terrible Scottish accent.

Great. Now he's quoting *Mad Max* at me. I stick up my middle finger behind my back and lose him halfway across the oval.

I've been walking a lot these past few days, to keep from sinking. It's exhausting, both the walking and the effort it takes to appear as if I'm not constantly looking over my shoulder.

Yesterday I had a mandatory six-monthly session with the school counsellor. Mrs Renfrey always says, 'Call me Connie', but I don't call her that and I don't tell her anything. She only acts as if she's interested because

85

it's her job, and this time she seemed relieved to mark me off for good behaviour and better marks. *Resilience is knowing that YOU are the one with the power to save yourself* says the poster behind her desk. And the one next to it: *Your biggest fears are completely dependent upon YOU for survival.*

You, you, YOU. It's all bullshit.

I've been watching the birds—you can hardly tell the sick ones from the rest. But look closely and you'll see they pretend—to strut, to sing, to eat—so the other birds don't know they're sick. *That's* how YOU survive. I want to write some real quotes for Call Me Connie and rip the lies from her walls.

Fear is not an unwanted pet you reluctantly feed; it doesn't come with reins and a bit. Fear feeds on YOU. It comes and goes as it pleases.

NINE

Three things I'm starting to know about the new me: I don't think like anyone else, I don't dream like anyone else, and I can't juggle. The last one is important. I used to be able to juggle five balls like a pro, but now I can't. Seems to me it's not the kind of thing you just forget—sure, I might be out of practice, but that's not it. It has something to do with the way I keep reaching for light switches that aren't there and having to take a moment to think about things that should be second nature—how to put on make-up, what my favourite foods are, how I take my coffee. It's like I have a faulty circuit, or I'm forgetting who I am.

My desk is covered with pencil shavings and coffee rings. It's six o'clock already and I'm only halfway through a sheet of algebraic equations. I still have four pages of notes to type up for Health and several quiz corrections, but I can't concentrate.

'What is it that you want?'

She's shifting, restless, in her corner.

The pencil shavings scurry and settle—it's only the breeze drifting through my open window. The days are getting cooler and the nights are getting longer. I dread going to sleep.

'Who are you talking to?' Cody sticks his head around the door.

'I didn't hear you come up,' I say. 'I'm not talking to anyone.'

'Dad says we're going out for dinner, so you need to put some real clothes on.' He nods at my tank top and boxer shorts.

'Out? Out where?' We never go out.

'Ruby's.'

Mum's favourite. 'Oh, no.' *No, no, no.*

'It's been two years, Grace. It's time.'

I throw down my pencil and swing back on the chair. 'Why is he trying to go back? It's not ever going to be the same.'

'It's only dinner. Get dressed.' He turns to leave and stops. 'What's wrong with your fish?' He nods towards the tank.

'They're amphibians, not fish.' I glance at the tank. Statler is floating. Sometimes they come up for air or they get bloated, but Statler is upside down. 'Oh, no,' I say again. I cross the room, lift the lid, reach into the tank and stroke his belly. His legs kick feebly. I brush his tail with my finger—if I give him a fright he might submerge. But he just floats. 'Waldorf is gone.' I lift the sunken ship and look behind the aeration rock.

'Maybe he climbed out.'

'He didn't *climb*, Cody. There's a lid.' I check the temperature gauge. It's twenty-five degrees. That's way too high.

'He's a walking fish, right? So why can't he climb?'

'You're not helping. Is it hot in here? It feels hot. Get me some ice?'

I switch off the tank heater and Cody goes downstairs. Waldorf has to be here; he can't just disappear. Maybe he did climb out. I look underneath the desk, bed and side tables. There's a wet track on the floorboards, but it could be drips from my hand.

'Here.' Cody comes back. He hands me a tall glass full of ice cubes.

I submerge the glass and let the cubes melt gradually. The temperature begins to drop and Statler flips over, slowly sinking. 'We can't leave until I find Waldorf.'

'Stop making...'

'It's not an excuse!'

'You weren't so worried about Rex when you swapped him for these two.'

I stare at my brother. 'How'd you know about that?'

He snorts. 'Gummer plus beer. I know about the pool prank, too, and the pipe.'

'Did you tell…?'

He shakes his head. 'No, I haven't told Dad. But I will if you don't stop giving him such a hard time. He worries about you.'

I sit on the edge of my bed. 'If you tell, you'll just worry him more.'

Cody points a finger at me. 'Forget this whole stupid war with Sacred Heart,' he says. 'It's been going on for generations, Grace, and people get hurt. You might get hurt. It'd be too much for Dad.'

'It's just a bit of fun. And I'm good at it.' I peer into the shadowy corner. She's not here right now. Where does she go?

'What?' Cody's looking at me strangely.

Just then I see Waldorf, lying near the door like a flung toy. He wasn't there just a second ago, yet it would have taken him forever to move a few metres.

I pick him up. He's limp, but alive. Axolotls have been known to leap from a tank, but mine has a lid and Waldorf has never been in a hurry to go anywhere.

Cody watches as I gently hold him underwater until his gills flare and turn pink. He slides gracefully from my palm and joins Statler on the substrate floor, as if two minutes ago he wasn't close to death.

'Lucky,' Cody says.

Ruby's is exactly as I remember it: eighties decor with faded plates and scratched cutlery, but filled with warm light and amazing smells. Dad's wearing a dress shirt.

It's as creased as his face, but it's a revelation to see him wearing something other than hi-vis workwear.

The waiter leads us towards a table for four near the front window—the table Mum always booked for its view of the fairy lights in the reserve across the street. As we approach, I watch Dad change. In the car he wore an expression of grim determination, but now his face looks the same as the day the police came: hopeful, with a pained smile—hopeful that it won't be as bad as he thinks.

Me—I just know the location might change and the food might be good, but we'll never get used to a table with only three settings.

I sit in the seat Mum would have taken, facing the reserve. I rearrange the cutlery and fold my hands in my lap. We order drinks. Dad and Cody spread their knees and elbows, taking up enough space for three.

'Well,' Dad says.

Cody picks up the menu. I know we're all thinking we used to order without looking, but if we read the menu we're spared the small talk, at least for a few minutes. The waiter brings our drinks to the table—beer for the boys, lime and bitters for me—and we're relieved to have something else to do.

'Hmmm.'

'Well.'

Cody asks Dad about an engine part they ordered, both of them spinning their beer bottles in unison. I can't stand to see the defeat in Dad's expression as he tries to keep up an ordinary conversation. I look around the restaurant, at the cute couples and happy families—and the needle scratches off the record.

Amber and Noah Wentz are sitting close together at the back of the restaurant. With Noah's parents. Sharing a plate of pappadums and raita. Talking and laughing.

I sneak glances at them, watching the way Noah's parents interact with Amber as if they know her well and like her a lot. Amber is so completely focused on Noah; she hasn't noticed I'm here.

Dad taps my arm. 'Grace.'

'Sorry?'

'Your order. What are you having?'

I order a steamed rice and side of vegetable bhaji. Dad and Cody go back to spinning their beer bottles; I go back to staring at Amber. I know we've grown apart lately, but now the distance is too great. She has a whole other life, like Kenzie.

Amber leaves the table and heads for the shared corridor between Ruby's and the cafe next door. I follow her into the ladies' toilet. She's leaning into the mirror, putting on a fresh ring of pink lipstick.

'Grashe Oley,' she says without moving her lips.

I turn the cold tap, rinse my hands and shake them, flicking droplets onto her flawless foundation. There are freckles under there, somewhere.

'I don't know, Amber. You never call, you don't write.' I grab her hand and stare into her brown eyes. 'You don't bring me flowers anymore.'

Smacking her lips, she says, 'It's not you, babe. It's me.' She flashes her teeth. She has lipstick on them.

'Well, shit, I know that.' I drop her hand and hoist myself onto the vanity unit. 'I vote to bring back the freckles.'

Silence. She takes a long time reapplying wings of eyeliner. 'You've just got to make room for Mitch. Move over. It's that simple. Kenzie's not ditching you because you've changed—you're ditching her because she has enough room for both of you, but you don't.'

I pull a face. 'We weren't talking about Kenzie.'

She twists her body to look at herself in the mirror again. 'Okay, let's talk about me. See, we've known each other since we were eight years old, and you still see freckles. I haven't had freckles since I was eleven.'

'Are you sure? Did you bleach them? Does that really work?'

She gets up beside me, swinging her bare legs. 'They disappeared. They can do that, you know. I no longer have the largest collection of shoplifted nail polish in the Southern Hemisphere either, but that's still the first thing you tell everyone about me.'

'That's because it's funny.'

'Funny has a use-by date,' she says, and lifts a foot to show me her pink toenails. 'See? Bought and paid for. Shoplifting isn't on my CV anymore.'

'So what are you saying? I'm stuck in some sort of eternal childhood, is that it? Wow, Amber. How does a canoe like Noah Wentz navigate your depths?'

She gives me a black look. 'Grace, our friendship group came with a set of rules and those rules haven't changed in almost ten years. Same with the whole Swampie versus Heart thing. I'm over it. It doesn't mean we're not friends, it just means the rules don't fit.' She spots the lipstick on her teeth and scrubs it away with her finger. 'Did you think we'd all be leftovers forever? Did you honestly believe we told each other everything?'

I nod. 'Yeah. I suppose I did. I *always* told you guys everything.' Every secret, every dastardly deed. Exclusion brought us together and made us exclusive.

'Did you? *Do* you?' Amber says. 'You're such an idealist. You think because we all have a history it means we automatically have a future.'

'Like I suppose you see a future with Noah Wentz?'

'Maybe.' She shrugs. 'Maybe not. Anyway, everyone knows there's a whole bunch of stuff going on with you that you're not telling anyone.'

Like *her*. My gaze slides to the closed door of the third cubicle. The latch says it's unoccupied, but that's hardly reassuring. I felt her with me in the car and again when I sat at the table. She's not in here. My head's clear and there's no buzz, just the echo of our voices and the unmarked grey tiles on the walls and floor.

'What are you looking at?' Amber says.

'Nothing.'

'Right.'

'Anyway, how do you know I haven't tried to tell you? It's not like you're around to tell.' I slide off the counter. 'And you wouldn't believe me if I did. Kenzie doesn't believe me.'

'Try me now.'

'No.'

'Everything is a front with you, Grace.' She scrapes her make-up into her open bag. 'Kenzie says you make so much stuff up, you don't know what the truth is anymore. She says you need professional help, and I'm inclined to agree.'

I know what's true—I just don't know what's *real*.

'Oh. You're *inclined*,' I say nastily.

'See, there it is. You're not even listening. You're trying to stuff me back into my trashy box. Screw you, McJudgy.' She's out the door.

I've been dying to say the same thing for weeks. I'm speechless because she beat me to it.

'Screw you!' I yell at the swinging door.

TEN

Dad's sitting at the kitchen table, reading the paper. Cody hasn't slept in his own bed for the last two nights— I assume he stays with one of the girlfriends he never brings home. It's 6.30 a.m. I hardly slept apart from a few hours of sweaty half-dreams. My hands are shaking as I make coffee, toast and fried eggs.

'You're up early,' Dad mutters. 'What gives?'

I shrug and pass him a plate. 'I've got work to do.'

'Work? It's the first day of the holidays. When did you ever surface before eleven?'

'I'm doing a project on urban legends. Swanston's urban legends.' I take a deep breath and say, all in a rush, 'Specifically the case of Hannah Holt and William Dean. You knew her, right? It's been over twenty years. Do you think the police would let me look at the files?'

'I knew *of* her.' Dad barely looks up from the newspaper. 'There was no case.'

'What do you mean there was no case?'

'There was no evidence of a crime.'

'But she was murdered.'

He sighs and stabs an egg yolk with his fork. 'There was no evidence of murder and William Dean was never charged. It was a rumour, and you know how damaging rumours can be when people give them too much oxygen.' He throws me a glance. 'As far as I know she's still a missing person. There was nothing but circumstantial evidence and talk.'

'But…'

'There are far more interesting urban legends for you to dig up, I'm sure.'

It's the longest conversation we've had in months. I want to keep him talking, but his lips are getting thinner by the second.

'Did you know her?'

'I told you, I heard of her. Everybody did.'

'So, if I was to interview anyone—for my project— if I had to ask questions, who would I ask?'

He wipes his mouth with the back of his hand. 'What kind of idiot would set a task like this?'

'Me.'

'You?'

'It happened a long time ago,' I say.

His head swivels slowly and he glares at me like he

wants me to shut up for good. 'There are people involved who are still living. It's been twenty-three years, to be exact, and that still isn't long enough. What, you think a bit of time goes by and it stops hurting?'

I sit in the chair across from him and set my plate down. The eggs are undercooked, swimming in grease. 'But what if I found something nobody else found? What if I got answers when no one else ever did?' *What if I had help from the grave?*

Dad suddenly pushes his own plate away, the breakfast only half-eaten. 'I know it won't be the first time anybody's told you, but your brother came out half-asleep and never really woke up, and you came out squalling and swinging your fists and you never stopped.' He hands me a knife and fork. 'I'll tell you something else that never stops, Grace. The sorrow. The pain. The missing. Get that through your head. You don't go opening wounds that aren't your business to open.' He stands, picks up his plate, slides the contents into the bin and slams it into the sink. 'Now, eat. Get some sun. You're starting to look like a ghost, and God knows we've got enough of those around here.'

Getting some sun is the last thing on my mind.

I spend most of the day in semi-darkness, sitting at my computer in my room, scratching up details, building a profile and a timeline of events beginning with the disappearance of Hannah Holt and ending with William Dean's suicide a year later. Though her story begins before and echoes long after those days, I have to begin somewhere.

I know what she looked like: tall and slim at five feet, ten inches. Fair skin, blonde hair, blue eyes. Straight, perfect teeth, apart from a chipped incisor. In all the cropped photos showing her wearing a school uniform, disembodied arms of fellow students are draped across her shoulders, and those shoulders are thin and rounded as if she had curvature of the spine or was self-conscious of her height. Every photo shows her smiling.

I know where she lived: Davey Street, South Swanston. There are pictures online of both houses—Hannah's, and William Dean's just a few streets away—along with a shot of her bedroom window. Reports say they knew each other, but they weren't friends. I find a few grainy images of a taped-off crime scene—it looks like a patch of generic bushland, but a different article tells me it's the steep gully behind the Holt house. Police had discovered a makeshift fort—the kind a child might make—high up in a tree, and they found evidence that William Dean had slept there. It was alleged that he watched the house. The police found pictures, and Susannah Holt said she knew someone was watching the house before her daughter disappeared. They were both afraid.

But the only solid evidence linking William to Hannah was the tip of a fingernail and a few blonde hairs found in his car—easily explained when William admitted he'd given Hannah a ride to school three weeks before she went missing. He denied everything. The investigation stalled. In desperation, Susannah Holt copied and distributed hundreds of flyers, placing them in letterboxes and under windscreen wipers, in an attempt to fan the dying embers of the case; it was not Hannah's Missing poster but a copy of a poem supposedly written by William Dean—the angry, bitter ramblings of a boy, about a girl, who didn't love him back. And although Susannah Holt is shown holding the flyer, her eyes black with grief, the words on the flyer are blocked out, censored by the newspaper. William Dean's parents are pictured below, scurrying away from the camera, their arms crooked over their faces.

The stories rehash the same details over a period of about nine months, dwindling away from front page news and double spreads to a few sad lines on the back pages. Then, nothing—until William Dean jumped.

Each time I pencil in another detail, I picture Hannah's scattered bones, rising from the earth, brushed clean of dirt, skittering, clattering, reassembling and locking into place; I imagine her shadow in the corner grows longer. In a way, just thinking about her is bringing her back to life.

She's not with me, though. Not today. When I'm looking for her, she disappears.

I uncurl the portrait I drew and spread it out on the desk. The charcoal is starting to smear as if she's been left out in the rain. The movement of her arm makes her appear as if she's waving goodbye. She isn't smiling.

I know what she looked like, where she lived—all these scattered bones. But it's near impossible to find out who she was.

*

On Tuesday, I haul my dusty bike out of the shed, grease the chain, check the tyre pressure, and tie a folded tea towel onto the seat to cover a broken spring. Dad and Cody are at work. Dad has left a note in the kitchen instructing me to vacuum upstairs and downstairs, hang out a load of washing, and pressure-clean the oil stains that Gummer's truck has left on the driveway.

The stains will have to wait.

I haven't ridden since Kenzie and I were thirteen or so, back when we lived much further apart and our bikes were the closest things to freedom. Staying on isn't as easy as I remember. I wobble and stall. I panic, swerving away from passing cars. The bike's too small—my knees clip the handlebars—and though I'm taller now the ground seems further away. By the sixth or seventh block I'm sweating. The broken spring sticks into my thigh and I've grated the skin from both ankle bones.

On the newer, northern side of Swanston, where we live, the streets crisscross in a perfect grid and every road leads out of town. Here, to the south, about a twenty-minute ride away, the land rises ever so slightly and the roads are twisty-turny. There are no shortcuts, no alleys, just looping streets that end in cul-de-sacs and shallow gullies. The houses aren't grander but the yards are bigger, the fences low, and the gum trees have been allowed to stay.

I pull out a sheet of paper from my pocket: a pencilled

sketch of a map. I should have printed a copy—the paper is damp and the street names are smudged. In the middle of the road, in front of a block of units, a couple of boys are playing cricket.

'Do you know where I can find Davey Street?'

One shrugs; the other points away from the direction I'm heading. I turn the bike around.

I must be close. It's too quiet. Sparrows huddle together in a knot on a power line. A sharp burst of needle rain hits my face. Winter's coming. The scent of wet earth rises, and I get a sudden pang of homesickness. I miss the farmhouse. I miss knowing that my best memories are contained in one place, a place where generations of Foleys have carved their names in the skin of the same ancient pepper tree and swung across the same winter creek in an old tractor tyre. The cycle is broken now.

Twice I get lost, pedalling up winding streets that go nowhere, until I find it. Davey Street. About six houses along, it rises to a steep crest. The house I'm looking for must be on the other side. I stop at the end of the street and get off the bike. I have the brief sensation of falling, the way you do when you miss the bottom step. My nerves are humming, as if any second I might get caught doing something wrong.

It's ridiculous—nobody knows me here.

A blonde girl, three or four years younger, appears. She has an old canvas shopping trolley and a backpack. Her arms are filled with bundles of catalogues. She glances at me curiously, smiling as she passes.

I give her a small wave. It takes me a few seconds to realise she has come back.

'Are you okay?'

I wipe the sweat from my upper lip. 'I'm fine. I just overdid it.' I point to the catalogues. 'Does it pay?'

She shakes her head. 'It's slave labour. It takes way longer to sort and fold them than it does to deliver them.' She holds out her hands: her fingers are stained with ink, the tips of two covered with bandaids. 'I'm quitting as soon as I've saved up enough for a phone.'

'You deliver here?' I look up at the street sign.

She nods. 'Most of them say No Junk Mail, but I have to do it anyway. They check.'

'I'll do it if you like,' I say.

She steps back.

'It's okay. I live here.' *Pants on fire.* 'It'll save you the walk.'

She searches my face and what she sees seems to frighten her; she thrusts a bundle of catalogues into my hands and turns her trolley around. 'You're not joking? If you don't deliver and they check, I won't get paid.'

'No jokes here.'

'You sure you're okay? You look kind of...funny.'

I secure the catalogues under the snap-strap on the rear of my bike. 'Funny how? There are two kinds.' I was funny-ha-ha. Now I'm funny-peculiar. I smile but I want her to go.

She's already walking away. As I wheel my bike up

the hill she calls, 'Good luck to you,' in a tone that makes her sound older.

How does she know I might need it?

I check each letterbox and slip bundles of catalogues into those without stickers, working my way up the even-numbered side. After the crest, the street dips sharply. This must be about the highest point in Swanston, which isn't saying much. There's no one around and most of the driveways are empty. I feel a magnetic pull in my belly—at first I dismiss it as gravity, the weight of the bike dragging me down the hill, but as I approach the house I change my mind. It's dread.

I swing my leg over the bike and coast along slowly, clutching the handbrake.

It's the last house at the bottom of the cul-de-sac. I recognise it from newspaper photos, but it goes deeper than that: a prickling familiarity, as if I've been here before, many times, and I feel strangely desolate that it's not the way I remember it. The weatherboard planks are buckled, flaking grey paint, like a disease. The curtains are drawn. Where a smooth driveway once curved across the garden, there are broken chunks of concrete, as if giant hands were pressing them up from underneath. My eye is drawn to the smallest window facing the street. An enormous, twisted pepper tree stretches its limbs in all directions but one: the bough leading to the window has been hacked off. The Holt house slouches between two neat cream-brick buildings with tidy gardens: left behind, forgotten.

It looks like I feel when I'm between Kenzie and Mitch.

The handbrake grips and the front wheel wobbles. To avoid losing control and crashing through the front yard, I hop off and let go. The bike tips over and skids across the road. I pick it up, lean it against a tree, and pull out the other sheet of paper.

The photo they used on Hannah Holt's Missing poster shows her smiling, forever seventeen. It's hard to accept that this girl is the same girl I drew, but the proof is there. It's in her eyes, the way they slant at the outer edges; it's in the curve of her cheek and the set of her mouth. And the window: there was a photo in a news article, a close-up of the chipped frame to show a likely entry point for an intruder. I remember drawing the catch with its curved edge, just the right shape for a thumb.

It was easy enough to find the articles. Her disappearance was front page news for months: a young girl went missing and no trace of her could be found. The only child of a single mother—who worked two jobs to pay for the privilege of a Sacred Heart education—she earned a partial scholarship to university. It wasn't long before the news reports took a darker turn: in the months leading up to her disappearance, Hannah Holt had become withdrawn. She stopped eating and skipped classes.

Her mother said someone was watching the house.

The thought hits me like a punch to the chest, but it isn't fear—it's a sharp spike of fury, and it's not *mine*.

'What?' I whisper. 'You have to help me. I don't know what I have to do.'

A dense cloud passes across the face of the sun; a flurry of dead leaves dances around my feet. Something brushes past my cheek and my heart trebles its beat. *Caw.* A lone crow drifts in lazy circles above. Overhead, the power lines are humming, and the pitch is maddening. I cup my hands over my ears and lean against the tree. My vision is leached of colour, sepia-toned—it's as if I'm the only person breathing in an abandoned world.

It isn't safe here. But here is where I'm meant to be.

'I've been waiting for you.'

It's Hannah Holt's mother, standing among the weeds near the letterbox, where the beginning of the immaculate driveway used to be. She's wearing mismatched trackpants and a striped shirt, slippers on her feet. No bra. Her hair is as neglected as the rest of her: greying frizz with straw-blonde tips.

Where the driveway used to be? Waiting for me?

'I want my specials. You're a day late,' she says.

'Sorry.' I fumble with the strap on the back of my bike and hand her a bundle.

'You're new.' Her expression is sly, as if she knows a secret I don't. 'Catalogues come on Mondays and Thursdays. Don't force them through the slot or they tear, and don't leave them poking out or they get wet. Walk around and put them in through the opening. It's not locked.'

I nod.

'What's your name?'

'Grace,' I say, without thinking.

'Mondays and Thursdays, remember.' She taps a dirty yellow fingernail on the top of the letterbox. 'It's not difficult. Not like, say...riding a bike.'

She was watching me. She grins, but with her blackened teeth it looks like a grimace.

As I pedal away I think I hear the scuff of her slippers as she goes back into the house, but when I look over my shoulder she's still standing there clutching the catalogues, staring at her feet. It's as if she's forgotten why she's there; if she waits long enough it'll come to her. Or *someone* will come to her.

I wonder if a mother grieves longer for a child than a child grieves for her mother. I wonder if I should tell her she should stop waiting.

ELEVEN

I'm lying in bed listening to the steady hum of the tank's filter, staring at a patch of light travelling across the floor. It's proof that the world turns and time passes. I'm not sure what time it is—one, maybe two. Twice, I've fallen asleep only to wake again seconds later. *Falling.* It's exactly like that—a long, slow dive. But something always snags me on the way down. It's happening every night now. I've forgotten how to fall.

The headboard of my bed butts against the wall by the window. The bed is too heavy to move by myself. When I'm lying on it I can't help staring into the hallway—red-tinted black like the inside of a throat—and the yawning emptiness of the stairwell. If I close my eyes, it's worse. I could shut the door but it makes me feel trapped. I've tried sleeping on the couch, tried Cody's room, since he's rarely home, but when I'm downstairs Diesel stalks me like a silent shadow. Once, I woke to feel his meaty breath on my face.

I roll over. I want to be closer to Dad and his snores. I know he'll only shoo me away and tell me I'm too old to behave like this, if he even wakes at all. I want to call for Diesel but he'll only come as far as the third-to-bottom step now.

The tank filter stutters and stops working. The sudden quiet is unnerving.

I get up and reach for the power cord. It's still connected, switched on at the wall. Waldorf appears to be sleeping. Statler has crawled between the side of the tank and the filter, possibly blocking the airflow. I remove the lid and slide my hand along the glass to dislodge him. He resists, moving deeper into the space behind the filter. I plunge my arm into the water, up to the elbow, and my finger brushes Statler's cold skin. A jarring pulse surges up to my shoulder and into my jawbone. I clench my teeth and yank my arm away, sloshing water over the floor.

I look down. I'm standing in a puddle.

In the corner, the lamp flickers and fades, only to burn again with a hot brightness—too bright for a forty-watt globe. I launch myself across the room and onto the bed, shuddering and panting. I clutch my pillow for protection and watch as the puddle grows, creeping in a perfect circle, as if the water is being drawn from beneath the floorboards. It's bottomless as a well and inky, like old blood. The patch of light on the floor begins to move, as if time is in fast motion; the reflection travels metres in seconds, coming to rest in the centre of the puddle. Time stops. The water is no longer black but illuminated, with the rippling image of a white-painted window.

I swing my legs over the side of the bed, keeping my toes away from the water. I have to fight the urge to run downstairs. There's a snuffling, scraping sound. I muffle my breathing with the pillow and try to pinpoint where it's coming from.

The hallway. Near the stairs. Diesel? It can't be Diesel.

The light from the lamp takes the edge off the darkness, but not enough to carry to the top of the stairwell. I press up against the headboard. Whatever it is, its breathing is deep and laboured, and it's getting closer. Now I can see a pixelated shadow, low, crawling, and when it reaches the half-light I make out the shape of an arm flung wide, slapping down with a thud, fingers grasping at the carpet. Then the other arm, stroking like a swimmer's—*clutch, pull, drag, clutch, pull, drag.*

I let out a hysterical shriek. The thing stops moving. Downstairs, Diesel barks, and the thing lifts its head. In the darkness it looks at me; faceless, it looks *right at me*.

Her. It. She?

I keep still, holding tight to the hope that she can't hurt me—willing her to stop, trying to force her out of my head. I squeeze my eyes shut and hold my breath until my heartbeat slows and I grow dizzy. I tip sideways and curl into a ball.

Let me sleep. Please, let me sleep.

I hear the reply, clear as a loud whisper: *You're not listening.*

And she waits.

My skin crawls and itches all over; my fear smells like sour sweat and rusty blades. I open my eyes. The sheets are twisted into knots and I've left muddied marks on my pillow. But over the screeching in my ears and the drumbeat in my chest, I'm struck by the strangely calm realisation that I've been going about this the wrong way: ignoring her will only feed her hate, make her stronger, stretch my skin thinner, keep me awake until I can't function well enough to remember to breathe.

'I'm listening.'

The lamplight fades to a gentle glow. The well has shrunk to a puddle, my wet footprints next to it. Statler drifts to the bottom of the tank and the filter begins to hum like a lullaby; the hallway is empty, bathed in grey light. When I look out the window, Diesel is doing his morning business on the council strip, and the sky to the east is streaked with pink.

On Thursday, I leave the house after Dad and Cody have gone, just before eight.

I slip on my sunglasses and set off in the direction of Davey Street with a litre bottle of frozen water and a packed lunch strapped to the back of my bike. It might be a long wait for the catalogue girl. I have fear, curiosity and the usual hateful thoughts, but no plan.

Last night, Diesel started howling. He howled for a solid minute, on the hour, every hour, and Dad and Cody took turns getting up to yell at him. They tried to drag him outside, but he wouldn't budge from the stairs. Dad said he could probably hear sirens, but I know an old dog who's never howled in his life doesn't teach himself a new trick like this. He still won't come all the way upstairs, but he's made it to the sixth step. He lies with his chin on his paws and watches the space above, like it's the entrance to a tunnel and a fox is holed up inside.

I wonder if he can see her. I trust him to let me know when she's near. I still don't trust him not to bite.

I pedal south. It's overcast and a warm northerly carries clouds of topsoil from the plains, raining it down onto houses and parked cars like a dusting of cinnamon sugar. Dad says things are starting to go bad: it'll be a cold, dry winter. Mum used to call him the canary in the coal mine—if Dad predicted a bad season, that meant the whole of Swanston would soon be in a rotten mood. If she could see us now she would know that Dad's bad mood has hung around since she's been gone. It has nothing to do with the weather.

I pass junk food alley—McDonald's, KFC, Subway and Pizza Hut on opposite corners of the Murray Street intersection—and shoot through the laneway behind the BP service station at the last second to avoid a group of Hearts hanging around in the car park. When we lived on the farm, I could go the whole holidays without seeing anyone from school except my friends. Here, every exit

112

is guarded, and every route requires a detour to avoid passing the shrine.

When I think about Mum, I remember her failings. Her cooking was terrible: she'd ruin a hundred different recipes rather than perfect one; we'd choke on charcoal or raw fish and have to order takeaway. Dad said she made us kids tough by trying to kill us, regularly, either through her cooking, her lapses in concentration (like driving Cody around in an unstrapped baby capsule for the first two months of his life) or her homemade homework experiments, including the volcanic eruption that permanently damaged my left eye. She had the kind of manic energy that made people feel guilty for sitting still—she ran like a demon every night after dinner, refusing to believe anything bad could happen to her on a deserted road late at night. She went out of her way to break the rules: serving roast beef on Good Friday, granting Cody and me four free-choice days off school each term, and marrying my dad, a Swampie, when she was a Heart. She talked to strangers, made everyone's business her own, and lived like there were no consequences.

It's as if she travelled through life trying to be the opposite of who she was born to be.

I think that's what hurts most: she was minding her own business, standing on the corner, a shopping bag in each hand, waiting for the pedestrian lights to turn green. The trailer cut across the footpath when the truck driver misjudged his turn.

Dad read us the findings: the judge stopped short of calling it an accident, but that's what he meant. The driver had his licence revoked and received a two-year suspended jail term. Negligence. Driver error. A human tragedy. No mention of mother-slaughter. Dad says he understands and he forgives; he's a truck driver himself and it could have happened to anyone. Cody doesn't say anything in case it upsets Dad.

The driver's name was Dominic Aloisi. He came to her funeral. Apparently he cried. He is and she was and I don't know him, but he's alive and he's free and I hate him more right this minute than I did the day it happened. I didn't think that was possible, but since the night on the pipe I seem to have tapped a fresh vein.

This time I take a more direct route to the hill where the Holt house stands, dodging the intersection and the shrine by a single block. I'm pedalling so hard my hands are cramping. My calves are tight balls of pain. It's as if there's a storm building inside my skull, threatening to break.

At the bottom of Davey Street, I can't stop. I won't wait for the catalogue girl.

I crank the pedals until the bike hits the top of the crest and let it freefall down the other side. The handlebars wobble crazily, the wheels spin so fast that the squeak in the chain becomes one long *screech*. A branch whips my cheek. I savour the sting, the rush of wind, the inevitability, as the tyres hit a patch of gravel and lose traction. The bike skids and flips, sending me soaring. I land hard on my elbow and wrist and feel the skin sanded from my hip and anklebone, but I don't feel the pain yet—only the pure satisfaction of staging a spectacular, bullseye crash-landing in Susannah Holt's front yard.

The wheels stop spinning. It's quiet. Stunned, I sit up and run an inventory on the damage. My lunch is scattered; the water bottle has burst. The bike has hit the concrete and died, its frame buckled, and I thank my lucky stars that I didn't end up like it. I hold out my hands: they're shaking so hard, drops of blood spatter like paint onto my thigh. I've progressed from stupid thoughts to stupid acts.

Hannah Holt's mother takes a long time to come out of the house. She keeps her distance, as if I might attack her. 'Are you all right?'

'Brakes failed,' I wheeze, staring at the pieces of gravel embedded in my forearm. Now I hurt, and not only from the parts that bleed.

She looks down at me, arms folded. 'You'd better come inside,' she says, offering her hand. The palm is red and creased—did she keep it clenched most of the time? It's shaking as badly as mine.

For a moment, I contemplate not taking it. The ghost of her child is with me. There's a fresh cut on the ball of her thumb, exactly where Diesel's fang punctured mine. I can't help thinking our blood might mingle—until now the freakiness has been contained inside my head, but together we could complete some sort of circuit that might set it free.

115

'Come on. Stop you bleeding all over the place.' She snaps her fingers.

I give her my other hand instead, forcing her to switch. She hauls me up, shoves the bike out of the way with her slippered foot and leads me by my elbow to the door.

If the outside of 26 Davey Street is overgrown and forgotten, the interior is a tidy, polished shrine of remembrance. I expect the same creeping familiarity I felt when I first saw the house, but it's foreign to me. There's not much furniture, only two plush armchairs, a wall unit and a coffee table in the lounge room, a two-person dining setting, no television. Hannah Holt's framed face is everywhere: on the entrance wall, the top of an old piano, the mantelpiece, the sideboard—even the peach-coloured bathroom where her mother takes me. A black-and-white photo in a silver frame sits on the vanity unit, next to an unused tea-light candle and a vase holding a plastic daffodil. In this one, Hannah is probably only two or three years old.

Susannah Holt carefully moves the vase, the candle and the frame to a narrow wooden shelf under the window. She fills the sink with scalding water. 'You'll want to clean yourself up.'

When I look at the rising steam, my skin shrinks and stings.

'Shouldn't you call somebody?' she asks.

'I will as soon as I've cleaned up.'

go search up gift yo

1A

2A

2B

3A   3B

Shrugging, she reaches under the sink to pull out a white box. 'Here. You can put it all in the waste bin. It'll sting but it won't kill you.' She passes me a few packets of gauze, tweezers, a handful of bandaids and a bottle of Betadine. 'Grace,' she mutters, as if to remind herself that the girl with a death wish, bleeding all over her peach bathroom, has a name.

'Thank you.' I put my phone and purse on the windowsill and roll up my sleeves.

'I'll leave you to it.' She shuffles out. Drawers slam and china clinks in another room.

I peer in the mirror, checking my face and scalp for injuries: there's a vertical slash of blood on my left cheek, but when I clean it away there is no cut underneath. The blood must have come from somewhere else. Peeling away the waistband of my shorts, I discover a weeping graze the size of my palm, and from my elbow to wrist the skin is shredded. My ankle throbs, but it's only scraped. It takes twenty minutes or more to tweeze out the pieces of gravel, clean the wounds, and stick on layers of bandaids—twelve in all. The water in the sink is bright pink, a sediment of dirt and gravel lying on the bottom. I've left muddy tracks on the floor.

Even after cleaning up, I look like one of the walking dead. My eyes are sunken and bruised from lack of sleep, and my hair is stringy and dull.

I pull the plug and the bloody water gurgles down the drain. Susannah Holt returns. I'm sitting on the edge of the bathtub, leaning over, my hair falling around my face, when I hear her sharp intake of breath. I tuck my hair behind my ears and look up. She seems panicked.

'All done then?' She collects herself and gets busy: removing the bag from the bin, wiping the counter and sink, replacing the photo, candle and vase in the same position.

'I think so. Sorry about the mess.'

She pauses. 'It's been a long time since I've had to clean up after anybody but myself.' She continues wiping and points with her free hand. 'There's a cup of tea in the kitchen. I don't know if you like tea but...'

'Tea is fine. Thank you.'

I leave her, still scrubbing, and head down the hallway.

It's a bare, cramped kitchen, nothing on the counter except a basket of greasy-looking fruit and one mug of black tea. The fridge is covered with rusty scratches and several old Polaroid-style photos, all showing Hannah when she was younger—on a bike, with a friend, in front of a birthday cake with six candles—except for one class photo with about twenty others dressed in the distinctive Heart uniform. It's hardly changed in two decades: long, chequered navy and green dresses for the girls; white shirts, navy pants and a diagonally striped green tie for the boys.

I've felt nothing but surface pain since I walked through the front door and I'm not prepared for the violent surge of emotion that hits me deep in my belly. My nose burns with threatening tears. I feel seasick, as if the floor is rolling under my feet, and the pain behind my eye is back, worse than before.

I step closer to the photo.

Hannah is easy to spot, right in the middle of the back row, wearing a tight smile, her blonde hair loose. I can see the glint of braces between her lips. She seems gawky and less defined, as if she hadn't quite shed her baby skin. She must have been about fourteen or fifteen.

But the seasickness backs off when I look at Hannah. The room rights itself. It's not *her* this time. I don't feel anything for her baby face, apart from mild curiosity. She isn't here, with me—she's not in her house, in her mother's kitchen, or breaststroking along the carpet, or looking at me without a face.

You're not listening.

I don't want to listen to the sly, sing-song voice.

Susannah Holt bustles into the kitchen swinging a tied-off plastic bag full of gauze and gore. She takes in my glazed expression. 'Are you all right? Are you feeling faint?' She takes me by the shoulders.

I nod and hold her gaze because I don't want to look.

'Come on.' She frowns. She's had enough of my weirdness. 'I'll put your bike in the back of my car. Where do you live?'

Hannah is still smiling that rigid smile, and I still feel nothing for her. I glance over my shoulder at the photo as Susannah Holt leads me out of her house; I obey the sickening urge to drag my gaze to the bottom left of the picture. Though I'm moving away, her face is as clear and familiar to me as my own reflection used to be.

No, it's not Hannah. It's Erin Grady. The girl in the front row—dark-haired, slim, with a direct gaze that burns—she looks just like me because she's my mother.

TWELVE

I lied about where I lived and asked Susannah Holt to drop me outside Reilly's Auto. I thanked her, but she didn't speak to me—she seemed as dazed as I felt. I dragged my aching body and my wrecked bike home, and hid the bike in the gap between the shed and the side fence.

It's six o'clock. I've showered, changed into long pyjamas. I stink like eucalyptus oil from trying to remove the cheap bandaids and replacing them with decent ones. I walk downstairs, stiff-legged like a zombie, to find Dad sitting on the couch with a plate of beans and toast.

Dad's shoulders tense but he doesn't look away from the television. 'Have you eaten? Want some beans?'

'No, thanks. Where's Cody?'

He glances at his watch. 'Should be home soon.'

Diesel barges through the dog-door and skids to a halt in the lounge-room doorway. A ridge of hackles rises along his back like porcupine quills. I back away from him and perch on the end of the couch.

'What'd you do to him?' Dad says, his mouth full. 'Did you clobber him or something? Pinch his bone?'

I shake my head. 'Nothing.'

Dad eyeballs Diesel. 'Dog doesn't turn for no good reason.'

'Maybe he has a good reason.'

He looks at me then, picking food from his teeth with his fingernail, thinking. 'You eating? You feeling right in the head?'

He won't say it, neither of us will. Some words roll easily from our lips, but we struggle to say the ones that count. We won't recall the before-times when Mum ran like a demon or the days when she couldn't get out of bed; we don't speak of the dark days or the reasons why, sometimes, it seemed as if she hated us. We sure as hell don't mention the statistics: of two children born of a mother whose mechanics weren't working, one is likely to have a faulty carburettor, too. We just say, 'Are you feeling right in the head?'

'Dad, I need to tell you something. And I don't want to, but I have to, because it's eating me up inside.'

He angles his body towards me, crosses his legs, and throws his arm along the back of the couch. 'Shoot,' he says, but his eyes are dark and fearful.

Cody's right, none of us is equipped for tragedy. Dad least of all. I want to prepare him—to assure him it isn't me this time, it's something else—before I tell him why Diesel has his reasons. But as I think about where to start, I imagine a giant blank canvas; I start throwing ideas and happenings and recollections at it like paint, and I know it doesn't matter where I begin, the finished picture will look like a Pollock—twisted, maybe compelling, but ultimately, completely, absolutely batshit crazy.

'I just…' I falter.

Diesel gets up and barks at the window. A second later, Cody barrels in through the front door with a tall beanied person close behind: Gummer. My brother has a carton of beer under one arm and a Lumpy's Pete-za in the other hand.

Gummer bends over and kisses my cheek. I get a whiff of something spicy and clean. He bends over and scoops me up, pyjamas and all, and I don't have the heart to tell him his hand is pressing on the mother of all grazes on my hip. I ignore the pain and let him spin me around. He's a bit drunk. But he isn't stoned.

'Where have you two been?' Dad says.

Cody slaps the pizza down on the coffee table. 'Pub.'

Gummer says, 'We walked. It's okay, I left the truck.' He dumps me onto the couch and drops into the space next to me. 'Your brother is a good influence.'

And we eat. The boys drink. Diesel dozes peacefully under the table. Sometime after midnight, I fall asleep near Gummer, on the opposite end of the couch. The television stays on all night. I don't wake until morning. I don't remember my dreams.

'What have you been up to?' Gummer says.

He's watching me intently, his sleepy face and a spoonful of cereal poised over the bowl. He's wearing his usual baggy jeans and a black T-shirt that reads 'Bad Apple' in a seventies font. His beanie is lying on the table like a dead hamster.

I wonder what he suspects. 'Nothing. Most boring holidays ever.' I pop two pieces of toast and spread them with butter and strawberry jam.

'You look like shit,' he says, continuing his breakfast.

I almost choke on a mouthful of toast. 'You can talk. You always look like shit. I'm just too polite to mention it.'

'I'm sorry.'

'You will be.' He can't know anything; he can't see anything. My injuries are hidden under thick socks and acres of flannelette. 'Have you been studying?'

'A bit. Exams seem a long way off still. You?'

I shake my head. 'Have you caught up with the others?'

'Just Pete and Mitch. Who've you seen?' He tips the bowl to slurp the last of the milk and wipes his mouth.

'Nobody.' I don't want to ask but I can't help myself. 'Kenzie wasn't with Mitch?'

He shakes his head. 'Trouble in paradise, I reckon. Amber, on the other hand, seems to be levitating.'

I snicker. 'Yeah, I saw her, too. At Ruby's with Noah Wentz. She told me to go screw myself.'

Gummer's mouth falls open. 'What'd you say to her?'

'I said it back to her. *After* she left the room.'

'No,' he says. 'I meant what did you say to her to make her tell you to go screw yourself?'

I drop my toast onto the plate. 'You think I started it? Gee, thanks, Gummer.'

I'm silently fuming. Gummer usually eats and leaves but today he hangs around, playing with his phone. It's frustrating—after a decent night's sleep, I'm bouncing on the balls of my feet, itching to go looking for answers. It's not an extraordinary development, seeing my mum in Hannah's class photo, but I'm fascinated by the feeling I got as we were leaving the Holt house. It was…satisfaction. As if I was heading in the right direction; as if a bone had clicked into place.

'What time are you leaving?' I ask.

He looks hurt. 'I thought you might want to hang out.'

'And do what?'

'There's a pop art exhibition at the library and free face-painting at the mall.'

'Face-painting? Seriously?' He snaps an image of me frowning. I try to grab his phone. 'Delete that.'

'Only if I can replace it with one of you wearing a smile.' He sticks out his bottom lip. 'I've forgotten how that looks.'

I bare my teeth and he takes another photo. I get up,

huffing, and throw myself onto the couch.

'Weird.' He pushes his chair back and strides across the room. 'Total Freaksville.'

'What?' I stare at a stain on the ceiling. 'Those words have ceased to mean anything to me.'

'Look.' He's waving his phone in my face. 'What have you done to your teeth?' He leans over and tries to peel back my lips.

'Get off me!' I jerk my head away and smack it on the arm of the couch. 'Do you ever go home?'

'Just look.'

I focus. It's my face. I'm unusually pale, caught wearing a typically annoyed expression, but there's something off. It reminds me of when our Year Eight History teacher, Mrs Franks, got new falsies—we all kept staring at her, trying to figure out why she looked the same, but different. My teeth are all wrong. They're bigger, squared off and perfectly straight. Mine are rounded and slightly gappy.

I peer closer, squinting. It's disconcerting. Me. Not me.

'It's nothing. You're imagining things.'

He shakes his phone as if that might fix the problem. 'You must have moved your head. It's blurred or something.' He catches my eye as I turn away. 'This is not weird or freaky to you?'

'That's what I said.' I want him to guess because I can't tell him. I don't want to see that understanding expression people give me when I'm riding a bit loose

126

on my rails; it's not a big leap they take from calling me a risk-taker to calling me crazy. *Oh, poor Grace, she isn't coping. Her mother was hit by a truck. She saw the shrine. She ate a bad prawn.* Like everything has a simple explanation.

'Hey. Tell me what's going on.' He sits next to me and lifts my feet onto his lap. 'What's this?' He touches a fingertip to the light graze on my leg and peels down my sock. He gasps when he sees how many bandaids are stuck to my ankle. 'What have you done to yourself?'

'I didn't do it. Not really.' I pull my foot away. 'Anyway, you wouldn't believe me if I told you. It's complicated and…weird.'

He laughs. 'Sometimes I park my car in the middle of a paddock and lie in the back, waiting for flashing lights and little green men. Tell me.' His fingers are gentle as he pulls up my sock. 'I'm the weirdest person you know.' He sees my hesitation. 'If you tell them you need them, they'll come. Kenzie and the others, I mean. You know that, right?'

'I don't know anything anymore.'

Diesel sidles into the lounge room, his ears back and his tail tucked between his legs. He takes a detour around the couch to get to his water bowl in the kitchen.

I sigh and lever my sore body from the couch. 'I crashed my bike. I'll show you.' It'll be a relief not to keep so many secrets, and he's right: he'd be the last person to judge. 'I just…you really think I started it? With Amber?'

He says solemnly, 'You start everything, Grace. Always have.'

We walk to the pub and pick up the Ford. Still in a haze of pain, I realise I've left my phone and purse at home, so Gummer buys me a sushi roll and a Coke at the mall— we call it the mall but it's just an outdoor food court next to the main shopping centre—and he waits for ages to have an alien painted on his cheek.

I'm sitting at a cafe table, eating my sushi. I can't help but smile, watching him stand in line with a bunch of four-year-olds, his beanie pulled low over his forehead. I guess we should be studying, but I've missed this—hanging out with friends, nowhere to be, no worries, no agenda.

There's a phone ringing. I toss the empty sushi container into a bin and automatically rummage around in my bag. With a sick feeling, I remember: my phone is with my purse, sitting on the windowsill in Susannah Holt's bathroom.

It's Gummer's phone ringing.

He answers, and a strange expression passes over his face. He leaves his place in the line. 'It's you,' he says frowning at the screen. He hands the phone to me.

'Hello?' The line's open but nobody speaks. I take it away from my ear and the screen lights up. *DisGrace*. The call *is* coming from my phone.

Gummer's mouthing something at me. *WTF*?

I cover the phone and whisper, 'I lost it. It's just some-body trying to give it back.'

He nods and steps back into the line. It doesn't seem to occur to him, as it has to me, that my keypad has a password. It's locked. The only person who knows my password is Kenzie. We have the same code—unless she's changed hers recently, which she probably has.

I press the phone back to my ear. 'Who's there?' My hand is clammy, my chest tight. 'Mrs Holt?' There's a sudden shrill whine that makes my eardrum throb, followed by a heavy thud. A second later, a noise that sounds like footsteps on bare floorboards. 'Who's calling from my phone?' I stand up.

Gummer is gazing at me steadily, trying to read the situation.

'Who is this?' A sharp crack. 'How did you get into my phone?' I'm shrieking now. Pacing up and down. Mothers gather their children close and head off.

Gummer's hand is on my shoulder. He takes the phone and speaks. 'If I were you I'd hand the phone in to the police. It's been reported stolen and you're being traced.' He blinks and checks the screen, shrugging. 'They hung up. Calm down and think. Where did you lose it?'

'I don't remember,' I lie. 'It was yesterday sometime.'

'Where'd you go?'

I can't answer. My brain is scrambled. The mall is packed with pre-school kids—and mothers, mothers everywhere, holding tiny hands, wiping snotty noses. Ordinary people going about their ordinary lives.

'Grace, look at me. Did they say anything?'

I swing around. I try to breathe. 'Okay,' I say. 'Okay.'

If I keep saying it, maybe it will be.

'Should I call your dad?'

'No,' I bark. 'Just take me home.'

'Sure,' he says. 'But I'd kinda like to know what you've got yourself into.'

We start walking back to the truck. Gummer is raving on about the Hearts and the night I dyed the pool. He has a conspiracy theory for everything. That's what he thinks: it's someone playing a revenge prank.

I cut him off. 'Do you remember, when we were about eleven, I hid under the boardwalk in the swamp? You guys came looking for me and I jumped out at you?'

'Sure,' he says, nodding. 'You were covered in mud and leeches and your eyeballs looked yellow. Scared the crap out of us. Pete ran halfway home and Amber almost peed her pants again.' He fishes in his pocket for his keys. 'Those were the days,' he says wryly.

'Do you remember what you said?'

He shakes his head. 'Shitbiscuits, or some such? I don't know. It was a long time ago.'

'You said you thought your heart was going to beat its way out of your chest and the first thing that came into your head was some prayer about dying in your sleep. You said you were a goddamned believer, until you realised it was me.'

'Wow. I was a verbose little turd, wasn't I? Shitbiscuits would've covered it.'

'You called me the bogeygirl.'

'And you were flattered enough to remember it?' He

opens the passenger door for me. 'Or offended, in which case, sorry.'

'I'm being serious.'

He laughs. 'I know. It's out of character. Which is exactly why my heart's beating its way out of my chest right now. Feel.' He presses my palm to his ribs. 'Jeepers, your skin is like ice.'

'Jeepers?'

'Creepers.'

'I've seen her.' I snatch my hand away.

'Who?'

'The bogeygirl.'

He starts the truck, throws his arm across the back of my seat and reverses out of the car park.

'Why aren't you saying anything?'

'What do you want me to say? *Woo-ee-oo*? There's no such thing? You're crazy? If this is one of your games, I'm not playing.' He turns left into the main road and drives too fast in the direction of home.

Gummer never used to drive fast.

I say, 'That sounds like something Kenzie would say, not you.' He looks away. 'You have seen her, haven't you?' I glare at his profile.

He snorts. 'The bogeygirl? Not since the boardwalk.'

'No. I'm talking about Kenzie. Let me guess—she told you I was acting out again and you should pay me no attention, like I'm a naughty five-year-old, not pushing eighteen.' I catch his grimace and I know it's true. 'Something something "the girl who cried wolf". Am I right?'

'I'm here, aren't I?' he says, hardly moving his lips. 'Paying you attention.'

I have a lump in my throat like I'm a cat with a fur ball, and if I don't bring it up, I'll choke. 'You're. Not. Listening.' I clap my palm over my mouth. My voice is not mine. It's deep and grating, caked with dirt.

But Gummer hasn't noticed. He didn't hear. He only sees his childhood friend, who has a history of pulling pranks, who tells so many half-truths she believes her own lies.

I try to hold back the panic coursing through my blood. He's smiling. He's *humouring* me.

'Thanks. Pull over. I'll walk from here,' I tell him. 'I need to do something.'

He parks in the bike lane near the cemetery. 'Here?' he says, staring across the field of headstones. 'Oh. Right. Want me to wait?'

Shaking my head, I get out and slam the door. As I push through the wrought-iron gate, I turn around. He's still parked, watching. He wants to help me but he doesn't know how. That's the difference between us: Gummer desperately wants to believe in things he's never seen, but I've *seen* things I don't want to believe. And no matter how hard I tug at the veil between his reality and mine, he'll stay safe on the other side where everything is possible but not quite real, like watching a scary movie with a bucket of popcorn in your lap, the lights turned on.

Gummer can't help me.

THIRTEEN

I have a Hollywood-movie version of a cemetery in my head. My imaginary graveyard is set in New Orleans; it's lush and overgrown, with elegant marble crypts, a labyrinth of winding pathways and ancient trees draped with hanging moss. The crypts are haunted by the restless spirits of people taken before their time. The flowers on the graves are brittle and dying, and shadows lurk around every corner. It's a place of mystery and old magic.

Swanston Cemetery is nothing like that. I must have passed it thousands of times, but I've never been through the gate. I stop just inside the entrance, flip my sunglasses down, and wait. It's bright here. Spread out like the town itself, in a tidy grid, it's flat, dusty and exposed, and the lawns are brown stubble.

I should know which way to go. I should have brought flowers.

I spot a squat brick building and trudge along the path leading to it. The headstones are all similar: dirty grey, rough around the edges—probably cheap because they were mined locally. Most of the flowers are plastic, and the few crypts are hideous marble boxes in the oldest part of the cemetery. The paths are wide and straight, covered with a layer of white quartz. A couple of sad pines huddle in the centre—no place for a shadow to hide. It looks like the dead buried here lived to be old, old people. I don't feel sad for them. I don't feel anything at all.

A woman comes out of the building. She's dressed in men's clothing, carrying a bucket and one of those extendable claws we use at school for picking up rubbish.

'Excuse me?' I ask. 'Where's the memorial rock garden?'

'Up further, past Maria's angel,' she says, pointing. 'It's at the end of 4Z. Be careful where you step.'

I thank her and head for a big angel on a pedestal. As I get closer, I see one of the wing tips is broken and the angel's face has crumbled away, as if birds have been pecking at her nose. *Maria Rossi, 1896–1972. Beloved.* Next to it, a twin headstone and grave that looks like a stone-age double bed. It makes me shudder to think of the bodies inside.

Near the end of the row, the path leads to a low gate set between two dying hedges. Beyond the gate, there's a circular, paved walkway with rough granite boulders set around the edge, each boulder inlaid with a plaque. It's greener here, well tended, with clumps of native grasses and more recent dates on the stones.

This must be it.

I step slowly past each stone, reading the inscriptions. Some have none: a future grave? No—not a grave. These are for ashes. Cremations. Dad went against my grandparents' wishes—they're staunch Catholics who believe a body must be buried to be resurrected. They moved far away when I was younger and we haven't spoken to them since the funeral. Mum wanted to be cremated. She always said if she died she wanted her ashes scattered between the east and west coasts, so she could be everywhere and nowhere. Not stuck in one place.

Her ashes are here, under a rock, in one place. But where? What is it for, this unwanted connection with the afterlife, if I can't feel the pull of my own dead mother?

I leave the rock garden through the opposite side. It opens onto an area with short grass like whiskers and graves with glittery black headstones. These stones don't look cheap or local. I scan the names, but I'm not looking for Mum anymore. I'm looking for *her*. Then I realise: you can't bury a body that has never been found. Where does her mother go? She must go somewhere to leave flowers. She looks like a person who would leave flowers.

I flip up my sunglasses and take a step back. The ground gives way. My feet scrabble on loose gravel and I slide in slow motion, down, down. I have grit in my eyes and fistfuls of dirt. Before I even hit the bottom I've done the calculations—everyone knows a grave is six feet under—and I'm not scared. My feet touch. I'm still standing, and the top of my head is only just below the edge. This is only a hole in the earth; the earth is solid and real. I can see and I can breathe. I could climb out if I wanted to, but I stay there, waiting for the dust to settle, noticing the different colours in the layers of the earth and the way the oblong of sky looks like a postcard, it's such a perfect heartbreaking blue.

'Oh, my goodness,' says a voice. It's the woman in overalls. 'Are you okay? Is anything broken?'

I run my hands over my body—for her benefit, not my own. Nothing is broken. Down here nothing hurts.

'I'm fine.'

'I warned you about the open pits.' She peers down at me, her forehead wrinkled. 'Wait a minute. I'll be back.' She disappears and returns a few minutes later with a three-step ladder. 'Here. Grab the end.'

The moment I climb out of the pit, my head aches. The sun is beating down and there's a crow sitting on the wing of Maria's angel. *Crows are everywhere, common as clouds*, I tell myself, but I still feel sick.

'Sorry. I didn't see it.' I slip my sunglasses back on.

'I don't know how you could miss it.' She points to the tape barrier. I must have torn it when I fell: an orange streamer lies limp on the ground.

'What's the hole for?'

She laughs. 'It's waiting for a new one.' She notices

my bafflement. 'Disinterment. Exhumation. You know, dug up.' She tucks the ladder under her arm. 'You be on your way now.'

I head towards the gate. I'm careful not to look back too soon, but when I do she's still staring after me.

'Girl,' she calls. 'Mind where you step.'

Dad and Cody are working in the garage. The roller-door is up—Cody's top half is underneath the car and Dad is on all fours, his cheek pressed against the grease-caked floor, bellowing instructions. I pause at the entrance. I count at least a dozen empty beer bottles on the workbench and it's only two o'clock. Dad has no work again.

'Chores, Grace.' He must have eyes in the back of his head. 'And you went out this morning and left the house unlocked.'

'Sorry.' I look up at my bedroom window. I left that open, too. The curtain is puffing in, out, in, out, as if the house is panting.

'It ain't like being on the farm. Lock up. You should know that by now.'

Oh, I do. And it ain't.

Diesel is snuffling at the crack under the front door, waiting for a sock or a limb. Out of nowhere I remember one of Mum's old superstitions: enter a house the same way you left, or bad luck will follow. But I can't remember if Gummer and I left through the front door or the back. For a moment, I freeze. I know I'm being ridiculous— what I have following me around is far worse than the bad luck that follows breaking a mirror, walking under a ladder, or leaving new shoes on a table.

I open the front door halfway and reach for the sock basket. Diesel has gone. I throw the door wide open and survey the entry: a metre from the doorstep, on the plush cream carpet, there's a foul dark-reddish stain the size of a dinner plate. I step around it, sniffing the air. The stain looks fresh. Vomit? Blood? And still no Diesel. I check the ceiling. If I drew a vertical line straight up, directly above the stain is the spot in my room where the inky puddle appeared. And on the ceiling there's a familiar shape. A mad beat starts up in my chest again and I take a long blink—but no, it's real and it's still there.

It's not the stain, or the memory of the puddle, or the fact that Diesel is probably plotting an ambush that makes me back away.

It's the star.

A tiny, plastic phosphorescent star, like the ones Mum glued in a swirling constellation above my bed when I was little. One was always different from the rest: deformed, with a lopsided sixth point. *A factory reject*, Mum called it. I complained it wasn't like the rest. When the lights went out and the other stars glowed, I would fixate on the imperfect one; if I had been able to reach the ceiling I would have plucked it down and thrown it away, but by the time I was tall enough, the stars had stopped glowing and I didn't care anymore.

It's *the* star.

I turn around.

Dad's close behind me. 'Before you say anything, it wasn't me,' he says.

'How…what…?' I stammer. It's official. I'm losing my mind.

He brushes past, stepping around the stain. I'm so relieved that it's real, I almost cry.

'Your brother kicked over a container of engine oil. We didn't know what to use to get it out.' He shrugs, looking shamefaced. 'Figured you might.'

Somehow, I manage to sound completely normal. 'Baking soda and lemon juice.'

His expression softens; I know he's thinking about Mum. But he shakes it off and the crease reappears. 'Could you clean it up?' He leaves without waiting for an answer, before I can ask him if he can see the star too.

I stumble out to the garage. 'Cody,' I say to the legs.

'What?'

'Can you drive me somewhere?'

'Not now.'

'Then when?'

'Depends where you want to go.'

'It'll just take half an hour.'

'Not *now*, Grace.' He slides even further under the Celica until only his feet are showing.

I stamp my foot and let out a frustrated shriek.

Cody ignores me.

At the far end of the garage, Diesel materialises from behind a stack of boxes—boxes filled with stuff we don't need, and probably the things we couldn't bear to unpack. I tense up, ready to move to higher ground, but Diesel's hackles are down. His tongue's hanging out and his tail's swinging.

The healing wound on my thumb throbs. Dread has pooled in my stomach. There's something terrifying about a smile on a dog.

FOURTEEN

I've never stolen a car before. Technically, Kenzie stole the teacher's car—I only moved it. I could walk to the Holt house, or catch the bus, but Cody's car is right there and his keys are sitting on the table by the front door. He and Dad have gone out in the truck, so I figure I have at least an hour before they come home, if not most of the day.

I take the backstreets. There's not much traffic. It's a wet-dog day in Swanston. I can't explain why the town smells like that some days; the slightest drop of rain after a dust storm and everything stinks like sodden sheepdog—your hair, your clothes, your skin. Old boots on cold days, mouldy hay when it's hot. I'm sure there are towns smelling of pine forests or salty air or fish, but

Swamptown, for as long as I can remember, has only had three base notes and two kinds of people. I used to think those two kinds were Hearts and Swampies, but now I believe they've the living and the dead.

Last night, somehow, I slept through the night without waking. Before I got into bed, I knelt beside it and I made promises to Hannah Holt—like saying prayers, but with more conviction—and I climbed onto a kitchen chair, took down the star, and fell asleep with it under my pillow. A weight lifted. I thought: love, hate, desire, the trappings of the soul—maybe they don't exist on only one plane. What if ghosts are all around us, all of the time? What if they're not always stuck, unable to move on until earthly justice is done—what if they're just existing, loving, hating, desiring, like us? Maybe it takes someone like me—in the middle, not really living—to close the gap.

The star is safely tucked in the zip pocket of my jeans. Cody's car is almost out of petrol. Desperate to get my purse and phone back, I ignore the gauge, which is showing empty. I pull up just around the corner from Davey Street and park facing downhill, just in case.

'You're not really the catalogue girl,' Susannah Holt says when she answers the door. She's wrapped in a fluffy dressing-gown, slippers on her feet. Her eyes are flat and cold as a shark's. 'She came after I dropped you off. I asked her and she said she didn't know who you were.'

'I'm not the catalogue girl,' I confirm.

'You don't live next door to Reilly's.'

I shake my head. 'I just wanted to ask you…questions.'

Her eyebrows shoot up. 'Grace Alice Foley, born in the millennium, thirty-six Raymond Street. Swanston Public student.' She smirks at my expression. 'Your driver's licence and student ID card. I checked. I was going to return your things but then I had a funny feeling you might be back.'

'I didn't forget them on purpose,' I say. *Did I?*

'No?' She's weighing me up, running her sharp eyes over my face and body. 'Did you crash into my front yard on purpose?' She laughs. 'I take it back. Nobody's that stupid. Come inside, Grace Alice. I have questions of my own for you.' She steps away from the door, leaving me to let myself in.

I follow her into the kitchen. My purse and phone are on the counter. I'm already inventing excuses but she sits down at the kitchen table, leans back in the chair and continues her silent assessment.

I pick up my things: my purse is zipped, my phone screen blank, out of charge. It had a few hairline cracks in one corner before—now it's completely fractured, diagonally, with a spider web of smaller cracks almost covering the screen. 'Did you drop it?' I blurt.

'I did *no such thing*,' she says.

The hairs on my arms stand up. It's cold in here, a gully breeze gusting through the open window behind us. A baby's crying somewhere. Or perhaps it's the wind.

'Thanks but I need to get going,' I say. 'I took my brother's car without asking.'

Her lips pinch. 'You're not the first to try to sneak in here, you know. All those wannabe sleuths and journalists, thinking they've found a missing piece of the puzzle, thinking they'll be the one to find her. They snoop and lie and try to trick me. It gets so I hardly leave the house. And just when I think I've gone a couple of days without thinking about her, just when I think this town's forgotten her, someone like you comes along to bring her back.'

'I'm sorry,' I say.

I'm so ashamed—this poor woman, grieving her dead child. I want to tell her everything I know, but it doesn't make sense, even to me.

Unexpectedly, she smiles. 'It's important that we never forget, don't you think? When we forget, they're truly gone.' She gets up. 'Come with me.' She heads up the stairs, turning back once to make sure I'm following.

I'm following. I can't not.

Halfway up, the staircase turns ninety degrees, opening into a long hallway with five doors, all closed. It's dim up here and it smells stale, like the air has been sitting still for a long time. Mrs Holt treads close to the walls as if she doesn't want to mark the lines of vacuum tracks on the carpet. I do the same. The walls are bare, painted a flat, yellowish cream. There are no pictures of Hannah upstairs.

She stops near the last room on the left. 'I don't come up here often,' she confides, her hand resting on the doorknob. 'And I wouldn't have, but your phone started ringing and I came to see. It took a while, but I found it on the floor under her bed.'

'My phone?' I say, confused. 'But I left it in the bathroom, on the ledge. With my purse.'

'No.'

'But...'

'Don't lie. I can't stand a liar,' she barks. 'What I want to know is, how did you sneak up here? And did you find what you were looking for?' She throws the door open and a dusty shaft of daylight brightens the hallway.

'I didn't...'

She takes my elbow and steers me into the room. 'You'll have to forgive me,' she says. 'I was too upset to tidy up. Then I thought, *she'll* be back, *she* can do it.'

I wonder who she's talking about and realise it's me.

In the corner nearest the window, there's a single bed covered with a pale blue quilt and a white three-drawer cabinet. A matching bookcase and desk are against the wall by the door. Everything else, barring some posters on the walls, is in a pile on the floor. The drawers are open, empty. Mrs Holt blocks the doorway, flapping her hands at the mess: books, clothing, brushes and make-up, lotions and hairclips and sheets of paper. The make-up has crumbled and spilt, leaving streaks of colour on the carpet. As I stand gaping, the last corner of tape holding one of Hannah Holt's posters rips free; the poster sails off the wall and curls up on the bed. We both jump.

She thinks I did this.

'I can't do it anymore,' she says, holding up her palms.

I'm motionless, mouth hanging open, unable to say anything to defend myself or to make her feel better. Truth is, I'm waiting, too. Waiting to sense her presence; Hannah Holt should be here, in her bedroom, with her possessions, the things she loved.

With her mother.

I bend down and start picking up lipsticks and eye shadows, placing them carefully in a cane basket. When I've finished, I shuffle the loose sheets of paper into a neat pile and place her battered paperbacks on the bookshelves. I leave the clothing until last, holding my breath as my fingers touch a lace bra with tiny blue flowers. I expect it to be soft and delicate, but the lace is hard and brittle.

Mrs Holt bites her lip. Her hand twitches at her side. I don't feel anything except sadness for her.

I put the bra away in a drawer and close it gently.

'You can stop,' she says, staring out of the window. 'It wasn't you. I can tell by the way you're touching her things. I'm sorry. I know it wasn't you.'

'But my phone…'

Her eyes dart my way. 'It was under the bed. Down there.' She points. 'I've no reason to lie. I can't stand a liar.'

I get to my feet. Mrs Holt moves away from the doorway and I tense up, ready to flee.

She raises a shaking finger. 'He watched her. He would sit on the branch and watch her.'

A shiver travels up my spine.

146

She climbs onto the bed, unravels the poster, and tries to put it back on the wall. The tape won't stick. Her hands battle to smooth the curling paper, losing, until she gives up and just holds it there, her hands leaving dirty black smudges on the white wall.

The poster is in direct line of sight of the tree, where the branch used to be. It's not a poster after all. It's a drawing—a simple charcoal sketch of seven crows, like musical notes, sitting on a power line.

I park Cody's car exactly where I found it and let myself into the house, still buzzing with adrenalin. Diesel's outside, barking at the back fence. I rush to the laundry and bolt the dog-door before he can come inside, toss my purse on the dining-room table and plug in my phone. I need to see the call log: whoever moved it—and used it—is likely to be the same person who trashed Hannah Holt's room. But why *now*? She's been gone for so long.

I wait for my phone to start but the battery is dead. I need coffee, but the canister's empty. I should try to draw the crows now, I think, as I rummage in the pantry for our emergency jar of instant. Their shapes are still fresh in my mind. Of one thing I'm certain: Hannah drew the crows, and it was her hand guiding mine to draw her portrait. There was a strong similarity of style—the way the lines blurred, the smattering of light on the wings. But there was not enough time to study them. As I was leaving, Susannah Holt seemed to collapse in on herself. She kept muttering *sorry, sorry*, over and over, but I wasn't sure who she was apologising to. I got the feeling the room had been preserved when Hannah went missing, and now it would never be the same.

The emergency coffee is nowhere to be found. I turn around. The light from the kitchen window outlines a hulking shape near the breakfast bar. I throw up my hands in fright. I have nowhere to run. I grab the nearest box of cereal and launch it.

The shadow bats it away easily.

Cody is furious. 'What the hell, Grace?' He picks up the box and ditches it back, hitting my shoulder. 'You took my car?'

'I thought I could be there and back before you got home!' My voice is high-pitched with panic. 'Jesus, Cod-face, don't creep up on people. You scared me.'

'You could've asked,' he yells. 'That's the last time I cover for you.'

'I did ask. Yesterday.' I push past him and try my phone again. The screen lights up.

'You asked for a ride. You didn't ask if you could drive it.' He stabs his finger into my shoulder.

'Sorry.'

'Say it like you mean it. I was supposed to start work over an hour ago.'

'*Sorry!*' I have dozens of notifications and missed calls. 'I've got to check this.'

Six calls from Kenzie's number and two texts. My heart starts up a glad beat. I'll go up to my room and read them in private. But Cody yanks the phone out of my hand and holds it up high, too high to reach. I jump at it, but he bats me away as easily as the cereal box.

'Give it back. It's mine!'

He laughs. 'Go ahead, throw a tantrum, problem child.'

'It's important!'

'So is my job.' He grabs his car keys from where I left them on the table, slips my phone into his shirt pocket and scoops up the spare set of farm keys from a hook on the side of the fridge. 'You're coming with me.'

'The farm? Why?'

We go back occasionally to pick up things. It's always painful.

'This is for your benefit.'

'What benefit? You know I get sad when I go there.'

'It's only on lease, Grace. We might go back one day.'

I sigh and give in. 'Cody?'

'What.'

'Your petrol tank is empty.'

FIFTEEN

I believed Dad when he said a fresh start would be a good thing. He'd have more time to spend with us now Mum was gone. Cody wouldn't have to drive the deadly twenty-kilometre stretch of highway into Swanston twice a day, and I'd be closer to my friends and school. But I learned to tune in to the way Dad's tone hit a high note—*a good thing?*—and he said it too often, as if he was trying to convince us, and himself.

Later, after we'd moved to the estate, Cody let it slip that we had to give up the farm because Dad couldn't afford to pay the bills; our livestock were sick and underfed, and the dams were running thin on clay, leaking precious rainwater. The Johnson family next door were cashed up but land-poor; they offered to take a five-year lease. Dad accepted. We had our fresh start. But I knew there was another reason we left—long days on the land were long hours Cody and I were left to our own devices. I knew by the way Dad shouted for me if I was out of his sight for too long and Cody knew it, too, when Dad made him call ten times a day.

Dad was afraid.

When we left the farm I worried it would give up my secrets to the family who moved in: the Johnsons' farm manager Brett O'Malley, his wife Mandy, and their three children. Paige is my age. She goes to Sacred Heart. She has my room. She sees the faded constellation of stars above my bed and looks out over the house paddock where I took my first steps and learned to drive. If she's gone exploring she would have found my name carved into trees, concrete slabs, fence posts and rocks.

Cody has managed not to speak during the whole drive. He won't give me my phone and it's driving me crazy wondering what Kenzie has said.

'They've killed her plants,' I say. The driveway up to the farmhouse is two hundred metres long. The year before she died, Mum had painstakingly planted rows of English box seedlings along the last fifty metres on either side. They struggled to take root, but now they're really gone.

Cody finally speaks. 'They never belonged here. Fancy plants—they needed too much looking after.'

I jerk my head around but he won't meet my eye. He's not talking about the plants. 'You're talking about Mum.'

151

He shrugs. 'True.'

'I hate you.'

He closes his eyes for a second. It wouldn't matter if he closed them for a whole minute—we could both still drive this track blindfolded. Probably the entire property, all six hundred acres.

'She loved Dad. She loved us,' I say.

He turns the wheel sharply to hit the ditch he knows is there. 'Yeah. She loved us all so much she threw herself under Dominic Aloisi's truck.'

Now it's me who can't speak. I have to get out. I turn the handle and the door swings open. Cody has me by the back of my jumper and somehow I wriggle out of his grip and jump. He's braking, but I still hit the dirt hard enough to drop and roll into the shallow ditch alongside the driveway, taking out another few of Mum's seedlings.

I sit up, breathing hard, and throw a clump of dirt and roots at the car.

Cody stops long enough to make sure I'm okay and takes off again, leaving me to walk alone. Alone is where I want to be. I can feel tears making tracks on my dirty face and my chest is heaving with the effort to stop myself from running after the car and taking a swing at him.

I've never said those words aloud. Except, the way he said it, I know he has. And maybe Dad has, too.

He's gone for about half an hour. I wait, sitting on a fence post, watching the light change over the fields, my hand in a fist around the star in my pocket. The farm doesn't really belong to us anymore. I practise the words

I'll fire at Cody when he comes back—have them all lined up, ready to go, like a wave of soldiers. He can't be allowed to think that way; Mum's not here to tell him it isn't so.

A breeze picks up, carrying whirlies of red soil into the sky. We used to chase them when we were kids. We used to build castles out of hay bales and make crop circles in the paddocks; we'd wait for storms to roll in, lying on our backs on the hay shed roof, tempting the lightning—and fate—by holding star-droppers up to the sky.

Cody wasn't always my big brother—once he was my friend.

When he comes back to pick me up he looks miserable. He throws an engine part in the back of the car and slides into the driver's seat, handing me my phone.

I've had so much time to think that my words have deserted. All that's left is the ache and frustration of being alive—it must be the worst kind of hell to be dead, and not to be heard.

Cody heads straight for the garage. I let myself in as Diesel watches my every move from under the dining-room table. I bolt upstairs, wash my face, empty my pockets of dirt, and throw myself onto the bed.

Cody is probably regretting what he said, but there's no taking it back. He can stew in his juices until he falls apart, for all I care.

My outgoing log shows no recent call to Gummer's

number. The last one registered was the night of Tamara Fraser's party when I set up the pool prank. I don't know what I hoped for from Kenzie—an apology, or at least a 'we need to talk'—but her voicemail messages are disappointing. Her tone is chirpy but guarded, and I imagine Mitchell looming over her, holding a script.

'Hey, Grace. It's me, Kenzie. Just checking up on you.' And, 'You're not answering your phone? Well, okay then. Bye.'

The texts were sent yesterday afternoon, around the time Gummer and I were at the mall. She wouldn't have known my phone was missing.

Call me when you're free. Okay, not urgent. Half an hour later: *WHERE ARE YOU?* Genuine concern, or does she need to talk?

I log in to my Facebook but there's not much activity apart from the usual insults. Insta's full of pictures from last night's round of parties and car park hangouts. I check Kenzie's Facebook. The only recent post is a picture of Mitch and her from four days ago. They're lying on his bed. Behind their faces is a poster with one of those inspirational quotes like the ones in Call Me Connie's office.

Michael Jordan: 'I've failed over and over and over again in my life…and that is why I succeed'.

Mitch doesn't even like basketball.

I try to check Amber's Facebook and apparently we're no longer friends.

I send Pete a message: *Wassup?*

I call Gummer and it rings out.

154

If I could only speak to one of them *before* I call Kenzie—to see how the land lies—but it's like I'm the last person on earth.

'Just call her,' I say to myself.

I'm surprisingly nervous as I wait for her to pick up, but of course she doesn't. I leave her a message.

'Hey, Kenzie. It's me, Grace. Just checking up on you. You're not answering your phone? Well, okay then. Bye.'

It's the same message, word for word—but hers was chirpy, and mine sounds vicious. And there's no taking it back.

Dad's cooking liver and onions, dinner of champions. The smell makes me feel sick. Mum couldn't stand it either.

I close my bedroom door and open the window; outside there's a grating sound. My escape platform, the tree branch, has grown and it's rubbing against the gutter. If Dad truly wanted to keep me in he'd only have to lock my bedroom door and saw the branch off. It's a long way down. I'd be like Rapunzel in her tower.

I open my laptop. Did Susannah Holt cut down the branch outside Hannah's window herself? Was it before or after Hannah disappeared? Was it obsession that drove William Dean to climb the tree outside and watch her?

I trawl through articles and there's one common theme: William Dean wasn't right in the head, people said. He was smart enough but something was off about him. That's the word that keeps cropping up. Off.

Everyone knew he had something to do with the disappearance of Hannah Holt but there was no real evidence. Every clue led to a dead end. Her body was never found.

September is traditionally a month of dry, sunny days in Swanston, but on September 18th 1993, the night Hannah Holt disappeared, an unseasonal storm rolled in and it rained. When the rain stopped, the surrounding paddocks were hit by several thousand dry lightning strikes; dozens of spot fires broke out across a hundred-kilometre radius. Between the hours of midnight and three, Swanston burned and Hannah Holt vanished. Almost a year to the day later, William Dean took his own life to pay the debt he owed Hannah Holt—at the same time, he took the secret of her resting place with him to the bottom of the gully.

The story of a missing girl and her killer's suicide was spread through whisper and rumour. Even twenty-three years later, it still gathers details. It's difficult for me to find much in the way of straight reporting—it was a crime that divided the media and the community. An *alleged* crime. A *possible* murder. The only thing most people could agree on was that it was an undeniable tragedy for Hannah's mother.

Search parties continued looking for Hannah for months. Dams were dredged, houses searched, backyards dug up; cadaver dogs were brought in to scour the gullies and surrounding paddocks and ditches. William Dean was arrested twice and brought in for questioning over nine times, but there was no solid evidence apart from the samples taken from the back seat and boot of his car. But William had a reasonable explanation for everything—except his strange behaviour.

Nobody could say for sure why William Dean decided to jump. After Hannah Holt's disappearance he'd dropped out of school—out of sight, if not out of mind. His body wasn't discovered for two days until a crop duster spotted his car, dumped, in the bottom of the quarry. He hadn't been reported missing—it wasn't that unusual for him to vanish for days at a time.

There are only a few photos of him online. Each one makes me shudder. His eyes, dark and empty, stare straight into the lens. His hair is long in the front and blue-black, so dark it looks dyed, the colour in stark contrast with his pale skin and the raw patches of acne on his neck and cheeks. He wears plain white T-shirts with tight black jeans, accentuating his skinny chest and legs. He looks at least six feet tall and his arms are unusually long, covered with coarse hair. In close-ups I can see tracks of blue veins under his skin.

'Grace,' Dad calls. 'Get down here.'

I print out several articles and photos, tucking them into a folder. As I close the flap to cover his face I almost feel sorry for him, except his appearance fits the profile of a damaged, psychopathic loner. William Dean wouldn't survive Swampie Public today. They'd tear him apart.

'Grace!'

'I'm coming!'

I take the stairs two at a time and, from halfway,

ride the banister to the bottom. I'm feeling energised and inexplicably happy. Dad looks up smiling as I hit the last step and bound into the dining room. Diesel has come around, his tail settling into a slow wag, his tongue hanging from the side of his mouth as if he's drunk. But Cody hasn't forgiven me yet.

'What's up?' I say, glancing between Dad and Cody.

'What do you mean, what's up? Dinner is what's up.' Dad pulls out a chair at the table. 'Sit.'

The blood leaves my face. 'You know I don't eat offal.'

Cody scowls. 'It's offal with *gravy*.' He picks up two pieces of bread and slaps them onto my plate. 'Sit!'

'I'm not a dog. A dog wouldn't eat that.' I fold my arms. 'And you're not my father.'

'Nobody would choose to be the father of a brat like you.'

'I'm right here,' Dad says quietly. He picks up his plate and moves to the couch.

'See what you did?' Cody hisses.

I flip him the finger and stuff a slice of bread into my mouth. As I pass under the light globe in the lounge room, it pops and goes out.

'Dodgy electrics,' Dad says. 'Bloody cardboard houses.'

Hannah Holt is standing at the foot of my bed. She's wearing white cotton shortie pyjamas, her face hidden behind a veil of matted hair. Her hands are cupped together—she looks like she's begging, or saying a prayer.

At first I'm not sure if I'm awake or asleep—if she's finally showing herself or if I've made her up, a composite of all the horrors I've ever seen or imagined.

Thump. Bump. Bruises blossom like flowers on her skin, only to fade and turn yellow, then bloom again in a different place. *Smack.* Her head snaps backwards like she's been hit, and she flops like a rag doll. *Click, click.* Her bottom jaw slips from side to side as if she's grinding her teeth.

I crawl across the bed, trying to capture one of her fluttering hands, but it dances out of reach. I still can't see her face and she's starting to fade. Desperate, I grasp handfuls of hair, scooping it aside. I feel like I'm swimming through a forest of seaweed, but the hair sticks to my hands and twines around my wrists. I pull back, and clumps of hair come away in my hands, leaving weeping patches of flesh on her scalp.

She claws at my face. Is she trying to get away? Or is she trying to climb inside my skin?

Her shape flickers. It reappears across the room, as if a group of stagehands had moved the props and set up a new scene. She's sitting quietly, chewing a fingernail, her arm hanging across the back of a seat, facing away. Rivulets of rain dance across a window and shapes streak past, illuminated by flashes of light: trees, fences, white lines. She's in a car, staring out of the rear window. Looking back. Leaving. She turns her head and spits out the fingernail.

Then, it's dark. She's curled up on her side, her hair

still covering her face. I smell dust, rubber, oil, metal, fear. Pinpricks of light flicker like distant stars and every few seconds she's jolted out of position. She can't stretch her legs. I hear her breathing—and mine. And I hear a wheezing engine followed by a sound like a gunshot. She jerks, and the darkness surrounding her glows red.

For too long, she's still. I'm sure she's dead. I'm no longer on the bed but in the dark place, with her.

Clunk. A latch releasing, a rush of air and moonlight. Hannah slowly turns over and her hair falls away. She looks up, and her features have changed—she's aged by twenty years or more, and she's staring into the face of William Dean.

This is where the scene ends. I'm awake, sitting up in bed, but my room still has the grainy light and blurred edges of a dream.

SIXTEEN

I wake early and spend the morning checking off the list of chores that Dad left pinned to my door: dusting, vacuuming, washing. Dad's and mine. Not Cody's. He can clean his own room. I shut his bedroom door. There's still so much to do, including a stack of work I need to finish before school goes back, but the bus to South Swanston leaves at 9.15. There isn't another straight run until 11.45.

Diesel's watching me, bemused. This new industrious Grace must be as confounding as the one he wants to bite. I keep him at bay by chattering to him and throwing treats.

I cart the vacuum upstairs to my own room. On the floor, right where I dreamed Hannah had curled on her side, there's a greasy outline and a fine layer of grit. I vacuum the grit and buff the grease away with a dirty towel from the bathroom. I've accomplished more in the last hour than I have in a month; it's like the night I wrote the essay—as if by letting fear run its course instead of trying to block it, I've tapped into a source of energy.

I realise I've spent most of my life marking dot points off an imaginary list, trying to prove I'm not afraid of anything. I've flown down steep hills on skates and skateboards, and played chicken with cars. I've walked the pipe and jumped off Morley Bridge to prove I wasn't afraid of heights or drowning. I take risks—breaking into Sacred Heart, sneaking out, stealing cars, playing pranks—to prove I'm not afraid of authority. I've stolen, lied, and cheated people for laughs, because if you're laughing, it means you're not afraid, right? My own mum died crossing the street, but sometimes I'll shut my eyes and step off a kerb because I believe nothing bad will happen if it isn't my time.

But I remember when I was small and Mum got her first mobile phone—she taught me to play a game called Snake. It starts easy: avoid running into walls and running over your own tail. But your tail becomes the main obstacle; every time you change direction, the space within your walls grows smaller as your tail grows longer and longer, until your tail isn't following anymore. It has become an entity of its own. It's *chasing* you.

I'm thinking I'm *this* close to crossing my own tail. All the fears I thought I'd faced down are back on the list, plus a few I've never acknowledged before, like being alone and seeing things that might not be real.

Now I know what Kenzie meant when she said she was suddenly aware of her own mortality, but the strange thing is: I'm not afraid to die. It seems like something I've done before.

The bus stinks like baby puke and exhaust fumes. It's standing-room only. I can't remember the last time I used public transport. I haven't missed it. Mornings during the holidays are always a seething mass of children; anyone between twelve and twenty is probably still in bed.

One boy says loudly, 'Does that lady have a disease?' and his mother digs her elbow into his ribs.

I smile, recalling the time Mum made me apologise for calling an old man a hunchback, but his wide eyes meet mine. He's talking about me.

'Can we catch it?' he says. 'Don't let her touch me.' She smacks his hand, mouthing an apology and recoiling at the same time. She switches seats with him, distracting him by playing Spotto.

I clutch the overhead rail, trying to avoid landing in anyone's lap, feeling like a creature from a different species. When the bus reaches Swanston Central, the midway stop on the line, everyone gets off, except for me and two women at the front with babies on their laps. I settle into a sticky seat at the back, pull out my phone and click on camera, reversing the view. I do look sick, gaunt, and my eyes are hollow and pouchy underneath.

My hair is matted, a nothing-colour, no gloss. A red rash has developed on my neck, as if I've been scratching, and my lips are so badly cracked it's a wonder they don't sting. Until now, I haven't noticed the flower-shaped bruises on my arms—some old, some fresh—a similar pattern to the bruising on Hannah Holt's skin in my dreams.

Are they from the bike accident?

I get up and peel down the waistband of my jeans. The edges of the graze are healing, but in the centre of the wound there's a deep hole, as if it's ulcerated. It looks like it should hurt.

Why don't I feel pain?

I'm standing in the aisle, jeans half down. The bus driver pulls up at a red light. He stares at me in his rear-view mirror and the two women at the front turn around in their seats.

'Is she okay?' says one.

The other woman looks familiar, but I can't place her. She gets out of her seat, holding out her hand. No, she's holding it up. The complicated language of a simple gesture: out says *let me help you*. Up means *keep away*.

'I'm fine,' I tell her.

The baby starts crying.

The seated woman covers her mouth but I hear her as clearly as if she was sitting next to me. 'Junkie.'

I button my jeans and press the bell for the next stop. The kid was right. Nobody touch me.

★

164

The gully behind the Holt house is wide and steep with plenty of cover, the trees thick and tangled with a dense mat of grass and weeds underneath them. I come the long way, following a well-worn path along the top of the opposite side, hoping I'll have a view of the backs of the houses on Davey Street. The path branches off about half a kilometre back. I follow my instinct, heading for the highest point, crossing over when I reach it. Dozens of tracks snake down the gully sides, and I stumble over sleds made from sheets of corrugated iron and rope, hidden in the grass. Kids.

I work my way along the rear of the houses, occasionally peeping over the top of the fences. I must be getting close. I lean over a low gate and a dog launches without warning, nearly taking a piece of my face; I'm so unsettled by its vicious bark, I run, skidding down the side of the gully to the bottom. There, I sit on a warm rock in a dry creek bed to catch my breath. I'm overheated and sweaty. It's secluded down here; quiet, but for the birds and the rustle of grass. A crested kite hovers overhead, searching for prey, and a blue-tongue lizard ambles past my feet, either unaware or unafraid.

Cody would have loved this jungle—so many places to hide. We grew up roaming flat yellow paddocks, hardly a tree in sight.

Did Hannah Holt play in this gully when she was a child?

Why did he kill you?

I survey the pattern of roofs above. From down here

they look like Lego houses. I find it on my second pass—the distinctive peak of the Holt house. I'm directly below it. I remembered the tiles being grey, but they're green, and the fence behind the yard is the only one unmarked by graffiti. Either it's been painted over or the local vandals have a conscience.

Where did he hide you?

I travel in a straight line up the side of the gully. I'm not sure what I'm looking for—am I seeking hard evidence or chasing a feeling? And I'm walking a twenty-three-year-old crime scene—after so much time has passed, what could I find that hasn't already been discovered?

What do you want me to do?

Twenty metres from the fence, I stop and hide behind a tree. Any closer and I risk being spotted lurking near the house. I can see through the kitchen window from here, but only a view of the upper cupboards and ceiling.

My fingers drum a beat on the tree trunk: *Why did he kill you—where did he hide you—what do you want me to do?*

A squalling breeze whistles through the gully. The sky to the north is red: the sign of a coming dust storm. I pluck strands of hair from my mouth and flick them away. My fingers are red, too. Sticky. I must be bleeding from somewhere. I lick my stinging lips—where my fingers have touched them, I taste the stickiness. But it isn't coppery like blood. It tastes like maple syrup.

Tree sap.

I look up, trace the oozing drips of sap on the tree. Heavy, rusting bolts have been driven deep into the trunk. At head height, a few pieces of rotting wood about a ruler-length wide are still attached. Are they part of a makeshift ladder? Higher up, I see the remains of a large crate, perched in the broad fork of the tree. The crate looks like it's been hacked apart with an axe—it's a broken skeleton of a thing, but it might once have been a lookout.

Or a *crow's nest*.

William Dean would have had the perfect vantage point from up there. From this side of the gully, and from the tree outside her room, he could have watched her without being seen. At the rear: the kitchen, dining area and lounge are visible through the windows. At the front: Hannah's bedroom and bathroom.

It's too high for me to climb without footholds, but this place is clearly no secret: the tree trunk is scarred with engravings, old and fresh. I'm no closer to finding out what happened to Hannah Holt. I haven't discovered anything new.

I catch my breath and prepare myself for the long walk back through the gully. I'm parched and I didn't bring any water. It occurs to me that I haven't eaten today, or yesterday, and that probably accounts for the way I look and feel. Who forgets to eat? What kind of person frightens children on buses, ditches her friends, and lies to a grieving mother? For what? To exorcise a ghost who doesn't exist, except in my mind?

I feel stronger, more myself than I have in a long time, except for the pain. Suddenly everything hurts—the bruises, my lips, the hole in my side. My head pounds, as if the blood vessels are set to burst.

I check the time: 12.30. I have less than fifteen minutes to catch the return bus, or I'll have to wait over an hour for the next one. It's a shorter route if I head back on this side of the gully, but it's steeper, with more trees and a less defined path. The wind has swung around and now it's coming from the north. I rub my watery eyes. Soon the dust storm will hit—they're frequent and predictable, unlike public transport in this town. It'll slow me down.

I break into a jog, stumbling on the rocky path. Some of the fences are low enough—I could easily hop over one and cut through somebody's yard. The sun breaks through the cloud, glinting on a metal post further ahead: a bike barricade, covered with twisting vines. I push through to discover a narrow alleyway between two houses, the ground deep in rubbish and dying leaves. Graffiti covers the fences on either side. It's a public thoroughfare, but I still feel as if I'm doing something wrong.

My phone pings. It's Pete. *Where are you?*

I don't know. Where am I? I open Maps.

The dust is here. It's in my eyes, my pockets, my shoes; the alley sucks the wind like a straw. I scuff through the layer of leaves, bottles and cans, making such a racket I startle a flock of birds from the trees and set the neighbourhood dogs barking. Ahead, the alley opens onto a residential street. I wipe dust from my phone screen. According to my GPS, I'm standing at the end of Edward Court, three streets away from the Holt house. Number

22 Edward Court is one of the places of interest I've flagged in my folder of notes.

Halfway up the road, I find it: a red-brick, single-storey house with a tidy garden and two parking spaces, side by side. I get a whiff of wet paint and wood chips. Everything—paint, garden, gutters, downpipes—looks fresh and new.

It's the Dean house. And it's for sale.

I've missed the bus. I'm too self-conscious to be one of those people who run after it waving their arms, trying to chase it down. *Dammit*.

I scrounge some coins from my pockets and buy a bottle of water from a service station. I guzzle the whole thing at the counter. Back on the main road, I pull up my hood and start walking. If I keep up a decent pace, I should be home in around forty minutes.

I stride along the footpath, arms folded, muttering to myself. *So, I'd rather feel pain than feel nothing at all. I'd rather be obsessed than bored. Would I rather be afraid than feel safe? Apparently, it's a yes. Am I slightly mad, like Mum? I don't think so—at least not in the same way. She knew Hannah Holt. But half the town probably knew her. Did my mother throw herself under a truck? No. I can't prove it, but I will never believe that*.

There's a car following me. It's crawling along in the bike lane, just a few metres behind. I'm not sure how long it's been there, or if it's really following me at all. I can't see past my hood without turning around, so I take a hard left at the next street and cross the side road. I'm facing into the wind; it's sandblasting my face. I speed up, blinking away the grit, covering my nose and mouth with my hand. I think I hear my name, *Graaa–aaace*, before the sound is snatched away.

I break into a sprint and try to cross the main road. A car beeps, passing close enough for me to see the shocked face of its driver. Then I'm yanked by the waist, pinned by my arms, lifted off my feet and spun around. I yell and kick out.

'Grace, it's me! Man, you're jumpy. Why'd you run off?' He lets me go. 'I was calling you.'

'Pete!' I shove him hard in the chest and whip off my hood. 'You idiot. I just lost ten years off my life!'

He yells back. 'Better ten years than all of it. You nearly ran in front of a car.'

I place my hand over my chest. 'I need to get my breath back. What are you even doing here?'

'I could ask you that,' he says, scanning my face. 'Jesus, you look like shit.'

I shove him again.

'Come on.' He spits in the gutter. 'Get in the car.'

If I had turned around I would have seen Pete's station wagon—it's pretty distinctive.

Automatically, I open the door and try to climb into the front seat, but there's somebody in it. Gummer. There's someone in the back, too.

'Hey. What is this? An abduction?'

'It's an intervention,' Kenzie says.

170

SEVENTEEN

'Annie saw you on the bus.'

Kenzie's eldest sister. Of course it was Annie.

We're sitting in Lumpy's in our booth at the back. Pete's got the CLOSED sign on the door and he's making smoothies. Gummer's helping. I suspect they're both happy to leave Kenzie to play diplomat—it's always been like this, any sign of 'girl problems' and the boys disappear.

Kenzie's trying hard not to stare at my face, and failing. 'She said you looked strange. Like, off-your-head strange.'

Kenzie looks different, too. Tired and softer around the edges. Older. She's taken out her piercings. I think about what Pete said—is that what happens when you do it? Do you lose more than you bargained for?

'Grace?'

'Sorry. What?'

She frowns. 'Are you doing drugs?'

It feels so good to laugh, but I go on for too long. I've hurt her feelings. 'I've never taken anything stronger than codeine. You know that. I guess I'm just not taking care of myself.'

'Well, you should. I think you need to talk to...'

'Why did you come and get me?' I interrupt.

She looks away. 'Because Gummer said we had to. He thought it was important. Is it? Or is it just you being the centre of attention again?'

I slump back in the seat. 'Right.' I stare down at my fingers, twisting them in my lap.

'I think you're depressed,' she says carefully.

My gaze snaps back. 'I think I'm possessed.'

'Please, not that again.' Her eyes fill with tears. 'Look, you're my best friend. Always will be. But I can't be around you when you're being like this. You make me feel angry and helpless and you used to make me laugh all the time, but now I'm anxious instead and I have this ball of, I don't know...*rage,* and I can't do it anymore. I can't fix it. I can't fix you. You need help, more than I can give.'

'You can't be around me?' We glare at each other.

Pete brings us both banana-berry smoothies. 'Ladies. Need anything else?' His head swivels from me to Kenzie, back again. He must sense we're at a stand-off.

'No? I guess that's it then.' He gives the table a brisk wipe and retreats.

I lean forward. 'Can we just be us for a little while? Just you and me? No Mitch. No Gummer or Pete?'

'What about "no Amber"?' she says. 'I saw her yesterday. She seems happy.'

'Amber's changed sides.'

She shakes her head. 'I just see her trying to have a relationship with a guy without all of us shouting her down.'

'She's different,' I say stubbornly. 'I don't trust her.'

'You don't trust anybody.'

I change the subject. 'Anyway, so if you're not busy on the weekend we could go out. Catch up.'

She fidgets with her straw. 'Actually, I have something on.'

'Oh? What?'

'A party,' she mumbles. 'Just a stupid party.'

'And I'm not invited. It's okay. I get it. Kenzie, please stop staring at my face.'

'I can't help it.' She blushes. 'You haven't touched your smoothie.'

'I'm not thirsty.' I push the smoothie over to her side. 'You have it.'

We run out of things to say.

We can hear Gummer in the kitchen, making his own abomination of a pizza. Pete's yelling at him for wasting toppings, saying the pizza is too loaded and the base will disintegrate before it has time to cook properly.

Gummer's telling him it will only be a waste if he doesn't put it in the wood oven, followed by something about necessity being the mother of invention. He goes off on one of his tirades about the kook who discovered penicillin, the nut job who researched germ theory in a cesspit, and the wacko who first thought of using a pig's aorta in a human heart. And then he backs out of the kitchen using a pizza tray as a shield, Pete is throwing dough at him, and Uncle Lumpy is swearing in Polish through the screen door.

Oh yeah. We're all mad here.

I catch Kenzie in a wistful smile.

She pushes the smoothie away and leans forward. 'Do you remember when we told our parents we were sleeping at each other's houses and we camped out behind the equipment shed on the school oval?' she says. 'I didn't sleep all night. It wasn't fun for me. I was so terrified we'd get caught, but you thought it was the biggest adventure. That's the difference between me and you. You always liked being scared.'

My first instinct is to tell her she's wrong, but it's true. I did like being scared. But it's different now. It's easy being scared when you have the choice to make it stop: turn off the movie, turn on the light, say you're not playing anymore.

Gummer comes out of the kitchen, covered in flour. 'Pete says he has to open up in five minutes.'

There's someone banging at the front door of the shop.

'Wow. Impatient, much?' I turn around, expecting a hungry customer, but it's Dad. He's peering through the gaps in the broken blinds, hitting the glass with the flat of his hand. There's only one reason he'd be here. 'Kenzie?'

'I called him,' Kenzie says, looking fierce. 'I'm sorry, Grace. I didn't know what else to do.'

In slow motion, I get up to open the door.

Kenzie's crying. Gummer has his arm around her shoulder.

I don't feel sorry for her.

'There's more than one difference between you and me,' I tell her. 'I would never ditch you because I couldn't fix you. And I would never, ever think you needed fixing.'

Dad is surprisingly gentle with me as he leads me to the truck. He doesn't seem angry. Just sad. He gives me a leg-up into the cab, making sure my foot is out of the way before he closes the door.

The dust storm has passed. The street is eerily quiet.

'I'm going to grab us a coffee,' he says. 'Wait here.' He crosses the road and goes into JoJo's Cafe on the opposite corner.

The truck is in dire need of a good clean. The dashboard's coated in a thick layer of red dust and dozens of empty takeaway containers and coffee cups are stuffed behind the seats.

Dad's not taking care of himself, either.

I remember when the truck was brand new and

smelled of vinyl and rubber. Mum said Dad had a new woman in his life and her name was Gina—I didn't speak to him for a week before I realised she meant the truck. When I was eight, he took me with him to Sydney, a three-day round trip; we lived on chips and gravy and glass bottles of ginger beer, driving through the night, counting how many rabbits and foxes ran in front of the headlights. I thought the ginger beer made me drunk. I think I was just deliriously happy.

I flip down the passenger visor. More dust. I can hardly see my face in the mirror. There's a photo tucked behind it. I pull it out. It's Mum: young, pretty, serious, with an arm around her shoulder. The photo has been cut in half. I've never seen this picture before. On Dad's side, tucked under an elastic band, there are individual photos of Mum, Cody and me. Mum's in fancy dress, wearing a slinky catsuit and holding a glass of champagne. She's laughing. Cody's about seven, smiling proudly, astride his first trail bike. Mine's a Grade Five school photo: my hair's pulled back in a severe bun and my ears stick out. Mum did it so Kenzie and I could be matching. Everyone made fun of us but we didn't care. A few days later, Kenzie and I had a massive fight about something stupid—Mum told me there was nothing that couldn't be fixed between two people, as long as one person was willing to be the first to give ground.

I think of all the times Mum said she wanted to live in a 'civilised' house, with a proper garden where flowers didn't curl up and die. She wanted a car that didn't constantly break down in the middle of nowhere, reliable phone reception, and good company, other than the cows and the sheep. She didn't love the farm like we did. She wasn't born there, like we were.

How much ground did *she* give? More than she could bear?

Dad's back, holding two extra-large cups. Quickly, I flip the visor back up. He gets in and hands me a cup. I take a sip—mine is hot chocolate, not coffee. I sigh.

'I need to price a job at the Morgan place,' he says. 'Want to come for a ride?'

The Morgans are rich, like Gummer's parents. They can afford to ride out a few bad seasons; they would never have to give up their family home to strangers.

It's not like I have a choice. I shrug. Dad takes it as a yes and does a five-point turn, stopping traffic. The Morgan property is about forty kilometres north of Swanston. This is going to take a couple of hours, at least.

'How's school?'

'It's the holidays, remember?'

He grunts. 'I mean, in general. Are you staying on top of things? Study?'

'It's fine, Dad. Everything's fine.' I stare out the window, focusing on the telegraph lines, flashing past.

He adds his empty coffee cup to the pile in the back and clears his throat. 'Cody told me what he said to you about your mum, and he's sorry. It's not something you need to be worrying about right now.'

'I'm not worried.' I lift my chin.

'I want us to get you a referral so you can start seeing Dr Nichols again—if you won't talk to me then you need to talk to somebody.'

'No, it's okay because I don't believe any of it. Mum wouldn't do that.' I hunch down in the seat.

'We'll never know,' he says. 'And it wouldn't change anything if we did. We have to move on.'

'Is that what we're doing?' I say, thinking of the way we used to be as a family, and the way we are now. He's wrong. It would change everything. It's not for me that I won't believe it; it's for him. If I knew for sure that my mother had killed herself, I would have lost both parents—I could never forgive him.

'We need to focus on you now,' he says. 'You're here and she isn't. I see you struggling but you won't admit it. I hear you wandering around the house in the middle of the night. You're hardly eating. We need to tackle this now, together.'

'It's not like before, Dad. I'm not like her...'

He cuts me off. 'It's more than that. Pills and therapy couldn't fix what she had. She couldn't outrun the demons in her head. What's going on with you is different, trust me on this.'

I go back over what he just said. 'What if I have demons, too?'

'No. Not like hers.'

'You know more than you're telling me,' I say, turning in my seat. 'I bet you tell Cody everything.'

He sighs. 'I can help you, Grace.' He lets go of the

gearshift and reaches out to touch my cheek. 'I couldn't help her.'

I start crying.

When we pull up at the Morgan farm, Dad wipes my tears with his shirtsleeve and encourages me to get out and stretch my legs. 'Sit by the lake, get some sun on your face. Take a walk, pet the animals,' he says.

I don't do any of those things. Instead, I wait in the shade by the truck. This place reminds me too much of the farm, even though it's very different. Dad's talking to Kel Morgan up by the house, a massive, modern ranch-style building with a wide verandah and a surrounding acre of green lawn. Their dams don't leak. Their live-stock are fat and friendly, unlike our mean, half-starved cattle that tried to eat your boots if you stood still for too long.

I pull down the waistband of my jeans: the hole in my side is gone, but a phantom pain is in its place. On the surface the graze is healing—it hurts somewhere deeper than that. I can't wait to get back to the estate, even if it's not my real home. I don't understand any of this anymore.

Dad keeps checking to see where I am; he'll check again tonight to make sure it's me under the blankets and not a pile of pillows. I'm pretty sure I've now graduated from grounding to full home detention with a GPS tracking bracelet. I'll need to work on my disappearing act—he's not going to let me out of his sight.

*

Last night, when I finally fell asleep, I saw Mum wandering through the new house, smiling and clapping her hands, until there was a low rumble outside and a truck crashed through a wall and carried her away, screaming.

I know it was a dream. This time I could tell the difference.

Cody's working on the car again. He's under orders to keep his eye on me while Dad's at work, and he's not happy about it.

'Want me to get you a drink?' I say snidely. 'It must be beer o'clock.'

'It's only eleven,' he says. 'Ask me at twelve and quit making such a mess.'

I've got *Grace Removals* packing boxes spread out all over the floor of the garage. Dad chose the company because of the name—I remember his finger scrolling through the Yellow Pages, coming to rest on the ad like he was grateful the universe had made at least one decision easy, when everything else was so hard.

I lift down another box. They're clearly labelled, but I'm opening all of them to be sure.

Grace: Foley/kitchen. *Grace*: Foley/dining. *Grace*: Foley/garage. I'm trying to find the ones with family photos, and failing. So far I've found Mum's clothes and a whole lot of kitchen appliances we didn't know what to do with, plus Cody's old school exercise books. I'm not the only problem child. He was barely literate in high school. It's no wonder he gets along with Gummer so well—Cody's books are filled with doodles of cars and monsters, too.

'Cod-face, do you know what happened to all the family photos?'

A low grumble comes from beneath the car. I think he said no.

'Does Sacred Heart have a yearbook?' In the movies, you can look through yearbook photos and find out everything you need to know about a person.

This time I get a definite no, accompanied by a greasy middle finger.

I discover yet another box of kitchen gadgetry. I could dice a carrot a thousand ways with the stuff I'm stacking up next to me, and the last two boxes are just old cooking magazines from Mum's subscriptions—either Dad has the photos packed away somewhere else or we left far more behind than I thought.

It takes twice as long to pack everything away as it did to make the mess.

'Hey, Cody?'

'What?'

'Are there any more moving boxes?'

'I don't *know*!'

'Want some lunch?' I wait precisely three seconds, long enough for Cody to slide out from underneath the car to give me the affirmative, before flipping him the finger. 'As if.'

For a moment he seems about to say something but decides against it.

I head inside, feeling mean.

It makes sense that Dad wouldn't leave precious things like photos to the mice and the damp—they'd be somewhere safe and dry, like the spare-room office or the linen cupboard.

I check both, but there's nothing.

Dad's bedroom is the smallest. His single bed is unmade, his clothes strewn all over the floor, and the narrow built-in wardrobe behind the door is tightly packed with heavy workwear and shoes. And one moving box.

Grace: Foley/Farm.

I haul the box out and peel away three layers of tape. I fold back the flaps, half-expecting mountains of paperwork to do with running the farm, but that's not what's inside. There are photos and ornaments, mosaics that Mum made from broken pottery she'd dug up from the garden, her jewellery, lotions and make-up. At the bottom, a stack of video tapes from parties, birthdays and holidays. The photos are of the farm and our family when we were four, all familiar, except one: an aerial image showing the entire farm, the dams mud-coloured smudges, the house a rectangle of grey.

I run my finger around the fence-line boundaries— they're barely visible in the picture, but I know them by heart. How is it possible to miss a place as much as a person? Or maybe it's just that I can't imagine one without the other—Mum and the farm, the farm and Mum.

There's nothing in the box that I haven't seen before, but Dad might as well have labelled it 'Pandora'. It's like he gathered all the objects that might tip me over the edge again, sealed them up, and buried them—a sleeping bomb, everything smelling of cut grass and Mum's brand of perfume—but seeing our lives exploded on the floor hurts less than I expected. Somehow, that makes me even sadder.

I put everything away, in order. Tucked between the last two photos, I find a yellow envelope. Inside, a bundle of newspaper clippings about the accident and the trial. About Mum.

Breathless, I take the envelope to the kitchen and lay out the clippings on the counter.

The papers used a cropped photo of the four of us taken about a year before she died: we were all sitting on the couch, and the camera was on timer delay. In the original, Cody, Dad and I were just blurs on either side of Mum, who was the only one patient enough to keep still until the shutter clicked. With us cut out of the image, it was a perfect portrait of her. But in reality it wasn't perfect at all.

My hands shake as I pick up each clipping. I can't imagine Dad doing this: sitting at the table, trawling through the pages, cutting carefully around the pictures of her face. It seems too sentimental—or calculated—for him. And I can't imagine why he would keep the pictures of Dominic Aloisi. One shows Aloisi leaving court, a jacket over his face; another is a full head-shot. He looks much older than a man in his early forties: greying dark hair, thick brows and lips, dimpled chin, a blank expression.

I grip the paper so hard it tears through the middle of his face. My brain's buzzing—Aloisi is familiar in some way. Recently familiar, not just recognisable because he stars in my nightmares since Mum died. All the chopped-up photos—these images are only half the picture. Hannah Holt's Missing photo was the same: an irrelevant person cut away, leaving only an arm around her shoulder. But the people around us are relevant— without them a photo has no story, no background, no context, like the newspaper portrait of Mum.

I put the clippings away. What else is Dad hiding from us? Or is it just from me? I'm already having trouble recalling Mum's face from the picture on Susannah Holt's fridge—is that why Dad kept the clippings, so he wouldn't forget?

Upstairs, a floorboard creaks. The kettle starts to whistle. I don't remember switching it on. The air ripples like a stream and I'm shivery all over.

I grab a pen and notepad from next to the phone, and it's just like before: my vision blurs until I see dots on the paper, the pen moves erratically, and the lines appear as if my subject is posing in front of me.

The first is a quick sketch of Mum's face, young again. She looks like me. I work over the top, adding lines and shadows, and she immediately ages by twenty years or more.

I tear off the sheet and begin again. Now it's Hannah Holt—fresh-faced, braces on her teeth, and then as I saw her in my room that night when she was lying on her side, her features fuller, wrinkles on her neck, hard lines around her mouth and eyes. More like her mother.

Rip.

The pen keeps scratching away. I'm fighting it, making the lines wobble, bruising the paper, but an image starts to take shape. It's Dominic Aloisi—a likeness of his newspaper picture, right down to the blank expression.

I think I'm done but there's more. I start again underneath. The pen slows, making careful marks with gentle shading, and the much younger face of a boy appears: black hair, dark and empty eyes. He's smiling. There's something strange about his teeth.

A wave of revulsion twists my stomach and I drop the pen. I arrange the drawings in a straight line, scanning the faces: Mum, Hannah, Aloisi, the boy. And I remember where I've seen him before.

EIGHTEEN

Dad's old-school: he still keeps paper receipts impaled on a spike on his desk, a manual book-keeping system, and a folder full of business cards in the top drawer. He's had the same shabby green address book for years—as messy as his truck and the rest of his life may be, he's meticulous about keeping that little green book up to date.

I run my finger down the index letters: G. For Grady, for grandparents, for gone away. *Terry and Jean Grady*.

Before Mum died and they moved, we saw them every few months, usually for dinner at the Swanston Golf Club. They drank too much and complained about everything—our manners, Dad's job, Mum's mistakes, my wild hair, Cody's dirty fingernails, the service, the weather, the price of milk. They were always overdressed, pushing food around their plates, sucking wine through their teeth. They didn't seem to like each other very much. I loved those dinners—I'm sure they gave Mum a glimpse of her other life and reminded her why she left it. At least that's how it seemed when we got home.

My grandparents' new phone number is written neatly under the old one, which has been crossed out. The area code tells me they're in the same state—not as far away as Dad led us to believe. I pick up the landline phone and dial the number. Calling them feels like a kind of betrayal.

It only rings once before my grandmother answers. 'Hello?'

'Grandma, it's Grace.' I wait for that to sink in.

Long seconds of silence. 'Grace. Yes, hello.' She sounds out of breath. 'Is there something wrong?'

'Nothing's wrong,' I say. 'It's just…it's been a while.'

'Does your father know you're calling?'

'No.' I twist the telephone cord around my finger. 'I thought it was time.'

'Well…' She draws the word out. She sounds pleased that he doesn't know.

'I'm sorry I haven't been in touch. I mean, I wanted to, but…'

'Your mother would turn over in her grave if she could,' she drawls.

'I know.' I leave it at that. Any more and I'll blow it. How can I ask her the questions I have swirling around without ending the conversation before it begins? 'I miss her so much.'

There's the clinking sound of glass on teeth, and a loud gulp as she swallows. 'Your grandfather has gone on a fishing charter. Imagine! He hates fishing. Could never stand the water. I don't understand it.'

Does he want to get away from you?

'I've been going through Mum's old photos. It makes me feel better.'

'Yes, you took it hard, didn't you?' she says. 'I hope your father got you the help you needed. It would have been better for you if I could have been around—it's not like I haven't dealt with it before. It's your grandfather's side—the women were all a bit flighty. It hasn't skipped a generation yet.' She gulps and swallows again. 'And it didn't help that your mother was stuck out there, away from her friends and family.'

It crosses my mind that my grandmother knows more than she's letting on. 'Did she have many friends? I never saw any apart from our neighbours.'

She grunts. 'Well, she was cut off, wasn't she? She said that was what she wanted, but I knew better.'

'So, her friends? I found an old school photo and—'

'How could you?' she interrupts. 'I have them all. She said she didn't want them. Your mother wasn't sentimental about things like that.'

'I saw a copy,' I lie. 'I was doing a project on the missing girl, Hannah Holt. Do you remember? They were in the same class once. Were they friends?' I suck in my breath and hold it. My finger has turned an alarming shade of blue.

'No, that's not right,' she says. 'They were in the same class three years in a row, but they weren't friends. Hannah Holt was a good student. Your mother preferred a different kind of company.'

She's talking about Dad. He never finished school; he was working the farm by the time he was my age and he started seeing Mum when she was just eighteen. I bite my lip to keep from answering back.

'I'd like to have some of her photos if that's okay, Grandma.'

She sniffs. 'I could have some of them copied, I suppose, but I'm rather busy right now.'

'Please? I just need…more of her.'

She lowers her voice. 'Your mother was never one to face things head on, Grace. Her solution was always to run in the other direction, like when she left school early and took up with your father. Why would she cut off all contact with her parents and her friends? Ask yourself *that*. Better still, ask *him*.'

I mutter a goodbye and hang up, slowly unwinding the cord to let the blood rush back into my finger. I can't shake the feeling that I've just been stuck with a poison dart.

Only two more days left of the holidays. It feels as if I'm stuck in a labyrinth with moving walls, no exit, and no way of retracing my steps because the entrance has mysteriously shifted.

Dad was gone before the sun came up. Cody has just

left for work. Diesel lives outside now, as if he can't bear to be anywhere near me. I have nausea and jitters all the time, so bad I can barely hold my spoon or swallow my cereal.

I wash the dishes and tidy the kitchen with the radio turned up. Chores keep me moving; when I stop, I get dizzy. Music drowns out the creaks, groans and rattles of the house. The whispers. Sunglasses help ease the ache behind my eyes, but I can only wear them inside when there's nobody else around.

On my way out, I stop when I catch my reflection in the hallway mirror. I wouldn't pass anybody's inspection. My cheekbones could be blades under the skin. My hair is greasy at the roots, frizzy on the ends, and I have a new rash, a mass of purplish dots across my chin and throat. There'd be no taking Kenzie and me for sisters anymore—not unless she was the before picture and I was the after.

I'm decomposing—a cadaver, rotting from the inside out. And it feels like I'm running out of time.

I dress in old loose jeans and a shapeless black hoodie to cover my bones, lock the house, and jog to the bus stop. This time the bus is empty. I have the back seat to myself. At the next stop, two kids get on but they're too busy with their screens to pay any attention to me. I write her name on the glass in the mist of my breath—Hannah, HANNAH, hannaH—wishing my name was the same backwards and sideways. Am I her? I don't feel like me anymore; Grace Foley doesn't fit.

190

No, I'm not her either. I'm just empty.

I get off at South Swanston shops and wait fifteen minutes while a techie fits a new screen to my phone. She watches me as I wander the displays, as if I might be a shoplifter. I had a friend who used to do that—shove bottles of nail polish down the front of her jeans. She used to say nobody would have the nerve to ask to check down a girl's pants.

Amber. That was her name. I clutch at the memory with relief.

The new screen is so clean and shiny it reflects the perfect blue sky above. I'm going to need it. I'll be putting my freedom at risk by doing what I'm doing, but the alternative is the labyrinth.

I have an angled view into Susannah Holt's kitchen from the gully behind the house, ten metres away. It's only eleven. There isn't a cloud in sight, but I'm wishing for rain clouds or a dust storm. I want cover. I hide behind the tree below the crow's nest. Very still, listening.

There's no movement inside the house for almost twenty minutes. I dare to move, and grasp the trunk of the tree; it's surprisingly easy to climb to the first fork in the branches about two metres above the ground. From there it gets harder. I have to swing my legs, scissor-style, to monkey along to the next horizontal branch. I lever myself with one of the ladder rungs on the trunk, but it crumbles, and I'm left dangling. I drop to the ground, exhausted. I don't have the muscle. My arms are dead weights and I have a fresh graze on my wrist.

I hear a noise, like a squeaky wheel.

I freeze, and my heart thuds. Susannah Holt is hanging washing on the line in the backyard; if she turns even slightly, she'll spot me over the fence.

I duck. I can still see the washing line and her hands, but not her face. She won't see me. She shakes and snaps a white sheet, pegging it in three places, followed by two blue towels. Then her hands shake out some smaller items—too small to be hers, and far too delicate. I recognise the lace bra, girlish underwear, and a pair of white shortie pyjamas. They're worn so thin the sunlight passes through, turning some patches brownish-yellow. They're not clean.

Why is she washing Hannah's clothes? What's the point? Who is going to wear them?

Her hands are still for a long moment. I hold my breath, worried I've been spotted. She snatches at the bra, yanking it by a strap, sending the pegs pinging off somewhere. She's dragging the clean washing from the line, stuffing it back into the basket, cursing. The squeaking noise starts again. I duck lower. I can see all of her now. She's pushing a trolley, carrying the basket up the steps, through the back door, into a laundry; she's stuffing the washing into the machine, still muttering. She pours about half a bottle of liquid over the clothing and slams the lid, turning the dial viciously, and disappears.

The back door is wide open.

I move closer to the fence. Through the kitchen

window, I watch her go upstairs. There's the sound of glass breaking and someone yelling. My skin prickling all over, I hoist myself over the fence and creep across the yard. More shouting.

Is there someone else inside the house?

I press close to the warm weatherboard planks, sidling along as flakes of old paint peel off and cling to my back. Up the steps, to the back door. The laundry reeks of bleach. Somewhere, a door slams. I tiptoe through the hallway and into the kitchen, pull out my phone, open the camera and snap four shots of the photo on the fridge, just as a shoe comes flying down the stairs to rest upside-down on the last step.

Someone screams. Every instinct is telling me to leave the way I came—now, before I'm caught, or caught up in something that's none of my business—but in the distance I hear a low sobbing and a crunch, like breaking bone.

I place one foot on the bottom step, next to the shoe. It's a stiletto, white, with a broken heel. The muscles in my calves are so tense they're cramping, and sweat makes my hoodie cling to my skin. I take nine quick, silent steps. I can see the door of Hannah's room: it's open, sunlight spilling into the dark hallway.

Another scream, this one ear-splitting, but with anger, not fear. Now I can make sense of the sounds coming from the room.

Susannah Holt's in there, alone, and she's trashing it: opening drawers, tearing paper, scattering bottles and throwing shoes. She's muttering. She's speaking to her daughter as if she's in there with her.

The hair on my arms stands up. I back away, one step at a time, until I've reached the back door and the clean air outside.

In the safety of the gully I scroll through the photos. The first two are out of focus, the next cuts off a third of the right-hand side of the picture. The last is clear and true, if a little dark. I edit, adjusting the contrast and light, and pinch the screen to zoom in. I drag my finger, moving past each face in the class, and when I zoom out again I can see the perfect triangle—middle top, bottom left, bottom right.

For once, my memory hasn't failed me. There are not only two faces I recognise in this picture—there are three.

Hannah Holt, with her guarded smile.

My mother, Erin Grady, challenging the lens with her stare.

And a young Dominic Aloisi, with his thick neck and his straight, square-edged teeth.

NINETEEN

On Sunday, I lie to Dad, begging him to let me meet my friends at the mall so we can hold a wake to mourn the end of the holidays. He forces me to eat a sandwich before he decides I can go, watching carefully as I go through the motions: chewing, swallowing, washing the plate.

'Want me to drive you? I've got a load to take to the dump. I'll be going right past,' he offers.

I shake my head. 'I'll walk. I'm meeting Kenzie halfway.' The fluorescent stripes on his vest hurt my eyes.

'Is there something you're not telling me?' He says it gently, but there's an edge.

I smother a wave of fury. There's a whole lot he isn't telling me, and I'm not allowed to ask in case I puncture this family-sized bag of hurt we're all protecting.

I smile. 'Of course not. I'd better get going. I'm late.'

Ten minutes later, he passes me in the truck on the main road. I've just arrived at the bus stop, but I keep walking, doubling back when he's out of sight.

To know Hannah Holt, I need to know William Dean, and the Dean house is open for inspection at two.

I get there half an hour early. The street is packed: there's no parking for three or four blocks, and a restless mob waits for the door to open. The worst part is the Deans are still inside, peering through the curtains. Are they too afraid to come out?

It's not as if the house is anything special—except it is. There's no such thing as a short memory in Swamptown.

I wait by the alley where I'm less likely to be noticed. Ten minutes later, both cars pull out of the driveway. The Deans hunker down; the crowd parts as though they might catch something, as though tragedy is a virus.

I know. I've experienced it.

The real estate agent's shiny BMW turns up at the same time that my phone pings.

It's Gummer. *At your place. Where r u?*

Out, I reply.

Out where?

He must be hungry. Either that or his clothes need washing. I ignore his last message.

The agent puts a flag and a yellow sign at the end of the driveway, not that there's any confusion as to which house is for sale. People are queuing at the front door already. When it opens, I wait fifteen minutes to see if the

crowd dies down. But the queue remains steady, so I join the line, trying not to make eye contact with anyone.

'Would you like a brochure?' the agent asks the woman ahead of me.

I hold out my hand and he dismisses it. He's sweating, red in the face—excited about the number of prospective buyers or annoyed because he suspects we're all 'just looking', I can't tell. He waves me through.

I follow the woman into a lounge room. She's breathing heavily and gives off an odour like cat pee, or perhaps the smell is coming from the threadbare carpet. The lounge room is stripped of everything apart from large items like the couch, and the table and chairs. There's nothing personal on display—no photos, ornaments or books on the bookshelves. It's colder in here than it is outside, and dim, even with all the lights switched on.

We wander into the kitchen and dining room. Again, it's bare except for a wilting bunch of yellow roses in a blue vase on the table. The first and second bedrooms are large but empty; the third is a cluttered haven for dust and a stack of empty moving boxes. The house is a warren of rooms with tiny windows. I step into a sunken family room at the rear—only a combustion heater and a single armchair. Cat-pee woman turns a slow circle, gazing at the ceiling. Her thin lips turn down. I brush up against a wave of people and they're all wearing a similar expression: disappointment. This house is ordinary. Ugly, even. Suddenly I feel like laughing. Were we all expecting a house of horrors? Evidence of devil worship? An

evil, ageing portrait of William Dean?

There are more people leaving than arriving now. Across the room, I see a familiar face: Lucy Babbage, one of our old neighbours. As if I've called her name, her head turns and she shoots me a questioning smile. I duck into the hallway, through a door, into the laundry. The back door is open, the screen door latched.

I flip the latch and dash down a flight of concrete steps to the backyard. A dented garage takes up the length of one side, and a washing line squeaks as it spins, its arms bowed just like the one at the farm that Cody and I used to swing on. All the way to the back fence, the weeds have been recently cut, exposing thick yellow roots like worms, raising the sweet smell of hacked grass, and around the yard there are indentations and humps of dirt as if the ground had been dug up a long time ago.

It was, I remember from the newspaper clippings. They looked for Hannah Holt here.

I check down either side of the house, searching for another way out, but the side gate is padlocked and the roller door under the carport is down. I'll have to wait until Lucy Babbage leaves—or I could jump the back fence and escape through the gully. But before I can move, the screen door bangs. A family of five are heading down the steps into the yard.

I try to make it look as if I'm casually inspecting the garden as the children run around, leaping from hump to hump. Their mother tells them off. The man turns the handle on the garage side door, and appears surprised

when it opens. I move closer, peering past him, and a rush of air escapes, prompting the man to pinch his nose and slam the door. The family head back inside the house.

I turn the handle and inhale. The smell is a blend of dust, dampness, ammonia and wood. It's not unpleasant. Inside, there's barely room to move: teetering stacks of chairs, piles of bulging boxes, and racks of old clothing left to rot. Some of it, I realise—T-shirts, ripped jeans, a leather biker jacket—must have belonged to *him*.

I step further inside and run my hand across a scarred tabletop, leaving tracks in the dust. A green BMX dangles from a wire above my head—I reach up to flick the lever on the bell and it makes a strangled, grating noise, setting off a scurry of movement. Mice. Or rats. The afternoon sun slips lower and a beam of light pours through the glass slats of a window, giving shape to the shadows. I can just make out a bunk bed, a pile of empty picture frames, an acoustic guitar and an easel in the far corner, as well as several pieces of exercise equipment covered with cobwebs.

It's as if the Deans packed away their lives—not recently, but a long, long time ago.

My nerve endings are thrumming with recognition and something else. Not fear, but longing. I dance my fingertips over the keys of an ancient typewriter, a square wooden box with a brass catch, a cloudy jar with a blueish residue in the bottom—everything I smell, everything I touch, it's all eerily familiar.

I check my phone. It's nearly 2.45. The inspection was over fifteen minutes ago.

I back swiftly out of the garage, close the door behind me, and dash up the steps into the laundry. Voices. Two men, one the agent and the other, a tall, grey-haired man I assume to be Mr Dean. They're in the kitchen. I manage to tiptoe past without either of them turning around, but as I bolt down the hallway to the front door, I run smack into Mrs Dean.

She gasps, winded, and stumbles back. Her eyes widen and she flings out a hand to stop herself from falling. She's clutching something to her chest, holding it underneath her cardigan like a baby; even as she slides to the floor in slow motion, she doesn't let go.

'Oh God, I'm so sorry!' I grab her forearm and haul her up, steadying her against my body. A shudder passes between us—hers or mine, I'm not sure. I check her over for injury. The whites of her eyes are bloodshot, the skin around her mouth an unhealthy shade of blue, and she's so thin she might have broken in two when she fell.

I stammer another apology, holding on to her frail shoulders.

'Jeanette?' One of the voices from the kitchen.

She twists away. Her free hand joins the other to cradle the thing in her arms. Without a word, she steps away. Her gaze is vacant, and she doesn't seem shaken or upset; she doesn't seem conscious of anything at all.

I obey the urge to run and keep on running until I'm as far away from the Dean house as my legs can take me.

I'm almost halfway home before they give out. I walk the rest of the way, haunted by the texture of her eyes, like shattered mirrors, still rattled by the sensation I felt as I held her.

It was as if we shared a heartbeat.

There's a black Ford 250 on the front lawn, parked like it was stolen and dumped, and, from the wet patches on the tyres, it looks like Diesel has marked his territory. The door to the house is open and the television is blaring.

I go upstairs to find Gummer asleep on my bed.

'What are you doing in my room?' I kick his foot. There's a half-eaten apple on the side table.

'What day is it?' he mumbles. 'Are we late for school?'

'It's Sunday. School's tomorrow.' I sweated buckets running home. I need a shower, but not with Gummer here. 'How'd you get in, anyway?'

'Door was open,' he says, sitting up. He has sheet wrinkles on his face. 'Nobody was home.'

'So you just let yourself in, ate an apple and fell asleep like Snow freaking White?'

He gives me a quizzical look. 'Why are you mad?'

I flinch at his word choice. 'I need to take a shower.'

'Seriously. Why are you angry all the time? You're so different lately.'

Pointedly, I go into the bathroom, yank the dirty towel from the rack and throw it in the corner. I get a clean towel from the hall linen cupboard and come back with it draped around my neck.

Gummer's standing with his hands in his pockets. 'I know you're probably still upset, but Kenzie said it was like before. You know, like with your mum and the accident. We were worried. We didn't know how to handle it.'

Against my will, I tear up. 'Like, how? Like I was sad? Of course I was sad then. Anyway, this isn't the same thing. I don't need all this Dr Phil interventionist bullshit. How about you guys just be there to hold my hand and feed me and laugh at my jokes like you used to? Oh, wait, you're right, that was before. When you were my friends.'

He shakes his head. 'You were more than sad back then, Grace. We didn't know how to handle it then, either. It's hard to understand you when you're so hell-bent on being misunderstood.'

'Screw you.'

'Right,' he says. 'Is that your default setting now?'

I don't answer. I just want him to leave. I open drawers and grab clean underwear and clothes.

'So where are the little green guys?'

'I don't know. You tell me. You're the star-gazer.'

'No, I mean the tank dudes.'

I turn around slowly. The tank's empty. The water line is down by a third at least, and Waldorf and Statler are gone. 'Did you let them out?' I say.

'Yeah. I took them for a walk.' He laughs, then realises I'm serious. 'Of course I didn't.' He's crawling on the floor, checking under the bed and behind the

202

curtains. 'For real? They can't just disappear.' He looks up. 'Why are you just standing there?'

I feel suddenly, desperately sad. 'Gummer, why don't you ever go home?'

'Huh?'

'I'm not trying to be mean. I'm just asking the question.'

He stares down at his scuffed sneakers. 'I'm not sure what you're getting at.'

He has a new tattoo on the inside of his wrist, in some kind of script. It's not really his style.

'I never thought I'd say it, but Amber's right—we all keep secrets from each other. We used to tell each other everything.'

He's giving me the strangest look, like he's grappling with a mammoth equation and nothing is adding up. 'But, Grace,' he says. 'I do go home. There's no big secret. I just like other people's food and couches.'

'Stop making fun of me.'

'I'm not!' He lowers his voice. 'You're acting paranoid.'

My head aches with frustration. I rub my eyes with my fists.

'You have to talk about it,' he says gently. 'Whatever it is.'

I smile. I know it's a horrible smile because it feels as if my mouth is splitting. 'You see that corner?' He looks to where I'm pointing: the dark corner of my room. 'There's something awful there, waiting for me. You can't see it, but that doesn't mean it doesn't exist.'

His eyes widen. 'How do you know I can't see it?'

'Okay. What do you see?' I put one hand on my hip.

His eyes slide left. 'A dirty towel.'

I push him across the room. 'You have to go.'

'Don't you want to keep looking? There has to be an explanation.'

I shove him through the door. He has his foot wedged in the gap. I kick it, stubbing my toe. 'I *am* looking! There is no explanation! People disappear all the time and never get found. She's just gone, okay?'

'Grace, I'm talking about the dudes. Who did you think I was talking about?'

'Please go.'

'Fine,' he says, pressing his nose to the gap. 'I'll go. But think about it—maybe no one tells you anything because you don't listen.'

I don't hear his footsteps on the stairs which means he rode the banister. I wait until I see the Ford pull away and tear my room apart looking for Waldorf and Statler.

After an hour of searching and crying, and no result, I take a long, hot shower. The water stings where my skin's still not healed. I close my eyes and concentrate on the sensation of the needles of water hitting my scalp, praying for another shift in reality: when I step out there will be a full tank, drifting axolotls, and Gummer was never here.

But Gummer's beanie is lying on my bed and they're still gone.

TWENTY

I hope something will happen so I won't have to go to school. A natural disaster before breakfast—it's not much to ask. But it's a clear, cool day outside and Dad's made pancakes with lemon and sugar; he's even ironed my uniform and packed me a lunch.

'You have an appointment with Connie Renfrey straight after school,' he says. 'Don't forget.'

'I won't.'

'Did you ever find a new topic for that project you were working on?' He hands me my lunch box.

Now he's showing an interest in my schoolwork. 'Yeah. I did.' He raises an eyebrow, and I'm scrambling to come up with something to put him off the scent. 'Germ theory,' I tell him, because Gummer once did a revolting, hour-long presentation about cholera that I still can't get out of my head.

Cody comes into the kitchen rubbing his eyes. 'Morning.'

'Interesting that you brought up Hannah Holt,' Dad says. 'I've heard a rumour the Dean family are moving away from Swanston.' He's watching me a little too carefully. 'Their house is on the market.'

'So?' I busy myself with packing my bag. 'I told you, I gave up on that idea.'

'Then there must be a very good reason why you'd go along to the open inspection.'

Shit. Lucy Babbage *did* see me. 'I was just curious, Dad. Curious and bored, that's all. There were about a hundred other people there, too.'

He frowns. 'That house has been vandalised countless times in the last twenty-three years. No doubt they're moving away because of *curiosity and boredom* just like yours.'

'You're talking about the Deans?' Cody butts in. 'They're moving because the old man's retired.' Dad throws him a warning glance, but Cody keeps going. 'How's this—they've had to replace their son's headstone *seven times*. So they dug him up recently and had him cremated. They're taking him with them.'

My stomach begins a slow, queasy slide. They exhumed William Dean?

Dad smacks the egg flip down on the counter and Cody and I jump. 'We know what it's like being on the receiving end of the muckrakers in this town. I expect better from both of you. Cody, quit flapping your gums, and Grace, that folder of clippings I found on your desk—get rid of it.'

'You went through my stuff?' I snap.

'Damn right I did.'

Cody slinks off to his room.

I drop my head. 'I'm going to school.'

Dad nods. 'Counsellor. Three-fifteen.'

My skin is prickling with aftershocks. I'm furious that Dad's been through my desk, but I'm more disturbed by what Cody said.

I fell into William Dean's grave at the cemetery—I touched the urn containing his ashes when I bumped into Mrs Dean. I'm sure of it.

Nobody pays me any attention as I wander past the wall. I'm yesterday's news. I throw my bag in my locker and grab my Biology book and pencil case, ready for first class.

Amber's already in homeroom when I arrive. She has moved from our shared desk and is sitting by herself at the back of the room. She gives me a darting glance, dismissing me the way she dismisses everybody else, but her legs are jiggling underneath the desk and she appears to be studying the poster of the periodic table of elements. I know her well enough to read her expression as deliberate disdain, not her usual innocent scorn.

'Just a reminder for those of you in Mr Geddes'

History class, you have a triple external study session tomorrow morning. Bring your bus passes and a hat, please,' Mr Hamley announces. 'And Friday you're supposed to have completed your first-person interviews for English. I'm telling you because I know at least half of you haven't started.'

Shit. It's one of those assignments I put off.

Amber's phone trills in her pocket.

She doesn't even twitch, but Mr Hamley taps the container on his desk. 'Amber Richardson, come on down. Anyone else? No?'

I slip my hand into my pencil case and switch my phone to silent.

Amber wanders over to his desk and drops her phone into the container. 'I'm waiting for an important message. My aunt is sick.'

'If your sick aunt calls, I'll be sure to let you know,' he says. 'You can collect your phone after school.'

She groans. For some reason, she turns and gives me a desperate look.

What does she want me to do about it? I can't do anything.

As I pick up my stuff and move out with everyone else, there's a tug on my sleeve. 'What?'

'Can you meet me at the toilets in ten? I have to tell you something.' She's flushed with drama. 'What have you got…Maths? Ten, okay? Bring your phone.'

I brush her hand away. 'So now you want to talk?'

She flashes her best poisonous smile. 'Stop being so

self-centred. This isn't about you.'

I'm intrigued. And nervous. At ten past nine I ask to leave class, tuck my phone in the folds of my dress, and run down to the Year Twelve toilet block.

Amber's waiting inside, sitting up on the basin, her back to the mirror. 'I wasn't sure you'd come.' She wiggles her fingers. 'Did you bring it?'

'You want to call your aunt?' I say, handing it over. 'This better be good.'

'Shut up. We don't have much time.' She logs in to her Facebook. 'This is going around. You probably haven't seen it because…'

'You blocked me. Yeah.'

'I was going to say because you're living on another planet, but whatever. Check it out. It's everywhere.'

'Jesus, Amber, what is it?'

She passes my phone back. 'You've noticed Kenzie's not here today?'

'We're not really talking.'

'Right. Well, this is why she's not here.' She points. 'I thought it was you at first, to be honest. It seems more your style.'

I scroll through a series of pictures. Kenzie's lying on the ground near a white letterbox. She's wearing one of our matching dresses, a high-waisted, blue flouncy thing I only wore once, to the Year Eleven school formal. The dress is riding so high you can see her knickers and the skirt is stained with vomit. So is the grass. The shots are taken from all angles, including one close up underneath her skirt. In this light, her hair looks as dark as mine, and you can't see that it's much longer because it's tucked underneath her body. Her tattoo is hidden. She's completely out of it.

It could be me, except I know it's not.

'Is she…okay?' I say. 'Is she…?'

'As far as I know, the only thing she's suffering is total humiliation and an epic hangover.' Amber slides off the basin, pulling down her dress. 'Oh. Don't read the comments.'

I shake my head. 'How did she get like this? She hardly drinks. Who took the photos?'

'I don't know. I wasn't there. They've been shared so many times and nobody's owning up.'

'And where was Mitch?'

'I wasn't *there*, Grace. Let me log out.'

'You don't trust me?' I say.

'No, I really don't. Anyway, I thought you should know about Kenzie.'

She slips out through the door before I can ask whether Pete or Gummer were at the party, too. I'd say not—they wouldn't have let her get in that state. But Mitchell…I'm furious. Because of him, Kenzie's today's news.

I head back to class, and get my third blue slip for being late. Another detention.

Detention, or counselling? Or Kenzie? It's a no-brainer. During afternoon homeroom I scribble a quick note for

Call Me Connie and, after the bell goes, I stick it on the notice board outside her office door. As for detention, well, I'm no stranger to a double. I hit the road and start walking. As long as I'm home by four-thirty, Dad won't know I'm missing unless either he gets a call from the school or another local busybody outs me. Spies, spies everywhere.

Kenzie's parents might as well be my grandparents. Her house is as familiar to me as the farm. When the last of her sisters moved out, she graduated to the detached rumpus room and turned it into her bedroom. She has a welcome mat outside her own front door, a fridge, a kettle and a sandwich-maker. We used to joke we could survive the apocalypse out here, living on cheese toasties and cans of Coke, but that was before Mitchell started sleeping on my side of her bed.

I slip through the garden gate to avoid knocking on the door and wasting precious minutes talking to Kenzie's dad. Baxter, their fox terrier, shoots around the corner and gives a warning bark, but shuts up when he realises it's me. I scratch his ears and throw his ball, making him skitter sideways into the back fence.

The faded curtain in the rumpus room twitches.

'It's me,' I say.

I let myself in, closing the door behind me. Kenzie's madly scooping up clothes and debris from the floor, still wearing her pyjamas. She has her back turned to me. One side of the room is a wall of plastic storage containers and old suitcases, stacked so high they cover a window. Her bedroom makes it look like she's a chronic hoarder, but it's mostly things her sisters left behind.

'Since when do you feel the need to clean up when I come over?'

'I was doing it anyway,' she says. 'I didn't know you were coming.'

Not so long ago I would have thrown myself onto her bed, but that seems too awkward, too intimate. I move a stack of sheet music from her piano stool and sit down instead. 'How are you?'

She pauses, still not turning around, a bundle of dirty clothing hugged to her chest. 'Not so good.'

'Amber told me today at school. I'm going to find out who did it.'

'You're talking to each other? That's good.'

I snort. 'Not exactly. Let's just say we're both united in our disgust.' Her shoulders tense. She's taken it the wrong way. 'Oh God, not *you*, Kenzie—whoever posted the pictures.' I cross the room and wrap my arms around her waist. I rest my head on the back of her neck. 'I know it's humiliating, but it won't be as bad as you think. That's what you told me, right?'

'I lied.' She disentangles herself from my arms and pushes me away. 'See?'

Her nose is red and swollen. Both eyes are black. She bursts into tears and covers her face. 'I drank too much and I passed out. I face-planted.'

'Now we both look like shit,' I say, shocked. 'Whose party was it?'

She sits on the edge of her bed. 'Just some random from Heart. One of Mitchell's parents' friends' sons or something...It doesn't even matter. I was mad with myself for calling your dad, and for saying those horrible things to you, and Mitchell was acting weird and ignoring me, so I got messy drunk.'

'They weren't that horrible.' I hand her a tissue. 'And where was Mitch during all of this? Didn't he come looking for you?'

She holds up her hands. 'It wasn't his fault. Don't look for another reason to hate him. It was my fault— my fault for calling your dad even when Gummer told me not to, my fault for drinking too much, my fault for those pictures.'

'No. Not the last one. You're hardly the first person to get drunk and fall on your face.'

'I wore our formal dress,' she mutters. 'And heels. Everyone else was in jeans and sneakers. I'm so *stupid*!'

'I hate that dress,' I say. 'On me, I mean. On you, it's beautiful.'

'Even up around my ears?'

'Especially then.'

Kenzie laughs, and winces. 'Ouch.' She goes to her desk, opens the top drawer, and takes out a sheet of paper. 'I need to ask you something and I want you to tell me the absolute truth.'

'You're freaking me out,' I say.

She's serious. 'I talked to my mum about you that night. I was worried after and I couldn't sleep. I kept

213

playing over something you said.'

'When? After the pool thing? We didn't speak.'

'No. Not the pool. Before. The night I rang and asked your dad to go upstairs and check on you. Do you remember? You said, "My heart is a room with an unwelcome visitor." Have you ever heard that before? Have you seen it? I need to know. Cross your heart.'

I remember saying it.

I cross my heart. 'I've never, to the best of my knowledge, seen or heard that before. Hope to die.'

Her face turns white. 'This is a copy of a letter found in Hannah Holt's bedroom after she disappeared. When they failed to arrest William Dean and the case went cold after a year, apparently Hannah Holt's mother went around door-knocking and sticking these flyers on windscreens and in people's letterboxes. When I told Mum what you said, she remembered where she'd heard it before. She said you were probably mucking around again.' She taps the paper. 'Tell me you aren't messing with my head.'

'I'm not.'

She passes me the paper. I scan the first few lines. I'm winded, as if I've been punched. It's *the* flyer, the one the newspaper blacked out, and it's not a letter—it's a poem, written by William Dean.

'Where did you get this?'

'Mum said it was in our letterbox. Like, years ago. Before I was born.'

'And she kept it?'

Kenzie gestures at the wall of containers and suitcases. 'She keeps everything.'

'Why didn't you show me this before?' I snap.

She takes a step back. 'Because I didn't want to get caught up in your...' She stops. 'It doesn't matter.'

Outside, Baxter barks.

'Then why are you showing me now?' I say quietly.

She looks away and shrugs. 'Because part of me wants to believe you.'

There's a tentative knock at the door. 'It's Mitch.' She holds out her hand for the paper. 'I haven't told him any of this.'

'I need to keep it for a while.' I tuck the flyer into my pocket. 'I won't stay. Three's a crowd and all that. Will you be okay?'

She nods and opens the door.

Mitchell is standing there, leaning against the doorframe. 'Grace,' he says.

'Hey.' I can see the appeal: Mitch has grown up nicely—broad-shouldered, thin but athletic, a nice, even smile—but out of the boys he was never my favourite. There was always something judgmental about him. 'Look after her,' I threaten. 'Better than you did on Saturday.'

His mouth twists and he shoots Kenzie an aggrieved smile. *See what I put up with for you?*

When I go outside, Kenzie follows. 'I need some time to think,' she says. 'I need to get back on track with study and fix things with Mitch.' She blushes. 'And you.'

I grab her hand. Two of her fingernails are broken. 'Kenz, that night at Tamara Fraser's…I didn't kill those birds. You might not trust me right now, but I'm begging you to believe that. I didn't hurt them. They were already dead.'

She yanks her hand away. 'What birds?' she says, her eyes wide. 'Grace, what birds?'

TWENTY-ONE

After leaving Kenzie's house, I jog the short distance to Swanston Cemetery. My backpack is weighing me down, but my whole body is vibrating like a tuning fork and I feel as if I could run forever. I'll be at least an hour late getting home, but it's a risk I'm willing to take.

Like the cropped photographs, the missing images—without context I couldn't understand what was happening. We see what we want to see. We reach for the familiar. I haven't been reading the signposts: my strange behaviour, craving different foods, fumbling for light switches, doing my buttons the wrong way and leaving the toilet seat up. Forgetting how to put on make-up. Diesel's sudden aggression. I took the quantum leap from drawing stick figures to creating detailed sketches—I built a skeleton from the scattered bones, but I put the pieces together all wrong.

I drop my bag at the entrance and tear through the cemetery gate, skidding on the loose quartz on the footpath. An old couple laying flowers on a grave look up in alarm.

The man holds up his hand as if to slow me down. 'Show some respect for the dead, girl.'

I think the dead would understand.

Overhead, hundreds of swallows fly in perfect formation like a dancing black cloud, and Maria's angel gazes down solemnly as I pass. Above the noise of traffic out on the road, I hear the rustle of leaves. But there aren't enough trees here to make that much sound. It's voices. A chorus of whispering—real, or imagined, I can't tell— that only gets louder as I approach the barrier of tape.

I stop at the edge of the grave. The cemetery is a dustbowl, but here it smells of moisture and decay. The bottom of the pit has flooded with muddy water; the sides are damp and loose. It's just a hole in the ground now, but I don't know where else to go to say the things I need to say.

'I know it was you.'

My voice carries—the man and woman are holding hands and staring at me with pity. I turn my back to them, shrug off my backpack, and sit down.

'You want me to find her, don't you? You want me to find her body before they take your ashes away.'

The swallows swoop and settle in the trees in the

centre of the graveyard, making it seem as if the trees are writhing.

I pull out the flyer and unfold it carefully. The handwriting is spiky and uneven, the words both beautiful and ugly. It's a love poem. It's a threat. It's evidence. It's a premeditation, or a confession. It's proof of obsession. I may never know what the poem truly means, but it's signed with a tiny sketch of a bird, and that has changed everything.

My heart is a room with an unwelcome visitor
every song is a ballad to her.
She walks with a lilt and she talks with a swagger
locks the room from within
leaves me raging outside.
She: careless, shrugging, restless, wild
gathering moonlight
soft glow
pale skin
painted with madness
the window her frame.
She.
Her.
Me,
raging outside.
Every song is a ballad to her.

It's not Hannah Holt under my skin—it's William Dean.

'Tell me where to find her. I'm listening.'

A chunk of mud breaks from the edge of the grave and falls, crumbling, into the hole. The scent of death is in my nostrils, my lungs, leaching from the pores of my skin. I'm shaking all over and the ground feels unsteady, as if any moment the grave could turn into a sinkhole.

I grab my backpack, stand up, and back away—at the same time I'm fighting the urge to crawl into the hole. I feel rotten on the inside. His rage, his guilt, his despair: mine.

'I'm listening now!' I shout.

The sound sends the swallows in the trees screaming, scattering in all directions, and the old couple scurry through the gate.

Our triple study break is supposed to take place at either the library or the museum, but since we're unsupervised, most of us sneak away for an extended morning tea instead. I left home without my bus pass and Gummer had to lend me money again. We're sharing a seat on the bus, and I have William Dean's poem and Mum's plastic star in my pocket.

Kenzie texted me before school to say she wasn't coming. Amber's up the back of the bus; I can hear her voice, the way it gets high-pitched when she's telling a tall story. I suppose I should be grateful Gummer sat with me, but I was hoping to be alone.

'So, what happened to the dudes?' he says. 'Did you find them?'

I shake my head. I've had dreams about finding their shrunken little bodies under my bed, like those rubbery toy dinosaurs that swell and hatch from plaster eggs when you soak them in water, and shrivel again when they dry out.

'Maybe Diesel ate them,' he offers. 'Or they escaped outside.'

'Diesel doesn't come upstairs.'

He raises his eyebrows. It's my flat tone—he thinks I don't care, but how can I explain why I'm so accepting of their disappearance without telling him about the cracks between this world and the next? Without sounding crazy?

He pushes up his sleeves and I catch a glimpse of his new tattoo. The script runs up the inside of his pale forearm, from his wrist to his elbow. We're not supposed to have exposed tatts at school. Getting one on his forearm means he won't be able to wear T-shirts, and Gummer lives in T-shirts, even in cold weather.

I grab his hand with both of mine. 'What does it say?'

He glances down. 'There is hope and a kind of beauty in there somewhere, if you look for it.'

'Giger?'

'Of course.'

'Beauty in where? What does it mean?'

'Beauty in terror. He's referring to his work. You know, how most people see his creations as monstrous. I think he's saying that we need our monsters to know what it is to be human.'

I shudder.

'Have you seen your bogeygirl?'

She's a he. 'I know you think I'm nuts.' I press closer to the window. 'I'm so tired. It's getting too hard pretending to be like everyone else.'

Gummer pulls down his sleeve. 'I don't want you to be like everyone else, Grace. I just want you to be happy.' When the bus pulls over, he puts out a hand to stop me from getting off at the mall with the others. 'Let's go to the museum instead.'

I frown at him. 'Aren't you taking this new commitment to study too far?'

'It's not that.' He seems distracted. 'I want to show you something.'

Amber brushes past in the aisle. She gives Gummer a fist bump, ignoring me, but just before she gets off the bus she stops and turns back, waving to get my attention. The crowd behind nudges her forward and, as the bus pulls away, she's standing at the mall entrance, watching us.

'What did she want, do you think?'

Gummer shrugs.

I wonder how we were ever friends. I *rescued* her. I *made* her. I broke that stick and handed her the pieces like it was a freaking metaphor for her pathetic life. That's got to be worth something. She *owes* me.

'She's trying,' Gummer says, as if he can read my mind.

Only a couple of other students get off at the museum.

222

They head inside, but Gummer leads me down the side street that runs between the museum and the much newer glass-fronted Police Station and Law Courts buildings.

'Where are we going?'

'It's a surprise.'

'I'm not in the mood for surprises.'

'Fine. I'm taking you to The Bog of Eternal Stench.'

'Oh. Yay.' I pinch my nose.

The boardwalk starts at the rear of the museum, winding for about three hundred metres through the man-made wetland, or what we call the swamp. It's slush at this time of year, just several inches of black muck. We often used to play here, when we were younger and we didn't mind the mosquitos; at almost two acres of dense reeds and pathways and holes, there were so many places to hide. The reeds make it look pretty but the smell is foul.

'You could hide a body here.' I follow Gummer down the left fork, which leads to a rotting gazebo at the edge of the main wetland. A dragonfly buzzes my head. I duck, swatting it away.

'Not for long,' he says. 'Everything floats, eventually. Anyway, this would be the first place they'd look.' He darts forward and slaps my arm.

'Ouch!'

He holds out his palm. 'Mosquito. Got you good.'

'So, Kenzie's not back yet,' I say. 'Neither is Mitch.'

Gummer nods. 'Yeah. She's not used to being the centre of attention.'

'Not like me, you mean?'

'I didn't say that.'

'The sooner she struts into school, the sooner it'll be old news. If it had happened to Amber, she would have had badges made.'

'She's not as tough as Amber.' He gives me a wry smile. 'Or you.'

'I'm not tough.'

'Beg to differ.'

'Sometimes you sound like an old man,' I say. 'What are you doing?' We've reached the gazebo and he's upending one of the weathered park benches. 'Hey, is that...?'

'Our time capsules from Grade Four, yeah.' He pokes his finger into the metal tube leg. 'It's stuck. Come here. You've got smaller hands.'

'We should wait for the others before we open them.'

'We'll only open ours.'

To be honest, I can barely remember what I wrote. I pinch my fingers, shove them into the tube, and grasp the end of a plastic bag. I pull it out. Inside, our tiny scrolls are squashed together.

'You first,' I say, tearing the tape.

'Dibs last.' He plucks his scroll from the bag and clenches it in his fist.

I untie the string around mine and scan my scribbled, childish words before I read them aloud.

'Okay, so bear in mind I was, like, ten, okay? Okay...I, Grace Foley, swear I will love and protect my friends forever because they are the best things in my life and even when we get old and married my friends will always come first. Pinkie swear. Amen.' I snort. 'Holy shit. *Amen*?'

'It never hurts to chuck a prayer out there.'

'Read yours.'

He unravels his scroll, squinting. 'I can't.'

'Give it here.' There's nothing written on the paper. I hold it up to the light. Not even an indentation. 'You cheated!' I smack his arm.

He laughs. 'It's partly your fault. I sat there for ages trying to think of something profound to write. You were pretty hard to impress, Grace. We were all exhausted from trying to keep up.'

Another mosquito lands on my arm. I don't feel the sting until after it has flown away.

'And now?' I say quietly.

'Now we feel like we're leaving you behind and you're making no attempt to catch us. It's like you only ever run if you're in the lead.'

That's not it. *Is it?* 'I've had some setbacks.'

He nods. 'And nobody's leaving you behind. We're all waiting.'

'Amber's not.'

'Amber would carry you if you asked.'

I scratch at the bite; the swelling spreads. 'Why did you bring me here?'

He shrugs. 'I thought there might be something there to remind you of the way you used to be.'

'You'. Not 'we'. Like I'm the only one who changed. We share a long, uncomfortable silence.

I sit on the opposite bench and busy myself retying my scroll. I can picture ten-year-old Gummer pretending to write his note, his earnest face, his glasses with the missing lenses perched on the end of his nose. I run through his various incarnations, from his *Where's Wally?* phase to now, what I've always thought of as the Shaggy look—but then I realise he's moved on from that, too. He hasn't smoked since before the holidays. I know that much. His hair's shorter, tidier; he still wears a three-day growth, but he's finally grown into his wide shoulders and slim hips.

I look down at my pale, bony hands. My bitten nails. I blink away tears.

He takes the scroll from me, bundling it up with the others, and stuffs the bag back into the pipe. He turns away, and I don't know what to say.

We head back to the museum in silence. At the bus stop, he says, 'Let's walk the rest of the way.'

I shake my head. 'I'm tired. You go. I want to be by myself for a while.'

Gummer looks as if he might argue, but he doesn't.

I sit at the stop waiting for a bus, any bus, to take me anywhere. I watch him leave: he's perfected the rangy, loose walk that made him look sloppy and double-jointed when he was a kid.

I'm not the same girl anymore: funny, brave, loyal. That Grace is gone. Gummer is growing up, growing into his skin, and I feel as if I'm crawling out of mine, like some creature from the bottom of the swamp.

A blue Commodore with dark windows and a crumpled rear bumper crawls by, its wheels almost in the gutter. I tuck my legs up and rear back. It does a complete turn at the roundabout, and drives past slowly on the opposite side of the road. A few minutes later, it cruises past again.

Unsettled, I get up and start walking. It swings wide around the roundabout a second time, belching smoke. By the time I've reached the next bus stop, I sense the car is behind me, following at walking pace, but when I turn around there's no car there.

I call Kenzie that night before I go to bed. It goes straight to voicemail. I type a text message telling her about opening my scroll and being sorry for breaking promises and about the bones of William Dean being exhumed. After I press send, I realise the message doesn't make much sense.

I'm sorry for everything. I should have left it at that.

I turn onto my side and burrow under the quilt. I'm so cold. So tired and confused.

It seems like no time has passed before I'm awake again. I'm coughing and wheezing. There's a crushing weight on my chest. My arms and legs are dead. I try to turn my head. I can't. I'm choking, trying to suck air through a pinhole, wanting to thrash and scream, but my body is paralysed. Above, a deep vacuum of space begins to spin like black water being sucked down a drain and my hair lifts from the pillow, snaking around my face. My heart seizes; my wheeze becomes a death rattle. All I can do is roll my eyes from side to side, cold tears leaking down my face and into my ears, seeing everything but feeling nothing, willing this thing to let go.

Just as I feel myself falling, it does let go, like a door slamming shut against a howling wind. My throat opens and my lungs expand, filling with air. It leaves me gasping, barely conscious. Slowly, sensation returns, a tingling warmth in my fingers and toes that spreads like a drug through my veins. I command my body to move, testing each part of me one twitch at a time: arms, legs, hips, shoulders.

And my voice. 'This isn't real.'

I sit up. Outside, the streetlights are shrouded in mist and somewhere a drain drips a relentless, crazy-making beat.

I crawl out of bed and slide up the window. Icy air creeps into the room. I swing my bare legs over the windowsill and sit there, shivering, my toes just reaching the slick iron roof below. The same gleaming grey roofs stretch in a grid pattern for as far as I can see, everything silent and still. I look down. There's something blue stuck on the iron sheets. I hook it up with my finger: a dirty, sodden denim baseball cap with a band of silver sequins. It's Amber's. I think of how I've been treating her lately—another thing to be sorry for. It's time for me to stop feeling paralysed and do something.

I stay there long enough to believe I'm alive, only crawling back under the covers when my teeth are chattering and my feet have turned blue. I lie on my side, drifting in and out of a light sleep, never quite going under; the drip becomes a woodpecker, rapping at my brain, *tap-tapping*, typing lists, endless lists.

TWENTY-TWO

Amber's regarding me from her chair at the back of homeroom, chewing a pen, while our teacher marks off the roll and hands out notices. She's wearing a Sacred Heart boys' tie knotted loosely around her throat.

Nobody calls her a traitor. She has transcended.

When I got Kenzie's text this morning before school, I decided there was one thing I could do to make this all go away for her. Nothing anyone can say or do to me will change the fact that my collision course is set, but Kenzie is on a different track. She deserves better.

I get up and place a plastic bag on the table in front of Amber. 'Just returning this.'

'What is it?' she says, recoiling.

'Your cap. It was on my roof.'

She makes no move to open the bag. 'How do you know it's mine?'

I nudge it towards her. 'Of course it's yours. You must have dropped it the night you helped me get back up to my room.'

'Oh,' she says, rapid-blinking.

'It's not a prank.' I scratch at the rash on my neck.

Slowly, she takes the bag and shoves it into her backpack. 'Well. Thanks.' She checks me out, noticing the rash and the bruises on my arms. 'You look awful. What's that rash? Are you okay?'

If we were still as close as we used to be, I'd tell her the truth. As it is, I don't feel bad for lying. I sit down next to her and lower my voice. 'No. I'm not.'

'Is it Kenzie?'

I cover my face with my hands. 'Oh God. I've done something awful and it's making me feel sick. I don't know what to do.'

I make it to the count of three before her arm is around my shoulders, her breath in my ear. 'You can tell me. What is it?'

'It's me in those photos. Not Kenzie.'

She gasps and pulls away. 'Why is she covering for *you*?'

'She thinks I can't handle it,' I say. 'I feel so terrible. I got a message from her this morning and her parents have been called to the school. They're probably here right now.'

Amber's furious. 'You have to tell the truth, otherwise

she might get suspended. It'll affect her record.'

'I can't,' I whisper. The first bell rings. I slide out of the chair. 'Amber, please don't tell anybody.'

I look back at her, just once. She's coiled and ready to strike. I was counting on it; Amber has a passion for drama, but she has an even stronger desire for justice. I am a hateful, gutless ball of misery wandering through the halls between classes for the rest of the day, and Amber is a shadowy avenger. She gives me way longer to come clean than I expected; it's afternoon homeroom before I get the call from the office, and by then the story has wings.

In this town, a rumour travels about a hundred kilometres per second faster than the truth.

Principal Moore is short and bald with smiley eyes and Groucho Marx eyebrows. Normally I get the impression he likes me, though I waste far too much of his time.

He doesn't like me today.

'This is a fine mess, Grace.' He leans back in his chair, tapping his fingers. 'I mean, it was plainly out of character for Mackenzie Collins, but I didn't expect you to let it go this far before you took responsibility.'

'I know. I'm sorry.' I hang my head. 'I wasn't thinking straight.'

His eyebrows are meeting in the middle. 'I will, of course, be trying to find out who took the photos to hold them to account. But this conduct, along with your absences from detention and counselling, well, I'm putting a full suspension in place for the rest of the week.'

Suspension. That's a first. At least it'll back up the story: the few people who saw Kenzie at the party will willingly drop that chewed-up bone and swap it for something juicier.

'I called your father but he said he couldn't get here until five. I suggest you make your way home—your suspension begins tomorrow.' He stands up, buttoning his suit jacket. 'And now I have the delightful task of explaining to Mr and Mrs Collins that I was wrong.' He smiles. 'You may leave. You have plenty of thinking time ahead.'

I cross the office, pausing at the door. 'Kenzie will deny it. She'll tell you I'm covering for her, but it was the other way around.'

He nods and dismisses me, waving his hand.

Kenzie and her parents are waiting in the administration lounge. They seem old and tired. She's sandwiched between them on the couch and they're all looking anywhere but at each other.

'Hey,' Kenzie says. 'What's going on?'

Principal Moore is standing in the doorway, beckoning. 'Come on in, folks. Grace and I have just finished. There's been a development. It appears there's more to this story than we thought.'

'Development?' Kenzie blinks. 'Is this a joke?' she asks me.

I pull her into a hug and whisper, 'No. It's an intervention.'

How easy it is for people to believe my lies; how hard for them to listen when I tell the truth.

Dad and I face off across the kitchen table over cold plates of spaghetti. Dad's chopping the strings into precise inch-long sections; I'm twirling them around my fork, making a nest that keeps getting bigger and bigger.

'I don't get it, Grace. You lied. I know you weren't at that party.'

'Yeah, but it's a good lie.' I cross my arms over my chest. I'm not backing away from this. I haven't felt this determined in ages.

'There's no such thing as a good lie,' he says. 'If you needed time off school, you should have asked. You have to talk to me.'

'It's not that. Anyway, we're not so good at talking, are we?' He flinches. I want to press the crease between his eyes with my fingers, like smoothing out a lump of Play-Doh. 'I'm not like before, if that's what you're thinking. Look! I'm up, out of bed, going to school. Well, I was. I'm functioning.'

He takes in my sloppy appearance—the way I'm playing with my food. 'Maybe you just have different symptoms of the same thing.'

'I'm telling you it's not the same. You're not listening.'

Dad gets up and scrapes his leftovers into the bin. Diesel watches and drools. 'I'd really like you to see Dr Nichols again.'

'I see Mrs Renfrey at school.'

'According to her, you don't turn up. And where do you go when you're not home?' he asks. 'Tell me the truth. I know you hardly ever see your friends. Where do you go?'

'You won't give me answers, so I go looking.'

'Looking where? What questions, Grace? Do you mean about your mum? Can't you accept that I don't have all the answers?' He takes my plate, too, except he throws the plate, cutlery and all, into the bin. He doesn't notice.

'I think you do.'

'Try me.' He leans on the kitchen counter, his mouth a grim line.

I take a deep breath. 'Do you think she threw herself under that truck?'

'No.'

I believe him. 'Did you know she knew both Hannah Holt and the driver of the truck, Dominic Aloisi?'

'They were the same age, in the same classes at Heart, yes. I knew that.' He clocks my expression. 'It's a small town, Grace, relatively speaking. Don't think I haven't wondered. But there's no connection other than two old classmates being in the wrong place at the wrong time.'

'Did Mum know William Dean?' The air is suddenly charged, like the minutes before a storm.

But Dad says, 'Not to my knowledge.'

'Why did Mum want nothing to do with her parents

and her old friends once she started seeing you? Why did she marry you so young and move out to the farm when she was so lonely out there? Did you make her do it?' I feel sick asking him this, but I have to know.

'You've been talking to your grandmother.' It's not a question. Dad rubs his big hand over his face. 'She assured me it was what she wanted. Nobody ever made your mother do anything. She was driven, one-hundred-per-cent committed to me, and you, and Cody. She wasn't happy, but it wasn't us who made her *un*happy. Whatever was going on in her head—it happened before. I know that much is true.'

'And she never told you what it was?'

'No.' His voice breaks, but he carries on. 'She said it wouldn't change it, and I would stop loving her.' Diesel has his nose in the bin, snorting up spaghetti. Dad nudges him away with his foot. 'Is that all of your questions?'

It's killing me to hurt him, but I stand up and take a step forward.

Diesel pushes between us.

'Did she ever see ghosts? Did she talk to them? Dream about them?'

There's a sharp intake of breath. He stares down at Diesel, who's watching us both in his silent, protective stance. Dad seems smaller somehow.

I've brought this on. I'm destructive. I hold out my arms. I want to wrap them around him, but I know I'm not strong enough to hold us both together. Dad's

236

looking at me as if I'm a stranger, and Diesel won't let me pass.

'I'm sorry.' My arms fall to my sides. I walk away.

Dad speaks so quietly, for a moment I think I made it up. 'She said they were everywhere. She said at least out there she could see them coming.'

TWENTY-THREE

The Deans are moving out. There's no SOLD sticker on the sign yet but it looks like they're leaving anyway.

I'm standing in the alley, watching their neighbours wander across the road to help carry boxes and chat. There's a pod, like a giant shipping container, parked on the street at the front of the house, plus a rubbish skip on the lawn. In a way, I'm relieved. It's over for them. They'll pack their things into a truck and drive away to a new place where it's peaceful and no one knows them and nobody paints their house without permission.

It's my second day home from school and that's exactly how I feel—suspended. Interrupted. Stuck in a holding pattern. My phone's buzzing in my jeans pocket—the messages have been coming in a steady stream of bile

and I've been avoiding Kenzie's calls. She's been passion-
ately defending me on every thread, trying to claw back
responsibility, but nobody's listening. She can't stop it
now. She should know that. I haven't responded—a silent
suspect is a guilty one—but I'm quietly playing along.

My life is exploding, and it's spectacular.

They're lugging boxes and furniture from the shed
through the roller door now. The moving pod's only half
full but the skip's already overflowing. Mrs Dean brings
a tray of sandwiches out to share with the neighbours,
waving, talking, balancing the tray on her hip. She seems
happy.

Maybe it isn't all bad. I get hours when I don't think
about Mum; maybe after twenty-three years you get
whole days.

The sky turns dark and a few drops of rain hit my
arm. We usually get either a short, sharp downpour that
runs off the hard ground before it can do any good or
a massive cloud that hovers over Swanston like an alien
mothership before it spins away to rain somewhere else.

I look up. A rolling band of cloud is moving south,
swallowing up the blue. I don't know why I've come. It's
not as if I can walk up to William Dean's mother and tell
her that what's left of her son has taken possession of me
and of the corner of my bedroom.

I pull my hoodie over my head as it starts to pour.
Mrs Dean makes a run for the house, beckoning to the
others, and they flee inside, abandoning a cabinet and
several boxes to the rain. I make a dash for cover under

the carport of the house next door and huddle against the brick wall.

A water spout starts shooting from the bottom of the rubbish skip. On top, there's something as shiny and blue-black as the wing of a crow, caught on a jagged piece of wood. It appears to flap—but there's no wind.

I swallow and step out into the rain, pushing through a gap in a hedge. My shoes squelch and my breath steams. I glance towards the front windows of the house—if I stay this side of the skip, no one will see. I curl my fingers over the edge and peer over the top just as something inside slides and shifts. I jump back. It's just the contents, settling: broken furniture, paint tins, books, toys and a sodden mass of old clothes.

I hoist myself up, balancing my belly on the edge of the skip, and lean across to tug at the wood. I lever it towards me. It's spattered with dried paint, smooth, apart from the splintered end. It's an easel, in pieces. Finally, it gives—as I drag the piece out, the junk underneath lets go with a groan and there's a hollow crash that seems to echo forever, followed by the tinkle of breaking glass. I'm holding the piece of broken easel in one hand, the fingers of my other hand jammed against the side of the skip, trapped by the weight of the junk slide.

I wait. Nobody comes outside; the rain must have drowned out the noise. But I'm close to screaming; the numbness in my fingers has given way to searing pain.

Fingers first. I let go of the easel. It springs back, and the crow's wing slithers over the opposite side of the skip.

Gritting my teeth, I push the layers of junk away to free my fingers, then crouch in the mud, holding my hand like a sore paw.

Shaking, I inspect the damage. My fingernails are blanched. An instant bruise has spread in a line across all four fingers and my little finger has a deep cut across the middle knuckle—white, where the skin has peeled away from the bone.

'Shit.' I curl my hand in the front pocket of my hoodie. *Shitshitshit.*

I stagger back under cover of the carport. I'm drenched and dizzy. Blood is already seeping through the pocket. I fumble for my phone. I'll just have to ring Dad or Cody—it's not like I can get on a bus looking like this.

I have two text messages.

We're watching you.

The second message is from the same unknown caller ID.

Tick tock.

I jerk my head up. Nobody can know where I am, only Dad, and he wouldn't suspect I'd come back here. I check up and down the street: it's empty and the rain has slowed to a drizzle.

Another one comes as I'm hitting delete and trying to block the number, my thumb slipping on the wet buttons.

Time's up.

I turn my phone to silent and shove it in the back pocket of my jeans. I start heading for the alley, but

241

decide it'll take me the long way around, through the gully, and I need to get to a place where there are people.

I turn around and walk straight up the street as if I've every right to be there—an ordinary girl, not bleeding all over the place, not swallowing the urge to be sick in the gutter. Not counting the huddle of crows on the power line above. Six of them.

Six means death.

I hurry past the Dean house. Out of the corner of my eye I can see the blue-black shiny thing lying on the ground, like a fallen bird. The seventh crow.

Seven for a secret never to be told.

At the last second, I dart across the lawn and scoop it up, cradling it to my chest. It's a leather jacket, not a bird at all, but it seems to me that it holds a faint heartbeat deep inside. It wants to be saved.

When I'm safely around the corner, I peel off my bloodstained, soaking hoodie and drop it in a wheelie bin by the kerb. I shake the water from the leather jacket and slip one arm into a sleeve. Teeth chattering, I push my sticky, bloody claw carefully through the other sleeve, letting the shoulders settle around my own. It has wide, pointy lapels and four fake pockets with tarnished zippers; in some places the leather is cracked or worn through to the lining, and the arms are too long, flopping like broken wings. Inside, the jacket is only slightly damp. It's warm. I notice the stiffness around the collar, the smell of mothballs and dust.

Mostly I notice that it feels like skin.

My injured hand feels twice its normal size, but it's turning numb. I keep walking—head down, arms folded around my middle, bleeding into the lining of William Dean's jacket—until another turn takes me along a winding, unfamiliar street and, finally, onto the main road.

A man barges through the door of a cafe, knocking me sideways and spilling his coffee. He's angry, spitting words through thick, rubbery lips, but I can't make out what he's saying. I huddle into myself, spinning away in a different direction, staggering past people, houses, shops, bus stops, cars—everything registers, but I'm lost and disconnected. I'm slipping away to another place.

Seven for a secret never to be told.

A bus zooms by, too close. I'm walking in the gutter. A rush of movement from behind.

Weightless.

Carried.

Rough hands and a breathless laugh.

Shhhhh.

I think I must be dreaming. The last thing I see before daylight is snatched away is a tiny patch of blue in the sky, like looking through a bullet hole in a dirty window.

TWENTY-FOUR

I've pinched myself hard and nothing has changed. My heart is pumping panic, not blood, and my breath comes in rapid, shuddering bursts—but there still isn't enough oxygen. I'm holding on to the image of that patch of blue sky; here, everything is grey.

I'm in the boot of a car. My wrists are taped in front of me. My muscles are so tense they're cramping. At every bump in the road there's bone-jarring impact through my left hip, shoulder and temple. It's not quite dark. Pinpricks of light flicker like distant stars and every few seconds I'm jolted out of position.

Using the index finger on my good hand I probe the swollen pinkie on the other: it's scabbing over. I can't stretch my legs. I'm curled up on my side, hair covering my face, and I can feel the hard rectangle of my phone in my back pocket, out of reach.

I've lived this before in my dreams. *Dust, rubber, oil, metal, fear.* But this is *real*, happening, right now—it's not a dreamscape or a figment or a hallucination. Dreamscapes don't have hard edges. Hallucinations don't hurt—not like this.

There's music coming from somewhere above my head. Speakers. A male voice, singing along to a song I don't recognise. The car brakes, the darkness glows red, and my knees ram against metal. A reply thud comes from the back seat. *Is there more than one person?* A door opens and closes. The volume of the music lowers and for long minutes the engine idles. The car is stationary.

I wait, expecting the boot to open. In my dream the boot opens. I see him, William Dean, and I hear the gunshot. I just don't know what comes next.

I scream and drum my feet against the back seat. Again, someone replies with exactly the same beat, and this time I hear voices and low laughter. More music. A different song.

And, '*Shhhhh.*'

The car takes off again, speeding up, sweeping right and accelerating. I use the momentum to roll onto my other side, feeling around with numb fingers for the boot release. I can't locate a cable—not near the catch or anywhere along the panel near my head, and I can't reach the opposite side without twisting around completely. The space is too small and we're moving too fast.

The speed has been consistent for a few minutes now. We must be on a long, straight road. Breathing hard, I pull my wrists apart. The tape stretches, but only so far; the more I yank at it, the less it gives. I bend my elbows and tear with my teeth. It's sticky and flexible. *Electrical tape?* Now it's dark inside the boot apart from the faint glow of the tail-lights. Finally, a piece of the tape splits and I keep sawing at it until I feel a blunt end with my lips. It starts to unravel: bite, stretch, bite, stretch. I can only unwind it so far before I need to start chewing at the next piece to separate another end.

The car slows and turns. The tyre noise changes from smooth to gritty. A dirt road.

Wherever we are, if we're off the freeway no one will hear me scream. My lips have split. I taste blood. Desperately, I shred the last pieces of tape to free my hands and waste precious seconds kneading some feeling back into them. I run my clumsy fingers over the lock mechanism, trying to work out which way it turns—find the catch, twist it, hear the pop. As the car pulls up I breathe in a sweet rush of night air.

Dust filters through the crack, and I smother a cough. My body wants to react, but my mind is telling me to wait. I'm shivering, head spinning, trying to catch hold of a single clear-eyed thought—and now one pulls me down like a stone: I'm here. How or why doesn't matter. If I wait, perhaps I'll learn what happened to Hannah Holt, but it might be the last thing I'll ever know—and it isn't worth it. Not for a girl I never knew.

I plant my feet against the metal. The engine cuts out. A door opens. I let go of the catch and kick out, sending the boot flying up. I swing my legs over the side, lever my aching body over the edge and start running.

I don't stop to look behind. I just run.

The car engine starts and revs. A deep voice calls out but I keep going, leaping over bushes and rocks, stirring up clouds of fine dust, darting and weaving like I'm dodging a spray of bullets. It's almost dark, barely a strip of luminous colour on the horizon and a hazy moon rising. About a hundred metres ahead, there's a silvery bridge stretching across a deep chasm.

The pipe. The quarry.

A chorus of voices now, yelling. I risk a look over my shoulder: one dark-coloured sedan and three, maybe four hulking shadows. My toe stubs against a rock, sending a jarring pain up my spine. My legs crumple and I fall, rolling almost to the edge of the quarry. Scrambling to my feet, I clutch at the safety grille and squeeze through the bars.

The gully is as good as a dry moat; from there I'll be able to defend. The pipe is my bridge to the other side.

I kick off my shoes and spread my arms for balance. The sleeves of William Dean's jacket billow, catching the breeze like sails. I step onto the pipe, feet turned out. No hesitation, cranking my own fear like a propellor. *Mississippi one, Mississippi two.* I take long, graceful steps, pushing off the balls of my feet and landing lightly on the arches.

247

Mississippi eleven, Mississippi twelve. I've reached the middle. The pink horizon is slipping away, and I can feel the ridges of concrete against my skin, the smoothness of paint. I imagine the softness of feathers where the birds should be.

I don't look down. *Twenty. Twenty-two. Twenty-six.*

Shouting. A horn blasts, but I don't stop. I finish the pipe at twenty-eight seconds flat, wrapping my hands around the bars of the grille to halt the momentum. I turn and raise my fist, feeling the warm trickle of blood as the knuckle splits.

The car is moving. They're not following—they're leaving. For a moment, the headlights are turned squarely on me as I stand there with my fist in the air; then the car is gone and everything's still.

I sit, straddling the pipe. My heartbeat slows. I can't think straight—my thoughts have scattered again. The night air is freezing, but it's warm inside the jacket. I pat my back pocket and my hand comes up empty. *Where did I drop my phone? Did I leave it behind in the car boot? Did I lose it in the dust?* I think I hear the rumble of an engine and decide to wait. I won't cross back until I'm sure they're gone.

I wrap the jacket tighter and tuck the loose ends of the sleeves over my cold hands. On the other side of the quarry, a mist is taking over where the dust has settled.

I'll wait ten minutes and start walking. It's not far to the freeway—there'll be a passing truck or car sooner or later. Dad will be getting worried, and there's zero chance he'll think of looking for me here.

The wind starts to blow from the north, spreading the mist until everything takes on a blueish hue. The colder I become, the more I begin to make out the true shape of the shadows in the night: the huddle of rocks at the bottom of the quarry, the rounded mounds of bushes, a lone bare tree leaning the way of the wind. I tense and suck in a breath. On the other side, near the edge where the quarry is widest, a faint flickering glow.

A campfire. And the outline of a car.

I rise, unsteady on my feet. How could I miss it? How could they miss *me*?

As I'm steeling myself to cross back, two more cars pull into the quarry, music blaring, churning up dust. Old cars. When they get closer one of them is instantly recognisable: Mum's red Celica. I'm struggling to make sense of it. Cody or Dad? Here? I realise the car is faded and banged-up, like it was *before*.

Three girls get out of the Celica. One is tall and blonde, wearing a short skirt and long boots, and the other has a boyish build and short, dark hair.

But the last girl, the driver—she's me. Or she looks like me, wearing unfamiliar clothes: flared jeans, a puffy red jacket and a grey scarf.

Mum. She's laughing. Mum when she was *young*.

I slip my good hand from the sleeve of William Dean's jacket and wave, calling out to her, 'I'm here! Mum, here!' I yell until my throat shreds, but my voice is coming from far away.

She doesn't react. My hand flutters and falls. It's like someone stuck a shank through my heart. She's so close, as real to me as she ever was when she was alive—but she can't be because she's dead, and I must be dreaming.

I crouch down, rubbing my eyes.

This isn't happening now. It was happening *then*.

Two guys get out of the second car, a dirty white ute with a tray top. They're both big and brawny, built like Cody. Mum and the other girls press closer to each other and fall silent. They've spotted the other car at the edge of the quarry, where a tall, thin person is kicking dirt onto the campfire, stamping it out. He gets into the car and slams the door. The engine turns over five times, whining. It won't start.

That's when I recognise Aloisi. Young Aloisi. He steps forward, staggering, pulling the other guy by the arm.

Mum follows, yelling, 'Leave him, Dom! It's not worth it!'

But Aloisi and his friend move up behind the car. They drop their shoulders and start pushing. The front tyres are less than two metres from the edge of the quarry, and though the car is hardly budging, the girls scream.

'Dom!' Mum runs. Her scarf flies off.

The door opens as the car slips forward a few inches, and William Dean tumbles into the dirt. He's precariously close to the edge, and without his foot on the brake the car slowly rolls forward and tips into the void. There's a groan, a crash, the sound of breaking glass. A

250

mushroom-shaped cloud of dust rises from the bottom of the quarry.

For a moment everybody freezes, stunned.

William moves first. He drags himself clear of the edge, and scrabbles in the dust, trying to get to his feet.

Aloisi kicks William hard in the ribs, lifting his entire body with one boot. He bends down and punches him.

Mum is hanging on to Aloisi's arm, trying to drag him away. 'Enough! You're drunk.'

'He deserves it. You know what he did to Hannah.' Aloisi spits in the dirt.

'Leave it to the police,' Mum says, still tugging his arm. 'We hardly knew her—I don't know why you...'

'The police? They aren't doing anything! You saw that flyer, Erin. Look at him—you know he's not right in the head.'

William stands groggily. He takes off, heading in my direction. To the pipe.

'Swampie piece of shit!' Aloisi pulls away from my mother and follows William Dean, his friend close behind.

William's face is white. He squeezes through the gaps in the grille and walks the pipe like an acrobat. He reaches the quarter-way mark without missing a beat, but then he looks down. I gasp as he falters and loses his grip with one foot. He recovers, arms flailing, and steadies himself side-on, but Aloisi is at the grille now, shaking the bars.

When William reaches halfway, right above the deepest part of the gully, Aloisi throws the first stone. It glances off William's right shoulder and ricochets onto the rocks below. The second hits the base of his neck. He ducks and touches his head. His hand comes away stained with blood.

Mum is kneeling in the dirt with her hands over her face. Aloisi picks up another rock, twice the size of the others. He raises it above his head and waits, as if he's giving William time to make a choice.

And William gives up. I see it, in his eyes, in his outstretched arms, in the way his body leans with the breeze like the windswept tree. If he's going to fall, he might as well fly.

I scream, at the same time as Mum, and stretch out my hand. Our voices unite, but he's already swan-diving, gracefully, the way the birds fell. It's too black to see where he lands. The darkness swallows him whole.

I use the sleeves of William's jacket to wipe tears from my cheeks.

Mum is crying too, her expression twisted with horror. Her friends are trying to hold her back, but she breaks away and sprints to the quarry edge. For a moment I think she might follow William Dean; even knowing the distance between us is far greater than the stretch of pipe, I still reach for her.

She collapses at the edge, scooping fistfuls of dust and hurling them at Aloisi.

Aloisi places the rock on the ground. 'He jumped,' he says without emotion. 'You all saw—I didn't push him. He jumped.' He looks around and, one by one, the others nod as if they've made some kind of pact. 'We just wait for them to find him, and we were never here.'

The girls pick Mum up and lead her to the car. She climbs in the back, blank-faced, and both cars leave.

I'm numb—without feeling in my body or my heart. I should go before I freeze to death, but I stay a little longer, just so he won't be alone—down below, up there, somewhere in the middle—wherever he is now. I don't know how much time passes. I listen to the sounds of the night: crickets, the whispers of the wind, the rustling of grass. Every sound is timeless and natural—until I hear a dry cough.

William isn't dead.

He's crawling up the side of the quarry, clutching at clumps of weeds, hauling his broken body over rocks. I watch, unable to move, though every part of me wants to climb down to help him. He reaches the top and staggers to his feet. He's hop-shuffling, unable to bear weight on one of his legs, making slow and painful progress towards the outer fence and Yeoman's Track.

I make a strangled sound in my throat. William turns. He looks right at me and slowly raises his hand, before he moves off, melting into the mist.

It takes me a long time to summon the strength and willpower to cross back. My feet are so numb I can only sit astride the pipe and shuffle, a painful half-metre at a time. William's jacket no longer feels like skin. It's how I imagine the sheep carcass in the bottom of the gully might feel—dry, stiff, paper-thin—and I resist the urge to shrug it off and let it fall, too.

As I slip through the bars of the grille, I hear the sound of tyres on gravel. Headlights flicker out on Yeoman's Track. *Help.* I start running towards the road, waving my arms, scared the car might pass by before they see me.

'Here!'

Something hobbles my ankles; I trip and fall, landing on my hands and knees. But the car turns, its lights sweeping over me and switching to low-beam.

I've been spotted.

Exhausted, relieved, I kneel and drop my head. A car door opens but nobody speaks, and I look up to see the white ute with only one occupant. My fear flares again.

Aloisi gets out of the ute and opens the tailgate. He scans the area, leans into the tray and hauls something heavy out, letting it drop to the ground.

William. He groans and curls in on himself.

Aloisi wraps a meaty forearm around William's throat. I can only watch as he pulls William Dean to the edge of the gully. He bends down, lifts William into his arms and throws him over the side.

A beat of silence, then a thud, dull and awful. Final.

There's mud in my eyes from mingled dust and tears. My hair hangs in a veil of tangles over my face.

Aloisi turns away from the gully. Again, he looks around.

Though I'm barely twenty metres away, I expect him to look through me, but his eyes stop. I push my hair away from my face and give him a stare that burns. I have no strength left. Only hate.

He rubs his eyes and squints. His mouth goes slack. He's shaking all over. He looks as if he's seen a ghost.

Aloisi jerks around and bolts to the car. He starts it up and takes off, circling twice to erase his footprints and the shape of William's body on the ground. He roars out of the quarry, spinning the wheels.

I try to stand but my ankles are still hobbled. I reach down to untangle my mother's scarf. It's real—I didn't make it up. Underneath the scarf is my phone, buzzing, lit up with an incoming call, but I don't answer; I stare at the screen, my teeth chattering from cold, while I struggle to connect the dots.

Dominic Aloisi killed William Dean. He went from committing a mean act—because he fancied himself a vigilante, because he was drunk, or because William was different, I may never know—to committing murder.

The thing I saw crawling in the ditch on the night of the pipe challenge—it was William Dean, twenty-two years before. He couldn't have made it far before Aloisi returned. And William may have murdered Hannah Holt, but he didn't come back to atone or confess, or to show me where Hannah was buried—he *used* me. It's not a huge leap to the final point of a terrible triangle: the ghosts finally caught up with my mother—perhaps her conscience demanded she speak up to make things right, but Dominic Aloisi silenced her before she could tell.

I'm light-headed. I try to stand but my legs have gone to sleep. Far away—or at least that's how it sounds—my phone keeps ringing.

William Dean has given me a curse *and* a gift. Now that I know how William died, I can show that Aloisi had a motive to kill my mother—I can begin to prove that she didn't step in front of Aloisi's truck. If I make my mother's killer pay, I will also give justice to William Dean, but he'll never be held accountable for what he did to Hannah Holt. It doesn't seem like a fair trade.

'It's not enough,' I whisper. 'You have to give me Hannah, too.'

I lift the scarf and run it through my fingers. It's so soft, still warm. I press it to my face to inhale the lingering scent of Mum's perfume, but my mouth fills with dust. My tongue is fat and dry. My throat is closing over, my lungs are screaming; when I stare down at my hands, they hold nothing but fine white ash.

TWENTY-FIVE

Kenzie is curled up on my window seat, flagging the pages of a textbook. She hasn't noticed I'm awake. She looks tired. Her eyes are puffy and bloodshot, and when she yawns the inside of her mouth is an unholy red.

For the past two days all I've done is sleep, pick at my food, and watch TV. Yesterday, I discovered I have four stitches in my little finger. My body has a fresh batch of scrapes and bruises, but the pain is distant and my head feels as if it's stuffed with cotton wool. I don't mind the feeling—I want to forget.

'Hey.'

Kenzie looks up and smiles. 'Sorry if I woke you. I was trying to be quiet.'

'You were quiet. I didn't know you were coming over.'

'Your dad asked me to stay with you.'

'What do you mean?'

'So you wouldn't be alone.'

I sit up in bed. 'Where has he gone?'

'He left a couple of hours ago. I think he's at the school, on the warpath. Then I think he's meeting Cody at the pub.' She closes the textbook with a slap. 'Sorry—I'm not supposed to talk about anything that might upset you.'

'Why the school? What for?' I swing my legs out of bed. They're wobbly and weak—I'm not sure I can stand.

'God, I'm so sorry, Grace.'

'Sorry for what?'

'For what happened to you…' She stops. 'I guess you don't remember.'

'I remember everything.'

'That's good.' She touches my shoulder. 'That's a start. Hey, are you up to watching a movie? I brought supplies.' She picks up a plastic bag, yanks my pillow from the bed, and leaves with them both tucked under her arm.

I follow, clinging to the banister rail with two hands, feeling as if I'm only moving at half-speed.

Downstairs, Kenzie has set up my pillow on the couch and arranged a pile of junk food on the table in front of the TV. I lie back down, search through the recorded programs and select *The Shining*. Ten minutes into the movie and I'm sleepy again, but Kenzie can't sit still—she's making me dizzy with her trips to the kitchen to make popcorn and pour drinks. Now she's jiggling her leg and winding her ponytail around her finger until it springs free. She keeps doing it.

'What's wrong with you?'

'I can't stand this film,' she says. 'It makes me feel dead inside.'

I frown and turn back to the screen.

'You shouldn't be watching it either.'

'It isn't real, Kenz.'

'I know that, but…'

She fidgets some more, so I turn off the TV. 'Sorry. I know I'm bad company.'

'It's fine. It's just hard to know what to talk about.'

I reach over and take her hand. 'You can ask me anything. I won't break.'

Her mouth twists and she pulls away. Her expression is a mix of helplessness and hopelessness.

I want to rewind my life—if not to a place where Mum is still alive, then at least to a point where nobody looks at me the way Kenzie is looking at me right now. I pull back my shoulders. 'You can go if you want,' I say. 'I'll be all right by myself.'

She ignores me and picks up a stack of brochures from the coffee table. 'What are these?'

'Dad brought them home. I think they're supposed to be conversation starters.'

'Pretty random,' she says, holding up one about drug addiction.

'He's covering all bases.'

'Or he's trying to understand.'

'I suppose. Maybe there isn't a brochure for what I have.'

'If there was, what would it say?' She bites down on her lip. 'Sorry.'

'Can you please stop apologising?'

'Sorry.'

'It's hard to explain.' She waits, so I tell her the only thing I know to be true. 'I have hateful thoughts in my head.'

'Doesn't everybody?' She snorts. 'Right now I hate my parents for suddenly acting like I'm the great white university hope for the Collins dynasty, when a year ago they couldn't have cared less. I hate my teachers. I want to set fire to those bloody textbooks. I even hate Mitch sometimes—' She cuts herself off. 'Wait. You hate yourself? Or everybody else, including me?'

Somewhere under the layer of cotton wool, I feel guilt for not being there for her. 'Kenz, the flipside of your hate is love. That's normal. It's different for me—I used to have plenty of hateful thoughts of my own, and that was normal too, but now it's like I have somebody else's. I don't know how much of me is *me* anymore.'

'I want you back,' she says after a pause. 'The way you used to be, even if you were getting me in trouble.'

I smile. 'I'm working on it. I promise.'

Diesel wanders out from underneath the dining-room table. He licks Kenzie's hand on his way past and flops down by the front door, ignoring me. His lack of hostility makes me feel as if I'm becoming invisible.

'I haven't seen Gummer or Pete,' I say.

'They want to come, but...'

'Dad.'

'Yeah.' She fixes me with a stare. 'And Amber has something to say to you. When you're ready.'

'She sent flowers.'

'I bet,' she mutters. She reaches for a brochure and holds one up about teen pregnancy. 'Grace Foley, is there something you're not telling me? Are you having an unexpected pregnancy?'

'No. I haven't even had unexpected sex.'

'Me either.'

We laugh. It feels good.

'It's nice to see you again.' Dr Nichols looks uncomfortable when she realises what she has said. 'Not here, obviously.'

She has a new office on the fourth floor—it has a nicer view, but the room looks the same: cosy, all-white furniture, the walls painted a soft green, and just a few certificates in black frames on the wall behind her desk. Dr Nichols is too smart to peddle inspirational quotes. She knows they don't mean anything.

This is my third appointment in a week. My voice is husky from talking so much—and from nerves, if I'm honest, because I know we're fast approaching the part where Dr Nichols talks back.

'It's not like before,' I remind her.

'What is it like?' she asks.

I think for a moment. 'A bit like before but minus the grief.'

'It can take a long time to come to terms with grief in its various forms,' she says. 'Tell me why it's different.'

'I'd rather say why it's similar first.'

She nods. 'Go ahead.'

'No appetite, nausea, anxiety, insomnia...Tell me if I've left anything out.'

'Risk-taking,' she prompts.

'Yeah, that.'

'Self-harm.'

'No.' I think of my bike sliding out in Susannah Holt's front yard. 'Not deliberately.'

'Delusions.'

I say nothing.

Her pen scratches away. 'You've had some trouble with your friends. You must feel very alone.'

'I've fixed that,' I say quickly. 'I was being a shit.'

She smiles. 'That's a very self-aware statement. It can be hard for people to understand what you're going through, especially the people you're closest to.' She taps her pen. 'So how is it different?'

In this room, the things I've experienced seem far away. I feel safe.

After the last time Dr Nichols helped put me back together, I remember thinking I was part of a game and the reset button had been pressed. Everything was the same, but slightly different. You have to navigate a familiar world—the same setting, armed with the same weapons—but you can only reach the endgame by making different choices. Except it's hard to make different choices with only a split second to react; you're relying on instinct, so you take similar turns. You fight—and lose—to the same monsters that beat you before. One wrong step and you're stuck playing out the game, watching your life run out, and the reset button is somewhere you can't reach.

More than anything, I want to start over.

'Are you sure you're ready to talk about this, Grace?'

'Yes.' I've chewed the tips of my fingernails ragged. My thumbnail has caught the tassel of Dr Nichols's blue scarf—one end of it is slowly unravelling under her desk. She hasn't noticed. 'I want to face it now.'

She pours a glass of water and pushes it across the desk. 'It's a slow...'

I tip back on my chair. 'I'm ready to listen to what you have to say. We've done this before, remember? Everything I've told you—you have the answers right there in front of you, don't you?' I lean forward and tap her notes. 'Devil's advocate, you said once. Let's play.' I sit back, pulling on the bright blue thread. Her scarf slips onto the floor.

'Right,' she says. 'You need to tell me if you feel agitated or upset at any time. Where would you like to begin?'

'The drawings...'

She runs her pen down the page. 'You're a bright

young lady. Your art teacher said it was evident the talent was there. She—and others—agree that you have an uncanny knack for mimicry and the ability to excel in any subject when you put your mind to it.'

'But I drew faces I've never seen before.'

She crosses something out. 'The subconscious is a powerful storage bank of incredible detail, so much more powerful than the conscious mind. It's likely that you have seen them before.'

'How about the night I couldn't move because some-thing was sitting on my chest?'

'Sleep paralysis is my theory. It's a reasonably common occurrence—harmless, but frightening.'

'What about the visions—the thing in the hallway and the person crawling by the side of the road? What about when I saw Hannah Holt in the boot of William Dean's car? And the birds in the pool?'

'An overactive imagination and catastrophic thinking can be symptoms of extreme anxiety. That thinking can result in you seeing signs and warnings—it's a way of convincing yourself that you can prevent tragedy if you follow a specific process. It can be a guilt-based response.' She pauses. 'We discussed this. You remember how guilty you felt that you didn't notice your mother was missing? You've been obsessed with looking for a missing girl—because she's still missing it means she isn't dead, and that fits with your need to avert another tragedy.'

I shake my head. 'But it was over twenty years ago. I didn't know her. I wasn't emotional about it—it wasn't *my* emotion. I was looking for her body. That doesn't fit with what you're saying…'

'And if it happened that you found her body by accident and sheer bloody-mindedness, Grace, there's no telling the damage it might have done. You'd have failed again, and the damage might have been worse. You convinced yourself you were moving forwards, but you were regressing.'

It's like I'm sending tiny, hopeful bubbles into the sky and she's shooting them down with cannonballs.

'If you were receiving thoughts and images from a ghost, ask yourself why the ghost didn't just tell you—better still, show you—where Hannah Holt's body was buried.' Her voice gets lower and lower the more she unpicks the stitches of my reality.

Under the desk, the scarf is coming undone. And so am I.

I shrug. 'I don't know.'

'Grace, it's because you don't have the information,' she says softly. 'And every motivation began with you, the source. You got so far on curiosity and, dare I say it, guts—but then you hit the same wall everybody else did.'

I wipe tears from my cheeks with my sleeves.

She passes me a box of tissues. 'Would you like to break?'

I know what comes next: phones get hacked and dogs have bad moods and the factories that make glowing plastic stars have faulty moulds that turn out a billion rejects—only one girl carries the reject around in her pocket and thinks she's special. I'm not sure which is worse—that none of it happened and my mind is broken, or that it did happen and I have to keep living in a world where nobody believes me.

'No. Keep going.' There are more things she has yet to cross from her list. 'What about my abduction?' That was real. I didn't teleport to the quarry; I didn't bind my wrists with tape. I couldn't have done that. *Could I?*

She covers one of my hands with her own. 'This is a truly awful thing with an earthly explanation. It was a prank.'

A *prank*? I'm cold all over.

'A girl...' She consults her notes. 'Amber Richardson—she has admitted she used her phone to trace yours that afternoon, but she denies being directly involved. She was under the impression they were planning a harmless joke, but of course it wasn't. As soon as she heard they had left you at the quarry, she called your father.'

'Who are...*they*?' I stammer.

'It was several Sacred Heart Year Twelve students. I can't reveal their names, but there will be repercussions. The police are involved.'

Whoever they were—and I'm willing to bet Tamara Fraser was the ringleader—they couldn't possibly have known that they were replicating the nightmare I'd had about Hannah Holt in the boot of William Dean's car. It was a freak convergence. And it was retribution, pure and simple, not a replay of the past.

'And Dad came to pick me up?'

She nods. 'He said you were calm and lucid—physically unhurt, apart from the cut on your finger, which you told him you had done yourself. He took you straight to the hospital to get checked out and stitched up.'

'I said that?'

Dr Nichols closes her notebook. 'Amber also took responsibility for breaking into your home and taking some things that belonged to you.'

Waldorf and Statler. Amber's cap on the roof—it proves she was there, and it sure as hell explains her expression when I gave the cap back.

Dr Nichols pushes away from her desk. 'That's enough for today. You've done well, Grace.'

While I wait for Dad to pick me up, I order a pot of tea and a slice of carrot cake at the cafe on the ground floor. I sit at a table outside in the sun.

My entire body is relaxed. I look down at my bandaged finger on one hand. I have the ball of scarf yarn still clutched in the other. I should probably feel confused, or angry, or bitter, but I don't. I feel relief. I don't remember anything after the ash: not Dad, not the trip to the hospital. Everything that happened *before* is in full colour, and the truth is grey or missing, but for the first time in months I have answers.

I'm ready to let go of the remaining questions.

TWENTY-SIX

I'm painting my bedroom walls green.

Dr Nichols said the colour green has a calming effect. She also said that, a long time ago, scientists believed germs couldn't travel across a green surface because the colour was on the sensitive end of the light spectrum. But that's not why I've decided it's time for a change—it's because of the ghost effect. Under fluorescent lighting, if the walls were painted white, surgeons would be distracted by ghostly mirror-images; if they painted the walls green, the ghosts disappeared.

Kenzie's helping. The floorboards are covered with sheets and we're spattered with paint. It's the first day of the mid-year holidays and Kenzie's dancing, singing along to a new song. I can only watch—I don't know the words.

I'm so out of touch. I've missed almost the whole second term of school. I'm resigned to repeating Year Twelve when I'm better. I glance at the corner: it's already painted over, and the shadows are ordinary shadows.

I *am* better. I'm just not ready.

'Do you want to do your wardrobe the same colour?' Kenzie has her brush poised over one of the doors.

'I guess so.'

She opens the doors. 'Ugh. I can't even look at this without wanting to throw up.' She pushes the formal dress aside, tucking it behind a heavy coat. 'I still can't believe you took the fall for those pictures of me with my face in the dirt. And I can't believe everybody fell for it. Get it? Fall? Fell?'

I snigger. 'Given what was going on at the time, it was really nothing.'

She blushes. 'I tried to put it right. Nobody would listen.'

'Forget it. It's done. My record was screwed anyway, but you, you are destined for greatness.' I rest the paint roller in the tray and wipe my hands.

She turns around, her expression serious. 'It'll be okay.'

'You keep saying that.'

She nods at the tank. 'Rexy got bigger. I bet you're glad to have him back.'

Rex is clawing at the glass. He's bloated. He was probably fed every time there was a class changeover. He's on a restricted diet, and that makes him cranky.

'I am. I miss the other guys, though.'

I'm talking about Waldorf and Statler, but I also miss Gummer and Pete. They haven't been around much— Gummer has a part-time job at EB Games after school and Pete has drifted in with a new crowd. Mitchell is ever-present, except for today. I'm learning to live with him. There's still a lot left unsaid between Kenzie and me, but we're working on it.

'Remember how we always used to dream about our apartment?' She laughs. 'And the boys?'

I try to think of something funny to say, but I can't. 'I don't think we dream the same dreams anymore, Kenz.'

Kenzie tucks my clothes away and closes the door. The hinge jams and, when she opens the door again, something falls off the hanger. She bends down to pick it up. 'I've never seen this. Very shabby-retro.' She slips the battered leather jacket on, flapping the too-long arms and giggling.

The shaking starts instantly. I didn't know Dad had brought the jacket home from the hospital. He must have assumed it was mine and hung it in the wardrobe. 'Take it off,' I say through clenched teeth.

She looks hurt. 'Sorry. Was it your mum's?'

'No,' I bark. I take a step towards her.

Annoyed, she shrugs off the jacket and tosses it onto the bed. 'What's wrong with you?'

'Nothing. Yes, let's do the wardrobe the same colour so it matches.' I pick up the roller and give the doors a few frenzied swipes. The only noise is the sticky splat of paint and the sound of an engine revving in the street.

Kenzie regroups: she arranges a smile, picks up her brush and starts on the edges of the door. 'Mitch and I were thinking we should get away for a few days. With you, too, of course,' she adds. 'What do you think? I know three's a crowd but no hanky-panky, I promise.'

I don't answer.

Dad's bellowing. 'Grace! Come down here!'

I sigh and put down the roller again. 'You coming? They probably want lunch.'

We run downstairs. Diesel's barking and turning circles. He accepts the sock I give him and shuts up, wagging his tail.

Dad's standing in the open front doorway with his hand on his hip. 'Are you ready?'

'Ready for what?'

Mum's old Celica is finished. It's parked in the driveway, engine running, and Cody is writhing on the bonnet like a model on the cover of *Autobabes* magazine.

It's so out of character, I laugh until my face hurts.

'What do you think?' Cody says.

I think I haven't seen him or Dad so relaxed and happy in a long time. 'It looks good. Different.'

Mum's banged-up red Celica is gone. This one is brand new and shiny, like a poisoned apple.

'It's yours,' Dad says.

I burst into tears.

★

271

Kenzie and I drive around town for hours. We've got the windows down. She's singing along to songs I don't know, but I don't mind.

It's Grace and Kenzie, Kenzie and Grace.

It's way past dark when I drop Kenzie home. I park the Celica in the garage, eat ice-cream on the couch, check my messages, and head upstairs to shower.

'I'm going up.' I kiss Dad, who's falling asleep in his armchair. 'It's been a good day.'

He mumbles goodnight, smiling. The crease in his face is less noticeable, or it could be the light.

Diesel follows me halfway up the stairs, and lies down. He's almost there—six more steps and he'll be wondering why it took him so long, and probably disappointed that there's no heaven at the top. I give him a pat, kick open my door, run the shower and get some clean pyjamas.

My room stinks of wet paint. I plan to sleep on the couch.

The bathroom fills with steam. Everything is so white. I sling a towel over the shower rail and step under the water, staring at the pale moon of my make-up mirror, letting the water run over my thin body with its old scars. I close my eyes and the ghost moon is there, behind my eyelids. When I open them, it's on the white tiles, too.

The ghost effect. Real. I smile.

I lather my hair twice to get rid of the paint; the second time the shampoo runs into my eyes and stings like hell. I tilt my chin under the spray to rinse, closing my eyes, thinking of my new old car, the unexpected sweet-sad emotion I felt when I got behind the wheel, and the expression on Kenzie's face when I misjudged a roundabout—for a second we were airborne.

I reach for the towel. My fingers touch cold glass. I open my eyes, batting at the steam, to find the towel on the floor and the image of a face on the wall: hollow eye sockets, a thin mouth, a shock of black hair.

Heart drumming, I wish it away.

There are tricks to keeping the hateful thoughts at bay. Over the past few weeks I've mastered them. It's simple: don't listen. Don't open my eyes if I hear noises in the middle of the night. Even if I miss feeling joy and misery, keep taking the medication, because it gives me an even-keeled feeling of *blah* instead. Go to bed early and try to sleep, even if I'm just lying there, pretending. The more I take care of myself, the less I lose myself. Screw up? Start over. It's like dieting or exercise—I can't let one bad day ruin the master plan.

It's turning out to be a bad day.

I dry off and put on warm pyjamas. Gummer has sent me a message: a simple, sweet *Goodnight, Grace.* I pick up a stray wet paintbrush and stand it in a jar of water, grab my pillow, and pull my quilt off the bed.

And William Dean's jacket falls onto the floor.

I kick it under the bed. It has no hold over me now—nothing from the past does. I know what's real and what isn't.

273

But as I'm passing through the doorway, the quilt in my arms grows impossibly heavy, taking the shape of a slumped body: a head, lolling over the crook of my arm, the curve of a spine against my ribs, long legs, banging against my own. I shudder. I try to blink it away, but this time it won't go. I can't hold it; I drop the quilt and stagger back.

Not real. Not real.

I think I hear Cody talking downstairs, but I realise the voice is coming from inside my head.

My heart is a room with an unwelcome visitor.

I put my fingers in my ears. 'Don't look. Don't listen.'

But I can't block it out. Supposedly there's a rational explanation for everything—surely it counts as progress if I go looking.

I unplug my ears and crouch, pressing my cheek to the quilt on the floor. I reach under the bed and touch the toothed edge of the zipper. I drag the jacket out. Cross-legged, I drape it across my knees and run my hands over the leather.

I put it on.

Every song is a ballad to her.

I feel around in the pockets. Inside the lining of the pocket closest to my heart, I find a square of cardboard the colour of tarnished gold. It's a label, torn from a packet of Dunhill cigarettes. I turn the piece over—on the reverse side, the word '*Saoirse*' is written in William's spiky handwriting.

I put it aside and slip my hands deep into the hip

pockets. In one, my fingers touch something soft, like powder; I take a pinchful and rub it between my thumb and forefinger. It's ash: fine and silvery, still smelling faintly of my mother.

TWENTY-SEVEN

I'm sitting at my desk, working on an overdue essay. I've been staring at the first sentence for over forty minutes. Most nights I try to stay awake until twelve; my first few hours of sleep are heavy and dreamless, but after that I slip in and out, waking every hour.

It's only nine o'clock.

I save the file and close it. It's no use; I'm too distracted. The push-pull of reality versus unreality is exhausting. William's jacket is hanging back in my wardrobe for now, but I know I'll have to get rid of it—that, and the pinch of ash sitting on the torn piece of cigarette packet next to my keyboard.

I sigh. My breath stirs the ash. I want to preserve it before it disappears.

'It's only dust.' I blow. The dust turns into a cloud and floats away. For a second I feel as if I've lost something precious, but my phone pings and it's Kenzie, texting goodnight. I smile. Except for Mum, everyone I love is still right here.

I smother a yawn and pick up the piece of cardboard. The word 'Dunhill' is embossed; the gold lettering catches the lamplight. A layer of fine ash has settled in the spaces in between. Nothing is ever really gone. Push-pull.

'Dunhill.' I turn the cardboard over. 'Saoirse.'

Surse. Say-urse. Sour-seh. However I say it, it doesn't sound right. And I'm talking to a ghost again, but William can't answer because he only exists in my mind.

Push.

Pull.

'What is a Saoirse?'

I type the sentence and run a search. *Seer-shah.* It's a name, of Irish origin, and it means 'freedom' or 'liberty'. It's also the name of an actress and a Celtic folk band.

Dunhill. I flip the piece again. *Saoirse.*

The lamp flickers. Dr Nichols's voice is in my head now and it's telling me to stop, but I'm not listening. I type the two words, transposed: *Saoirse Dunhill.*

My pulse begins to race. I wasn't expecting a hit.

Two people share the name: one, a musician who died in 2005, the other a Clairvoyant, Tarot Reader and Intuitive Healer who lives on the other side of the country in Broome, Western Australia.

A clairvoyant. I click on the link.

The website is kitschy, with an animated header showing a cartoon gypsy running her hands over a crystal ball. Saoirse Dunhill offers face-to-face, phone and Skype tarot readings, and prepares administer-it-yourself healing spells for faraway clients. She's only been practising for fifteen years. That throws me—if they were connected, why would William Dean have written her name so many years ago? Does he want me to contact her? Does she have a message for me? Or perhaps the two words are unrelated—I'm clutching at bones again.

I scroll through a page full of poorly written testimonials from people who have been cured of arthritis and diabetes, who have found missing pets and jewellery, or contacted loved ones on the other side. The same words cropped up over and over—*amazing, uncanny, brilliant, the-real-thing*—and I wonder if she wrote them herself.

But one testimonial stands out:

> *Saoirse brought my beloved son back to me for a last goodbye. I was stuck for so long, hanging on too tightly to his memory. He couldn't pass over. She told me things only he could know—she showed me how to find peace so that he could let go.*

Bullshit, Cody would say.
But that doesn't stop me.

The house is quiet. Dad and Cody are sleeping. I'm sitting on the window seat, laptop open, a rolled-up towel stuffed into the gap under my bedroom door, waiting.

An hour ago, I went downstairs and took Dad's debit card from his wallet to pay for a Skype tarot reading with the Amazing Saoirse Dunhill. I texted the number on the website, and I received a reply text to confirm my reading at ten-thirty—nine o'clock in the west.

I want her to be the real thing. If she turns out to be like that claw-fingered caricature on her home page, wearing a headscarf and strings of coloured beads, rubbing her crystal ball, I think I might start crying and never stop—I desperately need someone who believes to show me how to let go.

Outside, the wind is howling, the estate roofs glimmering with rain.

When the call comes, I nearly jump out of my skin. I make sure the volume is turned down low and adjust the screen.

'Hello?' I get a grey, fuzzy image.

'Oh. Are you there, Grace?' Her voice is deep, with a slight lisp.

I can't see her. 'I'm here.'

'Sorry, let me fix this…'

The image moves and sharpens. She's wearing a soft grey jumper. No tacky beads—no headscarf. She has dark hair, like mine, twisted up in a simple knot. Her eyes are blue and kind.

'Do you see me now?'

I see her. My mouth is instantly dry. It's like my heart is being squeezed by an invisible fist. A rash of goosebumps travels along my arms.

She's the real thing.

'Yes.'

'Hello, Grace. Where are you from?' She looks away and reaches over to one side.

'East coast.' My tongue feels twice its normal size.

Liar, liar, Cody's voice chants in my head.

'It must be pretty late there.'

'It is, but it's school holidays.'

She moves so close I can see a chip in her tooth.

'You've paid for a full tarot reading. What kinds of answers are you looking for?'

Shonk, Cody would say. *If she was a clairvoyant she'd know why you were calling. She'd know where you're from.*

'I…' I can't speak.

She leans back and opens a pack of cards. 'It's okay. Take your time. Why don't you tell me a bit about yourself while I get organised.'

I shift, turning around so the window is behind me. 'I'm in my final year at school. It's not going so well. It's been hard—my mum died two years ago.'

'Oh, honey.' She closes her eyes for a second. 'I'm very sorry to hear that. Let's see if I can help you. Is there a specific question or outcome you're looking for during this reading?'

The moment I picked up that Skype call, everything changed. It's not about Mum now. I have different questions—specific ones.

'I want to find somebody who's missing.'

She shakes her head. 'The tarot reading will only…'

'Her name was Hannah Holt.'

Silence.

Her blue eyes dart away. Eventually, she says, 'Where did you say you were calling from?'

'Swanston.' I let that sink in. 'Take your time,' I add, and there's a sarcastic note to it.

Her mouth pinches. 'Look, I think I should refund your money. I can't help you. Thank you for your—' She reaches towards the screen.

'Please don't hang up.'

'This isn't…' She stands. Her face disappears, then her body, as she moves away.

'Hannah.'

She's out of shot. The room is tidy but cheerful. Matching watercolour paintings on the wall: a pair of blue wrens on a branch, and a galah sitting on a fence post. On the bookshelf behind her screen there are photos of three children, two boys and a girl, but they're too far away to see the faces.

'Saoirse. Your name means freedom. *My heart is a room with an unwelcome visitor—every song is a ballad to her.* You are *her*. Please don't hang up.'

She speaks softly, off camera. 'He promised.'

'He kept his promise.'

'You're too young—you couldn't have known him. How is this possible? How did you find me if he was the only person who knew?'

Was. Past tense. So Hannah knew William had died,

and she probably knew he'd been accused of her murder—and still she never came forward to clear his name. She's sobbing, still out of sight. I thought I'd be the one crying, but now that I'm over the shock of seeing her—alive, twenty-three years older—I'm dry-eyed and clear-headed. And angry.

When she reappears, her eyes are red and her make-up has been rubbed away. She sits down and readjusts the screen. She looks like her mother, except for the colour of her hair. Her face is slightly asymmetrical, as if one side smiles more easily than the other.

'How did you find me?' she asks again.

I shake my head. 'You first. Why did you disappear? Why didn't you tell anybody?'

She sighs, folding her hands in her lap. 'I'll tell you what I remember, but it won't change anything.'

'It might,' I say. 'For a lot of people. For William. For me.'

She nods. 'William and I were friends when we were young. It was around the time my dad left, when I was nine. We used to play in the gully behind my house together. We would hide in the fort when things got rough for me at home and he drew pictures and wrote songs and poems. He was such a romantic.' That lopsided smile again. 'But when my mother enrolled me at Sacred Heart we grew up and just drifted apart. I fell in with a new crowd. It wasn't that we weren't friends anymore, it was just…well, it was complicated.'

She won't say it, but I know what she means. William

was odd. Different. And the two schools probably had similar unwritten rules about consorting with the enemy, even back then.

'He never stopped looking out for me, though,' she says. 'He was always watching, only I didn't know it until one night when my mother threw me down the stairs. She left me there and went to buy milk. Can you believe that?'

I believe it. I think of the way Susannah Holt tore her room apart—the way she spoke to me. *I can't stand a liar.*

'I saw William in the fort. I knew he knew. He always knew. He left me a note that night—he climbed the tree and stuck it to my window. It just said: *I'm here.* And that was enough to get me through for a while, but the last time, that woman nearly killed me over a packet of Dunhills. She found them on the ledge outside my room and woke me up by shoving the rest of the packet down my throat until I choked. *Eat them*, she said. *Swallow the whole lot and you'll never light another one.*' She smirks. 'Dunhill—get it? William and I had a good laugh about that.'

'Why didn't you tell someone?'

She gives a dry laugh. 'Who would have believed me? My mother was on the board of the local council. She clocked twenty volunteer hours a week at Sacred Heart, for years, just to get me on a scholarship. She was very careful—very charming.'

I don't mention that I've met Susannah Holt. Something tells me Hannah—Saoirse—wouldn't be shocked to know her mother still washes her clothes trying to get the bloodstains out.

'My mother was scared,' she says. 'I think she might have spotted William outside my bedroom window, watching, and she was worried about what he'd seen. I told her she was crazy—I said if she started spreading stories about a boy in the tree everyone else would know she was crazy, too. One night she hit me with a broom handle. I didn't wake up for three hours. When I did, one side of my face had dropped. See?' She touches a finger to one corner of her mouth. 'I waited another month. William, he had a box of money stashed in the tree. He said when it was time to go, I should take it—if I needed him, he'd come. I was only three months off my eighteenth birthday, but I didn't last that long. I thought I'd be carried out in a box if I waited, so I told William I was ready. I knew she'd come after me if she had any clue where I was. I went to bed that night, waited until she was asleep, and crawled out the window. I hid in the boot of William's car until we got fifty kays out of Swanston, just to be sure, and then I got into the back seat. I fell asleep, and he drove all night. In the morning, I told him to get some sleep and go home. I knew if we stayed together any longer, it would make it harder to completely disappear.'

'Where did you go?'

She waves her hand. 'A hostel. A train. Another hostel. I went as far as I could before I ran out of William's money. I ended up here and never left.'

'You left him without an alibi.' I stare at her hard, through the screen.

She stares back at me. 'It didn't occur to me that my mother wouldn't tell everyone I had just run away. She gave me a million reasons to leave. Maybe she did know—she must have known. And William—I knew he loved me, but I was so messed up. I told him to wait a year before he tried to find me, but he never did.' The tears start again. 'Local news like that wasn't a click away back then. I had moved on, and I didn't go looking until years later. By the time I found out he had killed himself, it was too late.'

I watch her cry. I'm torn between anger and pity, but I can't tell her that William didn't jump until I have proof. Hannah was just a girl—she couldn't have known that her 'disappearance' would set off a chain of tragedy, beginning with William and ending with my mother. Did she remember my mother, or was she just another face in an old school photo? Is there any point to any of this—any way out, any way back? How could Hannah even begin to comprehend how far the poison had spread after the night she climbed out of her bedroom window?

Maybe Dominic Aloisi would still have been a killer—only his victims might have been different people. That's the part I can't let go.

'I need to know—how did you find me?' She startles me out of silence.

'A piece of paper in William's jacket. Cryptic. Nothing anyone would notice,' I say flatly.

'That old thing. How did you get it?'

'A garage sale,' I lie.

'You seem like a very intuitive, together young lady. I only wish I was like that when I was young.'

'I think you might be the first person ever to say that.'

'I suppose they'll come looking for me now.' She sighs. 'It won't change anything. You know that, don't you?' She's begging, or praying, her hands pressed together like the night I dreamed about her.

I almost hate her then.

When Cody comes out of his room the next morning, he finds me on the couch, laptop open on my thighs. Dad has already left for work and Diesel is lying next to me.

I haven't slept. I couldn't.

William Dean took the secret of Hannah Holt's whereabouts to the grave, where it has been buried under dirt—and lies—for twenty-two years. Now that I hold the key, what will I do with it?

'What's going on?' Cody says. 'You okay? Have you been here all night?'

'I'm great.' I close my laptop. 'Are you working today?' I sound too perky.

'No.' He's suspicious. 'I was thinking I'd hang around here.'

'You don't have to babysit me *all* the time.'

He rolls his eyes. 'I know.'

I tuck my laptop under my arm. Cody switches the

kettle on and mooches around in the kitchen, waiting for it to boil.

'Cody?'

'Yeah.'

'If I show you something, will you promise not to tell?' He never could resist a secret.

But he frowns. 'That's not fair. You know I can't promise you that.' He pours himself a coffee and places it on a coaster on the table.

'Fine. Then I can't show you.'

He's dying to know. It takes him less than ten seconds to change his mind. 'Okay, but if I think you're in trouble, I might have to break my promise.'

'I'm not in any trouble.' I move to the kitchen table and open my laptop. Cody sits next to me. 'This is a Skype call I recorded last night. I'm talking to a clairvoyant called Saoirse Dunhill.'

Cody rears back. 'Jesus, Grace.'

'Wait. Listen to what she has to say.' I start Quick-Time. 'Are you ready?'

He nods, and I press Play.

When I log off, Cody is silent for a full minute. 'Are you sure it's her? She's not just some crackpot?'

'How much more proof do you need? You saw her. You heard.'

'It's old news. She's an adult now.'

'Yes. The same age Mum would be if she was still here.'

He flinches, as if I've caused him physical pain.

Sometimes I forget how much he misses her, too.

'Okay.' He's thinking. 'Let's wait a few days. It's not like it'll change anything.'

A loud thud makes Cody spin around. 'Something just hit the kitchen window!'

'A bird,' I say. 'It's probably just a bird.'

TWENTY-EIGHT

I'm on my way home from my weekly session with Dr Nichols. These July days are short and freezing. It's already getting dark. The Celica's windows are fogging up in the back and, even though Cody has worked his mechanical voodoo, she keeps stalling when the engine's cold.

Kenzie texted earlier to ask if I want to meet her, Mitch, Pete and Gummer at Lumpy's at six, so I have an hour and a half to kill. I drive around for a while, avoiding the one place my intuition is telling me I should go.

I haven't made up my mind whether to contact the police myself, tell Dad, or let Cody take the decision out of my hands. I should be elated, but I'm feeling flat and tired. Finding Hannah Holt hasn't changed anything. The only thing it proves is that William Dean is no murderer; it doesn't prove he was murdered, or that my mother didn't step out in front of a truck. It sure as hell doesn't prove that I haven't lost my mind.

Rational explanations are easier to come by, and harder to refute.

I fill up with petrol and park outside the cemetery. I want to go inside—and I don't. I'm constantly caught between doing what's right and doing what *feels* right.

The cemetery is deserted. At five o'clock on a Tuesday afternoon, I suppose that's normal. What is normal anyway? The goalposts keep shifting—it's like kicking with my left leg, trying to aim for the space between a pair of chopsticks, set an inch apart. And everyone notices when I miss.

I get out of the car, pulling a beanie low over my ears to keep out the cold. The lampposts dotted around the cemetery flicker and light up.

I was wrong. There's one other person here—a gaunt, broad-shouldered man wearing a hooded blue raincoat—but he's on his way out. We brush shoulders as we move through the gate; he steps aside, muttering an apology.

I follow the path towards the memorial garden, running my hand over the wings of Maria's angel as I pass. The pock-marked stone is surprisingly warm, like the star I have clasped in my other hand. It doesn't matter if it's the original star or it isn't—I figure there's more sentiment in that knobbly piece of plastic than there would be in any expensive bunch of flowers.

But first, I want to say goodbye to William.

William's old grave is occupied and freshly filled. A shiny black headstone stands perfectly upright, and a matching marble slab covers the trench.

I have mixed emotions. Sadness, anger, loss—but mostly a growing sense of peace. He didn't belong here. I'm glad his family didn't leave him behind. I can't feel him anymore—it's like Hannah was the last thread, and now that she's found, he's lost to me.

He doesn't need me now.

Mum's memorial is well tended, surrounded by glittery rocks and native grasses. There's a single rose, fresh and white, in a plastic vase on a spike—Dad must have visited today, or Cody.

I bury the star next to the rock with Mum's plaque, covering it with dirt and a clump of bright moss. I take the folded tissue from my pocket and sprinkle the tiniest bit of ash from her scarf among the grasses.

Mum isn't here either. I know I'd have more chance of her listening if I shouted into the wind, or called out to her in my dreams.

The Celica's engine has cooled and it struggles to start. I must have taken longer at the cemetery than I thought. I pump the accelerator and end up flooding the carburettor, so I text Kenzie to say I'll be running a bit late. I search through Mum's CDs in the glove box—Cody said he'd replace the ancient stereo, but I don't want a new one. I change the CD and flick the visor down. The photo of Mum wearing the catsuit is tacked to the inside; I blow on my hands and my cold breath curls around her face.

When the engine finally kicks over, I reverse out of the park and sit in the bus lane, revving, until I think she's warmed up enough. After a few more minutes, I pull out into traffic, take a right and head for Lumpy's. But, when I try to turn left at the end of Reginald Street, there's a council crew setting up a road block for night-works. *Dammit*. Ten minutes earlier and I wouldn't have to take the long way around.

Then I realise: the detour isn't necessary. It's just habit.

I do a U-turn and take the next right. Trimmer Road will bring me out at the corner of Waites and Blaine, and save me a trip through the dark, semi-industrial estate. I'll shoot through the intersection and hang left.

I won't look at the shrine.

The traffic lights are red—someone is crossing at the pedestrian lights. I brake hard and pull up. There are no other cars waiting. Mum's photo slips from the visor and flutters to land in the footwell underneath the accelerator pedal. The engine sputters and stalls. Swearing, I duck down and fumble around under my feet, trying to restart the engine at the same time. There's no slope, so I can't get a roll happening and drop the clutch.

I grab hold of the photo and jam it between my thighs. Turn the key, pump the accelerator, listen to the starter motor whine. The engine turns over, clicking.

'Come on, baby.' I check the rear-vision mirror but there's no one behind. 'Seriously? Come *on*.'

There's movement across the intersection, near the shrine.

I look up. It's the same man in the raincoat, the one I passed at the cemetery. He's frozen to the spot, staring at the car, holding a single white rose in one hand and a drooping clump of grass in the other. Our eyes meet.

In that millisecond, I know who left the white rose on Mum's grave—I know who tends the shrine.

A sick wave rises in my throat. Does he think that bringing flowers and pulling weeds and painting the cross makes him *free*? Knowing that I rubbed shoulders with Dominic Aloisi as I passed through the cemetery gates—and somehow *not knowing* it was him—is too much. It's a betrayal of my own intuition.

I'm willing the car to start. It's like I'm holding a gun with an empty chamber—I can point, but I can't shoot. And he's coming; he's crossing the road. Halfway across he drops the white rose and it's crushed under his boot. I'm shaking the steering wheel, turning the key, listening to the engine cough and choke in the silence between CD tracks.

It's no use.

I get out of Mum's car and slam the door. My legs are shaking. As he gets closer, I hold up her photo like a shield. 'Don't touch me.'

He cocks his head to one side. 'I know you,' he says.

I lift the photo higher.

He seems dazed, white around the gills, like Rex when he's out of water. His face is haggard, and he has a vibrant red rash along one side of his neck.

'I've seen you before.'

I'm trembling so violently my body aches. 'You've never seen me. You don't know me.'

His eyes flick back to the photo, narrowing, and his whole body slumps to one side. 'You look like her,' he says, and his voice cracks.

I stamp out a surge of pity. 'Like my mother.' I push the photo closer. 'You killed her—you ran her down. I know it and one day everyone else will, too. And you know what else? Hannah Holt is alive, so you can't cover your tracks anymore. You killed William Dean for nothing, and you killed my mother for nothing. That makes you *nothing.*'

A misty rain starts to fall. We face off, both of us crying, until I can't tell the difference between rain and tears.

'No,' he says quietly. 'No.' He runs his hands over his face, as if he's trying to blink me away.

He can blink all he wants. I'm not going anywhere. I won't move away first.

He steps back, clutching his raincoat around his wasted body. 'I know *you*,' he repeats. 'You were there. You're the girl in the dust. I *saw* you.'

I shiver.

I think of the way he stared into my eyes the night

he killed William. It's not possible—I wasn't born—and yet Dominic Aloisi is the only living person who might believe me about the dreams, the visions, the Swanston ghosts. He *knows*. He feels them, too. I want to scream at the injustice—stuck forever, sharing a mad dream with my mother's killer. But, as the rain stops, I realise something elemental—Dr Nichols would be proud. He can't hurt me. He's dying, rotting from the inside. I can see that. There's nothing I can do or say that could be worse than what's already happening to him.

'They're haunting you,' I say. 'They'll never leave you alone. You know that, don't you?'

He takes another step back, and it's enough for me. The mad dream is his now.

I get into my mother's car and she starts, first time.

Tuesday nights are quiet. Pete's got the CLOSED sign up on Lumpy's door.

I stand outside in the shadows for a while, watching my friends through the steamed-up windows. They're crammed into our booth at the back, a candle on the table, a single dim light on in the kitchen. Mitchell and Pete are leaning across the table, deep in conversation. Gummer's behind the counter, spinning a pizza base like a vinyl record, his finger poking through the centre. Amber is here, too. It's time we talked. Kenzie's resting on the back of the booth, chin on her hands, staring out at the street. I'm drawing out the moment —making sure I remember the details so I can file this memory away with the good ones.

I should be busting to share what happened tonight on the corner of Waites and Blaine, but something is warning me to hold it close. It's not a story I'm ready to tell, and I'm not sure they're ready to hear it. The next few months will be busy for them—they'll be getting ready for exams and making plans for the future.

I'll be on hold, and it might take me a while to catch up. But I'll keep going, even if I'm not in the lead.

Tonight feels like it's the final episode of a long-running sit-com: we'll kiss cheeks and fade out, leaving Pete to wipe the tables and turn out the light. I guess I thought the day we met was the way we'd always be—we were pieces that didn't fit anywhere else. There was no warning that we wouldn't always be together.

Or maybe there was—I just wasn't listening.

TWENTY-NINE

Kenzie brings me homework from school. She thinks I should try to keep up; she says if I fail (I say *when* I fail) it'll make next year easier. She's probably right. The problem is everything is so much harder than I remember—my focus, my memory, my commitment.

I try to focus on the equation in front of me, but the numbers make no sense. They're drunken ants, marching across the page. I pick up my phone—as usual it has no messages.

Everyone is moving on.

And we're going back.

The Johnsons are relocating in February and Dad has been offered the position of property manager at the farm. The lease stands—we'll basically be caretaking our own property until it runs out—but when Dad told me the news it felt as if I'd just been drained of poison. Like I had reached the endgame with full life and a freaking arsenal of weapons.

Dominic Aloisi's confession didn't come easily. On my own, my claims were discounted as ramblings, but one of Mum's friends—the blonde girl, Anna Foster—was interviewed and she admitted they were there the night William Dean fell. She said that she and my mother had wanted to tell the story, many times, but Aloisi had convinced them to keep their conspiracy of silence, and for a long time they'd agreed—telling wouldn't change anything. But they didn't know what Aloisi had done.

Anna Foster's statement established motive in my mother's 'accident'; detectives began to look more closely, and Aloisi's pack of lies fell in on itself.

Susannah Holt was advised that her daughter was alive and well, but Hannah had no plans to return to Swanston—neither to see her mother, nor to acknowledge the terrible price William Dean paid for keeping her secrets. And just a few months after they'd left this town behind, the Deans were told their son had not taken his own life twenty-two years before. I feel a sense of responsibility for that. I wonder if there was a moment of peace for them before their nightmare returned in a different form, if Mrs Dean still carries her son's ashes like a child. I wonder if we'll see each other again when Dominic Aloisi one day faces trial for the murder of their son.

I visit Mum's memorial every week, and one day I hope to have the courage to pull down the shrine. Showing grief is normal behaviour. But, like sick birds pretend to eat, I try to fit in, to not cause pain, but I feel as if I'm stuck in a halfway place. Sometimes I still think there are voices on the other side, but the voices of reason shout down the quieter ones I strain to hear.

Every Tuesday at four, Dr Nichols talks with me, crossing things from her list. Every morning, Dad lays out my pills with exaggerated care. Cody navigates around me like I'm broken glass, and Kenzie wears a resolute expression as if she's being forced to visit a sick relative. Gummer still thinks things through from every angle, but I suspect he's rapidly running out of theories about me. His visits are brief now—he never sleeps on our couch, and he leaves too much silence for me to fill.

Diesel is lying under my feet. He has finally beaten his stair demons; he made it all the way to the top. I sometimes believe he understands more than any of us about fear.

I lay down my pen and close my laptop, sighing. It's no good. I have a headache coming, and it's time for dinner.

I go downstairs, Diesel close behind. Cody is dozing on the couch with his bare feet hanging over the back, an open car magazine on his stomach. It's dark outside and starting to rain. So much for Mum's canary-in-the-coal-mine theory—it's been the wettest Swanston winter I can remember.

'Where's Dad?'

Cody shrugs. He doesn't open his eyes. 'Work.'

I pick up a pack of cards from the kitchen table and shuffle them absentmindedly. It's a trick deck: hidden in the intricate illustrations on the face of each card, there are tiny indicators telling you the card's number and suit.

Pick a card, any card. Let me read your mind.

'Where was he working today?'

'Fixing fences at the Morgan place.'

I try to snap and split the deck the way I used to, so fast people would think it was magic, but my hands aren't my own. They're shaking, the veins bulging like they did once before. The cards flutter across the kitchen floor. I bend down to pick them up and my vision goes dark, pixelated, like it does when you stand up too quickly.

An awful sense of déjà vu rises like a black wave. *My brother is asleep on the couch. I'm shuffling a deck of cards. Dad hasn't come home.*

'He should be here by now.' I'm trying not to let the panic show, and failing. Maybe I am seeing signs and portents everywhere, falling into that trap of catastrophic thinking, like Dr Nichols said.

Cody sits up and glances outside. Sleet hits the windows, turning them muddy. He puts his magazine down on the table. 'I'll call him. It's okay.'

I know he's just humouring me. I'm broken glass. 'Yes. Call him.' I wring my hands, squeezing the blood until my fingers turn white. 'Tell him he has to come home right now.'

My brother picks up his phone. He's moving too slowly. I watch him press the buttons, frame by agonising frame.

'He's not answering. Wait here. Don't wig out on me, Grace.' He goes to his room.

Wait. *Wait?*

The air ripples. I'm feverish all over. Diesel starts barking at the ceiling.

William is here. He doesn't show himself, but he's here—he's the darting smudge at the edge of my vision, the stabbing needle behind my eye, the worms under my skin. I brace myself against the kitchen table, digging my nails into the wood, taking great gulps of air.

The alternative is to pretend, and do nothing. And it's different this time, I realise. The panic is manifesting itself in a new way: a clear-headed, unshakeable belief. It's like I've been stuck in a dark room for years, moving around the indistinct, shadowy shapes of covered furniture—now, I'm racing around, stirring the dust, dragging the covers from the furniture and throwing up the windows to let the light in.

And I'm furious.

I did what you wanted. Why are you still here? You've taken everything from me! You have to leave me with something!

Cody's back. Shoes on and carrying a coat. 'No answer at the Morgan place, either. What do you think we should do?'

I hand him his keys.

★

Cody has the heat turned up so high our combined sweat and fear fog the glass. It's like it's raining inside the car. He uses his sleeve to wipe the windscreen and opens the window. A blast of freezing air takes my breath away.

'Did you call before...?'

'I called again, twice. No answer,' Cody says.

'He always picks up.'

'I know.' His mouth is set in a hard line. He keeps adjusting his grip on the steering wheel.

'Can't you go faster?'

'I'm doing a hundred and twenty.' He glances over. 'Are you okay?'

I nod, staring straight ahead, but I'm reliving the night I froze on the pipe, the terrifying ride home in Pete's car, the thing in the ditch on the side of the road. The seatbelt's getting tighter and tighter. It's choking me, bruising my shoulder. I loosen it, holding it away from my chest with my thumb. I don't know how long we've been in the car or how far away we are from the Morgans. I have no concept of time. The shapes and shadows streaking past—trees, fences, sheds—all look the same, as if we're living the same ten seconds, over and over.

There's ice on the road ahead. Cody sees it, too. He eases off the accelerator. Before I can scream at him not to brake, he does, too hard; we hit the patch, the tyre noise disappears and we're aquaplaning. Everything slows down. The tail end slides left and the car begins to spin. In the space of a heartbeat, I see a future where Cody wrenches the steering wheel in the opposite direction and the car flips and rolls like a tumbleweed; instinctively, I throw myself across to grab the wheel. The slack seatbelt lets me go. Using both hands and all my weight, I yank the wheel hard right, turning into the spin. Cody fights it, but I have the element of surprise and he can't stop it from happening. It's a carnival ride—a sick spinning, the starry sky a blur, the wind moaning through the open window, our necks snapped sideways—but eventually the ride comes to a stop.

The car is in the middle of the road, facing the wrong way. Nothing but the sound of our breathing and a humming in my ears. I peel my stiff fingers from the steering wheel, sit back in my seat, and close my eyes.

'Are you in one piece?' Cody says.

'I'm okay. You?' I look across at him.

He pulls over to the side of the road. 'I was thinking about Dad. I can't believe I did that…I *know* better. That was almost it for us.'

'Yeah.'

'You and I should never be in the same car at the same time.'

Cody has said exactly what I was thinking; it shocks me that he feels a similar responsibility to stay alive—for Dad.

'I think he's probably just as scared we'll lose him,' I say quietly.

He looks away, but not before I see tears.

The rest of the trip is made in white-knuckled silence.

Cody concentrates hard on navigating the slippery road. I'm repeatedly dialling Dad's number as if the sound of his recorded voice is a beacon, calling me home.

Ten minutes later, we pass the turn-off to the Morgan farm. Cody stands on the brake, turns around and pulls up at the entrance to the access road, the windscreen wipers still flapping madly, though the rain has stopped. From here, we can see a huddled mass of cattle, steam rising from their backs, and rectangles of warm light spilling from the windows of the house. Fifty metres ahead, the road splits three ways.

'We should go up to the house first. He might be there.' His voice cracks with indecision. 'But I can't see the truck. He's probably already at home wondering where we are.'

I squint into the dark. On the left side, the paddocks are a sea of tall, rippling feed grass; on the right, the grass is chewed down and trampled by cattle. I open the window and tip my face up to the sky. I close one eye—the good eye, not the one with the stabbing pain—and everything looks different.

'Take the left.'

'How do you know?'

'There's a light.'

'I don't see anything.'

I open the door and get out. The car can't take us where we need to go.

'Grace, what are you...'

I squeeze between the fence wires, ankle-deep in

sucking mud, running, heading for the blackest part of the landscape. Through one paddock and into the next, and the one after that. Cody's somewhere behind me, lumbering and yelling, but I can't wait for him to catch up.

I'm following a star—a single, flickering star that doesn't look like the rest.

But a moment later the star falls from the sky and disappears. I'm lost. I stop, blinking. My breath forms a curling mist. Gradually, my eye adjusts and the dark isn't dark anymore—it's layers of green. I turn around. Behind me, the grass parts, bending to a form—shoulders, hips and slender arms—and the stalks ripple like the plucked strings of a harp. The grass flings back as she passes, moving fast; she turns her head to make sure I'm following, but she has no face. She leaves no footprints, makes no sound.

I reach out a cold hand to find it suddenly infused with heat.

I run after her, sobbing, never quite able to catch her, like chasing the end of a rainbow. I ache with love; it's tearing my heart from my chest. Part of me wants to stop running—where we're going, when we get there, I'll lose her. I know this.

She leads me to the edge of the paddock. It's open here; nothing to hold her shape. She shifts through another fence, losing form, just quicksilver mist.

Cody's getting close. His voice is not far away, calling. I stop at the fence, holding out my hand, begging her to stay. 'Cody, here!'

He comes crashing through the grass, wet through, almost tackling me to the ground. 'Jesus, Grace.' He's gripping my shoulders, searching my face.

'Look,' I point. 'She's right there. Do you see her?' I'm smiling, my heart so full it might explode.

Cody turns around and his face lights up in an expression of sublime wonder. 'I see her!'

He lets me go so suddenly I fall backwards and land in the wet grass. He's off, hurdling the fence, sprinting, and I'm laughing and clapping my hands, trying to get to my feet. Cody's still running, up an embankment, skidding on his hands and knees in the mud. I swear he passes right through her—and keeps going.

He hasn't seen her. He's seen Gina, Dad's truck.

And she's gone.

I finally stand up, set my shoulders, put one foot in front of the other. My world is utterly normal again: black, cold, real. Frightening.

The twin beams of Gina's headlights cut through the dark and I can hear two voices: Cody's, pitched with panic, and Dad's, slow and deep.

I numbly accept the trade, and whisper goodbye to my mother.

Cody and I choose seats opposite each other in the emergency department waiting room. We're the only ones waiting. My brother is covered in mud and blood, from his hands and wrists to his jean-clad thighs, and his right foot is *tap-tap-tapping* on the linoleum floor. Harsh fluorescent lighting casts deep shadows under his eyes, turning his skin grey.

An hour passes without us speaking. Three times, the triage nurse checks to make sure Cody's not hurt. Twice, he says, 'It's not me. It's not my blood.' The last time he takes off his shirt, balls it up, and stuffs it in a rubbish bin. He sits there half-naked, shivering.

I stare down at my own hands. They're bloodless but steady, impossibly clean. I don't have a drop of blood on me, though Cody, Kel Morgan and I carried Dad all the way to the house to meet the ambulance. Dad's stricken expression is on loop in my head; I'm still feeling the scalpel edge of his shattered leg bone, still smelling the odour of sweet grass and leaking diesel, still wondering how we got through the last two hours and how we'll get through the next—yet, somehow, my pulse is slow and even.

'He's gonna be okay,' I say to break the silence. 'I know it. This is how it's meant to be.'

Cody's head jerks up. 'And how do you know, Grace?' His voice breaks at the end of his question. He clears his throat and tries again. 'Are you a bloody clairvoyant now? Can you see through walls or something?'

'I don't know,' I mumble. 'Something.'

He gets up, arms folded across his bare chest, and starts pacing around the rows of plastic chairs. 'Why aren't they telling us anything? I'm so cold.'

'You're in shock.'

'That's not it.' He shakes his head and completes another lap.

'You're not wearing a shirt.'

He stops. His arms drop to his sides. 'I don't understand you,' he says. 'Maybe you're the one in shock. You're so calm, it's scary.'

I shrug.

'You're not scared?' he says.

I'm not sure if he's angry or dumbfounded. 'No. Not anymore. I think all of it was leading to this.'

'This? You keep saying that. Why do you keep saying that?' He pulls away. 'My chest feels really tight.' He massages it with one hand. 'Lucky we're in the emergency department.' He sits back down.

'Guilt,' I say. 'That's what guilt feels like.' He didn't notice Dad wasn't home—he's thinking about what would have happened if he hadn't taken the keys when I handed them to him. Dad would have bled out in a hayfield.

Cody's face goes slack. 'Maybe.'

I get up to ask the triage nurse for news and, when she has none, I ask her for a warm blanket. I tuck it around Cody and take the seat next to him.

'I just need everything to be all right, otherwise this is all for nothing,' I say again, and this time he doesn't answer.

Together, we watch the clock tick around and around. I slip into a state somewhere between waking and sleeping, dozing to a persistent hum coming from another room.

★

It's after ten when the double doors swing open.

We both launch to our feet. This could go one way or the other. I'm ready for both, but Cody—he's shaking so hard the tendons in his neck look ready to let go, like the winch cable on Dad's truck.

'He's doing well,' the doctor says quickly. 'He's still heavily sedated. We've given him a transfusion and temporarily set the break, but he'll need orthopaedic surgery to insert a rod and pins sometime in the next few days. You can see him now for a brief visit, but he won't know you're there until the morning, at least.'

Cody's mouth is moving; he's asking questions.

I'm trying to focus on what the doctor is saying, but the faraway sound is getting louder: snatches of conversations, music, laughter, crying, the spit and crackle of static, like when you spin the dial between the stations of an old radio. The walls are breathing in and out, and there are winged shadows at the corners of my vision. Colours are brighter; Cody's smile is exquisite.

I want to tell him: *Don't you get it? She's everywhere. She's beautiful, Cody. I wish you could see her, too.*

But I don't speak. I smile. And just like that my big, brash, overgrown brother is crying into my collarbone— shivering, sighing, talking, all at once.

I put my arms around him, and they're stronger than I ever knew. I have the sensation of something bright and unbreakable settling into place at my core; at the same time, the final thread that holds me back—it snaps, like a rubber band letting go.

ACKNOWLEDGMENTS

With every book, the acknowledgements page is harder to write. It's not that I need more space, just fresh words to thank the same fine people.

As always, thank you to Penny Hueston and the team at Text Publishing.

To my early readers (who also happen to be big-hearted, gifted writers) Allayne, Bec, Paula, Kim, Simmone, Cath, Fiona and Emily—thank you.

There is always a dog—on my lap, under my feet, scattering pages and barking at the moon. It has been Banjo for every story but this one (miss you, mate), and Bowie had a huge dog-shaped hole to fill. He did. Thanks, nutter.

To my parents, family and friends, my love and gratitude for always being there.

To Mia and Roan, my beautiful creatures, thanks for yanking me back to reality when I need it. (Not so hard, okay?)

And to Russ, thank you. You're a keeper.